A SORE LOSER

Anticipating the reaction he was sure to see, Lacey, still grinning, replied, "Remember that feller you had a little go-round with back at Fort Pierre, in O'Malley's Saloon?" He got the reaction he'd expected. The big man's eyes narrowed and he snorted angrily through his bruised and broken nose. "Yeah, you remember him," Lacey went on. "Well, I just saw him and that feller he was with—I think he's his brother—eatin' dinner at Whitey's place."

Jake almost came out of his chair. "Where? Is he still at Whitey's?"

"Nope," Lacey answered. "He left Whitey's and took that trail up beside the harness shop. I followed the two of 'em up the ridge to see which way they was headin'. Then I hightailed it back here. Figured you'd wanna know."

"That son of a bitch," Jake growled as he got up and kicked the chair out of his way. He paused then when the thought occurred to him. "Why the hell didn't you shoot the son of a bitch when you had the chance?"

Lacey shrugged. "I thought about it—I sure did—but I figured that was a score you wanted to settle yourself."

"I don't give a damn who shoots him," Jake declared, still on the verge of exploding. "I just want him dead. Him and his brother, too."

THE DEVIL'S POSSE

Charles G. West

BERKLEY
New York

BERKLEY

An imprint of Penguin Random House LLC

penguinrandomhouse.com

ISBN: 9780451471987

Signet mass-market edition / March 2015

Berkley mass-market edition / March 2022

Printed in the United States of America

3   5   7   9   11   12   10   8   6   4

For Ronda

Chapter 1

"Here you go, boys!" Oscar Bradley called out as he approached the group of men waiting at the corner of the corral, their saddles and other gear on the ground beside it. "It's payday." He picked a saddle to sit on and set the leather bag, in which he kept his notebook, on the ground in front of him. "Like I told you when you signed on back in Ogallala, this is gonna be my last drive, and I promised I'd pay you a bonus if we made it here in less than twenty-three days." He paused to look around at the expectant faces. "Well, we made it in twenty-one, with the cattle in good shape. But the price for cattle is down, so I ain't gonna give you that bonus." He paused again to witness the looks of shock and disappointment, but unable to play the joke out any further, he cracked, "I'm just joshin' ya. I got top dollar for the cattle, but you oughta see the look on your faces." The silence that had descended upon the drovers immediately erupted into a burst of cackling relief. "Like I said, you can each pick one horse outta this bunch in the corral, too. Now, who's first?"

"I reckon I am," Smoky Lewis volunteered, and stepped forward. The cook on the drive, Smoky owned his chuck wagon and the team of horses that pulled it. He had a separate arrangement with Oscar, since he had come along as an independent contractor to do the cooking. "You might not really be japin', so I'll get my money before you run out."

His remark, made in jest, brought a few chuckles from the other men. Oscar Bradley was a fair man. Each of his drovers knew that he would lose money on the sale of the cattle before he would go back on his word to them. Their only regret was the fact that this was Oscar's last drive.

One by one, the men stepped up to receive their pay. Oscar marked each man's name off in his notebook with his pencil and shook the man's hand. He paused briefly when the Cross brothers stepped up. Billy, the younger, was first. He and his brother, Logan, had been working for Oscar since they were teenage boys, and they had proven to be his most dependable drovers.

"I'm sorry I don't have something else for you fellers, but like I told you, I'm headin' back to Omaha to sit in a rockin' chair on my daughter's front porch. I know I'd sure as hell give you a good recommendation, if anybody was to ask me."

"Thanks, Oscar," Logan replied.

"What are you plannin' to do, go back to Ogallala with the rest of the boys?" Oscar asked.

"I reckon so," Logan said. "We ain't talked about doin' anything else."

"Except gettin' a drink of whiskey first thing," Billy

piped up. "That's about as long as I wanna stay around this place."

He and Logan had already decided that there was no future for them in Fort Pierre. It seemed the only sensible thing for them to do was to return to Ogallala with the others in hopes of signing on with another cattleman. Herding cattle was all they knew.

"Hang around till I get everybody paid," Oscar said. "There's a little somethin' I'd like to run by you."

Billy glanced at his brother, and Logan responded with a shrug. "Sure thing, Oscar," Logan said. "I'm gonna go throw my saddle on that flea-bitten gray standin' over by the fence before somebody else has the same idea." The gray had been his favorite and the one that he had most often ridden. It was the only one he had named, calling it Pepper. Having already set his sights on a buckskin, Billy followed him.

After every man had selected a horse and saddled it, Smoky Lewis motioned to Logan and said, "We're goin' over to the Cattleman's Saloon. You and Billy comin'?"

"You go ahead," Logan said. "We'll be along."

When the others had gone, Oscar put his notebook away and picked up his leather bag. "I was talkin' to a feller at the cattle sale, and he said he was lookin' to hire a couple of men to help him drive some horses over to Sturgis in the Black Hills. He's got two men who work for him, but he could use a couple more, since he wound up buyin' more than he planned." Oscar smiled and winked. "I sold him the rest of the horses here in the corral at such a good price he couldn't pass it up." He paused for their reaction before continuing. "Anyway, I told him I knew two good men who might be interested. Whaddaya think? You wanna drive some horses over to the Black Hills? There's a helluva lot goin' on up that way ever since the government opened the hills up for prospectors. This feller said there's a heap of travel on the roads between here and Sturgis—mule trains, bull trains, wagons, and everything else that rolls or trots. Might be somethin' else over that way for you boys."

As usual, Billy looked at his older brother for his reaction. "How long a drive would it be?" Logan asked.

"He said it's about a hundred and fifty miles from here," Oscar said. "It'd take a week or more, I expect. I told him I'd see if you were interested."

Again, looking to Logan for his opinion, Billy shrugged and joked, "I don't recollect any appointments we've got. Whadda you think, Logan?"

"Wouldn't hurt to talk to the man," Logan replied. "Where do we find him?"

"He said he'll be in O'Malley's place in about an hour from now. It's that little saloon down the street from the hotel. His name's Matt Morrison—seems like a reasonable feller."

"Okay, we'll go talk to him," Logan said. "That all right with you?" he asked Billy. When his brother shrugged indifferently, he turned back to Bradley. "Much obliged, Oscar. We appreciate it." They shook hands again, and then he and Billy climbed into their saddles.

Oscar stood there and watched them as they rode off toward the town of Fort Pierre. *I wish I was as young as those two,* he thought. *I'd ride to the Black Hills with them.*

Fort Pierre was settled on the west bank of the Missouri River, on a level plain that provided easy access to the river. It was a pleasant setting for a town, but it held no attraction for the Cross brothers. They rode past the Cattleman's Saloon, even though there was plenty of time to have a drink or two with the rest of Oscar's crew before Mr. Morrison was supposed to be at O'Malley's. They both agreed that it might cause some resentment if the others found out that Oscar had favored them with his recommendation.

There were a few horses tied up in front of O'Malley's, though not as many as those at the larger saloon's hitching rail. Dismounting, they pulled their rifles from the saddle slings and walked in the door. They paused to let their eyes adjust to the darkness of the room, a sharp contrast to the bright summer sunshine outside. After a moment, they started toward a table against the opposite wall, thinking it a good place to watch the door and spot Morrison when he walked in.

They had taken no more than a few steps when they were stopped by the bartender. "Howdy, gents," he greeted them cordially. "If you don't mind, I'd appreciate it if you'd leave those rifles on that table by the door." When both men balked for a second, he continued. "I reckon you fellers ain't ever been in here before. We ask every customer to do the same." He smiled then to show he meant nothing personal.

Logan looked back toward the door. Like his brother, he hadn't noticed the table with half a dozen pistols on it. "Sure," he said, "seems like a good idea." He and Billy went back and propped their rifles against the table and laid their pistols on top. Then they proceeded toward the table they had selected.

"What's your poison?" Roy, the bartender, asked as they passed by the bar.

"Whiskey," Billy answered. "Just whatever you got—

rye, if I've got a choice." Neither he nor Logan was a heavy drinker, so it really didn't matter.

"I've got rye," Roy said. "And I've also got some smooth Kentucky bourbon, if you'd rather have it."

"Which is the cheapest?" Logan asked.

"Rye," Roy said.

"Then we'll have that, and two glasses of beer to chase it," Logan said, and stopped to wait for it while Billy continued to the table.

"Well, here's to another cattle drive behind us," Logan said after they were seated. He raised his shot glass in a toast. Billy raised his glass to meet it, and they tossed the fiery whiskey down.

"Whew!" Billy coughed. "That stuff burns all the way down."

Logan laughed. "It makes a difference when it's been a long time between drinks."

Working slowly on the beer, they looked around them at the sparse crowd in the saloon. Only three other tables were occupied. And of the three, only one had more than two men quietly enjoying an afternoon drink of whiskey. That table, back in a corner of the room, was occupied by three men and a woman. The two brothers had sat there for only a few minutes before the woman got up to take an empty bottle to the bar to exchange for a full one.

On her way past them, she openly eyed the two strangers, and on her way back, she favored Billy with a smile. It didn't surprise Logan. His younger brother had been blessed with the good looks of his mother, while Logan seemed to have inherited the brawn and strength of his father. Though, at times, he wasn't sure if Billy's handsome features might better be called a curse. The thought had no sooner occurred to him than he began to hear a raising of the voices at the corner table.

He turned to Billy and asked, "You smiled back at her, didn't you?"

"I don't know. I mighta," Billy answered. "Why?"

Logan gave his younger brother a tired sigh. "That's why," he said when the conversation at the corner table suddenly escalated into a loud argument.

"You don't own me!" the woman exclaimed indignantly, and rose to her feet.

"Set your ass back down!" one of the men demanded. "Countin' all the whiskey you drank, I sure as hell made a down payment on you." His remark brought a laugh from his two companions, who seemed to be enjoying the spat between the two.

"I'll set my ass where I damn well please," the woman replied. A large-framed, long-legged woman, with many miles etched into her not unpleasant face, she seemed capable of handling her rough company. "I've wasted enough time on you and your friends. You coulda got drunk without me, if that's all you were interested in."

"Set down!" the man demanded again, and grabbed her wrist.

Logan glanced at the bartender. Seeing that he was now aware of the potential trouble brewing at the corner table, Logan was satisfied that the bartender would handle the situation before it became violent. As he had figured, Roy walked back to the table where the woman was still standing defiantly before the three men.

"Hey, fellers," he began, "ain't no need to get your backs up. Gracie didn't mean nothin' by it. Right, Gracie?" Gracie didn't answer. She just continued to glare at the belligerent bully holding her wrist. Since Gracie was obviously not inclined to apologize, Roy attempted to appease the quarrelsome brute. "Let her go and we'll have the next round on the house. Whaddaya say?"

"I ain't takin' no sass from a broken-down old whore," the bully replied. He looked back at the woman and said, "I told you to set down." To enforce the order, he attempted to pull her down on the chair, but she fought against his efforts. The ensuing struggle knocked the chair over and landed Gracie on the floor, her wrist still captured in the brute's hand.

"Mister," Roy said. "I'm gonna have to ask you and your friends to leave now. I think you've had enough."

Fully agitated at that point, the bully clamped down as tight as he could on the woman's wrist while she strained to free herself. "I'll leave when I'm ready to leave," he roared, then threatened, "How'd you like it if I tore this whole damn place down?"

"Wouldn't like it," Roy replied.

To this point, the few other patrons of the saloon had watched in silence. Seeing that things had seemingly gotten out of hand, two of the men got up and made a hasty retreat out the door. "Damn," Logan cursed softly when it became obvious that Roy's efforts to defuse a situation already gone bad were not going to succeed, for Logan had no desire to get involved in the altercation. "You had to smile at her," he said wearily aside to Billy.

"Hell, I didn't know," Billy replied lamely.

By now, Gracie was desperate to free herself from the brute's clutches. When her struggles proved useless, she resorted to attacking his arm with her fingernails. "Yow!" her captor roared in pain, and struck her roughly with a backhand across her face.

That was as much as the Cross brothers could tolerate. Logan was the first to move. "That's far enough," he stated emphatically as he rose to his feet. "Billy, go over there by the door and take care of those weapons." He walked over to the corner table to confront the troublemakers. "All right, the man here asked you politely to get outta his saloon. Now I'm tellin' you that it's time for you to turn the lady loose and do what he says."

His statement was enough to cause the bully to release his hold on Gracie, but he got to his feet and kicked his chair back. "And just who do you think you are, big mouth?"

"I'm the feller who's gonna whip your ass if you don't get outta here like I said," Logan said.

"Huh," the brute snorted defiantly, "you gonna whip all three of us?"

"If I have to," Logan replied calmly. His assessment of the trio told him that they all appeared too drunk to put up much of a fight—that, and the fact that the man's two companions did not seem overly enthusiastic about joining in. And he was not discounting Billy's help after his brother finished emptying all the cartridges out of the weapons on the table by the door.

"He's talkin' mighty big, ain't he, boys?" the bully snarled with a sneer. "Let's see if he can back it up." He shoved Gracie's chair aside and stepped out in front of the table, only then aware of the effect of the whiskey he had consumed. Spreading his feet wide in an effort to steady himself, he took a wild swing at Logan, missing by a mile.

Anticipating such a move, Logan ducked down and answered with a hard uppercut under the brute's chin, which caused him to stagger backward onto the table.

Woozy from the uppercut, he managed to push himself up from the table only to meet a hard right hand flush on his nose that drove him down on the floor. The back of his head banged against the edge of the table as he went down, knocking him senseless.

With his adversary flat on the floor, Logan turned to face the man's companions. With a glance at the menacing figure before them, and another at his brother coming toward them now, carrying a rifle in each hand, their decision was simple. "We ain't got no quarrel with you, mister. Jake's the one with the problem."

Logan, still in position to attack, took a step back. "Well, get Jake outta here, and go sober up."

He took the Winchester Billy handed him and stood aside to give the two men room to drag their partner toward the door. Billy followed them and watched while one of the men settled up with the bartender. Then they picked up their empty guns and helped Jake outside. Billy remained in the doorway to make sure they got on their horses and left.

"Are you all right, ma'am?" Logan asked Gracie as she gingerly touched her cheek with her fingertips.

"Now, that's gonna be a pretty bruise," she complained, her face flushed with anger. "Yeah," she said. "I've had worse than that." Realizing then that she owed him a word of thanks, she said, "I appreciate you and your friend stepping in to help me." She managed a painful grin as she felt her face again and added, "It'da been even better if you'da stepped in a minute sooner."

"Sorry," Logan said.

"Least I can do is give you and your friend a free ride," Gracie said.

"Well, now, that's mighty sportin' of you, ma'am,"

Logan quickly replied. "And I've got to say that it's a temptin' thing to think about. But I'm here to meet a man about a job, so I'll have to take care of that. I truly wanna thank you for the offer, though."

"What about your friend?" Gracie asked, actually more interested in the tall, sandy-haired young man.

Logan smiled. "I reckon you'd have to ask him. He ain't my friend, though. He's my brother."

"Oh," Gracie responded. She shot another glance in Billy's direction. Without thinking first, she blurted, "You sure you had the same daddy?"

Logan couldn't help laughing. "You ain't the first to ask me that."

Roy, who had been standing there listening to the conversation between the husky stranger and the prostitute, was prompted to remark, "Gracie, you ain't got a lick of sense."

Realizing then how unkind her words must have sounded, she tried to make amends. "I hope you didn't think I thought you weren't handsome, too," she sputtered, causing Logan to laugh again.

"Think nothin' of it," he said. "Billy always was the pretty one. I'm the one with the brains."

Gracie turned her attention toward Billy, and Roy took the opportunity to thank Logan for ridding him of the three drifters. "You'd best be careful," he warned. "They came in here a couple of days ago. I never saw 'em before that, and I just don't like the look of 'em. That one you had the fight with especially. He looks like he's just got a natural mean streak."

"I wouldn't doubt it," Logan said, "but I don't plan to stay in town long enough to have another go-round with him."

Two men seated at a table on the other side of the

room got up from their chairs. They had sat, silently watching the altercation, waiting until the fight was over. One of them, a man of slightly more than average height and slender build, walked up to Logan. "Is your name Cross?" he asked.

Surprised, Logan said that it was. "Yes, sir, I'm Logan Cross."

"I was pretty sure that you were. I'm Matt Morrison. Oscar Bradley said he'd send you over to talk to me about helpin' me move some horses to Sturgis."

"Yes, sir," Logan said, somewhat taken by surprise, since Oscar had told him it would be an hour before he could expect to meet Morrison. "I'm sorry you had to see that little scrap we just had with those fellers. Me and Billy ain't normally troublemakers."

Morrison smiled. "To the contrary, seein' how you handled that son of a bitch made me sure I wanted to hire you and your brother. Tell you the truth, I got here early so I could look you and your brother over before we talked." He turned to a gray-haired man behind him. "This is Red Whaley. I reckon you'd call him my foreman. He's been working for me for so long I don't know what his job is."

Red smiled at his boss's attempt at humor. "Logan," he said and extended his hand.

Billy joined them and the introductions were repeated. Morrison got down to business then and made his proposition. "I'll pay you three dollars a day, each, for eight days' work. It shouldn't take longer than that to make the drive. Whaddaya say?"

"What about grub?" Logan asked.

"We ain't got a chuck wagon," Morrison said, "so you'll provide your own grub."

Logan glanced at Billy for his reaction, knowing

already what it would be. Compared to their usual pay while working for Oscar Bradley, Morrison's offer was almost a month's pay for eight days' work. And they would have to feed themselves whether they took the job or not. Since leaving Oscar's employ, they were drifting anyway, so he said, "Looks like you've got yourself a couple of hands."

"Good," Morrison said. "Let's sit down and have a drink on it and I'll tell you all you need to know." He went on to explain that he had come to Fort Pierre to pick up twenty horses, which he thought he and his two men could manage. But thanks to Oscar Bradley's ridiculous offer, he found himself the owner of over twice that number. After examining the remuda, he decided the deal was too good to pass up, but he felt more comfortable with a little more help.

Before they had finished their drinks, Morrison's other man joined them. "They're all bunched up in that lower corral," he said to Morrison as he walked up to the table. "We'll be ready to push 'em out in the mornin'."

"This here's Percy Walker," Morrison said. "Percy, say howdy to Logan and Billy Cross. They're gonna help us take those horses home."

"Glad to meet you, boys," Percy said with a cordial grin. "I could handle 'em all by myself, but I'm always glad to have a little help." He pulled a chair over from another table and pushed in beside Red. "Move over, old man, and pass me that bottle."

"Why, I didn't know you was a drinkin' man," Red joked. He looked at Logan and said, "Boss forgot to tell you that Percy's so full of hot air and horse shit that we have to tie him down in the saddle to keep him from floatin' off." Red's remark brought a chuckle from Percy.

Logan and Billy could see right away that they were going to fit in just fine.

"Tell you what, fellers," Morrison said, "meet us over at the hotel after you've got your supplies and possibles ready to ride, and I'll spring for supper. About five o'clock, all right?"

"Yes, sir," Billy said. "That suits me." He winked at his brother, already thinking that by the end of this short drive, Morrison would possibly offer them permanent employment. Logan smiled and nodded.

"Well, I reckon we'll see you at suppertime," Logan said, getting to his feet. "Come on, Billy, we need to buy a little grub to take us to . . ." He paused to ask Morrison, "Where'd you say we were goin'?"

"Sturgis," Morrison said.

"Right. Come on, Billy." They left their three new partners and headed for the door.

"Much obliged," Roy, the bartender, said as they passed by the bar. Both brothers nodded in reply.

With Billy following, Logan stepped out the door onto the small platform of planks that served as a porch. He paused to stretch his arms in an effort to ease a stiffness in his back, the result of his brief tussle with the brute called Jake, he supposed. His arms were stretched up over his head when he was suddenly knocked off his feet by a driving tackle by Billy that sent them both sprawling. A moment later, he heard the rifle shot that sent a slug whistling over their heads.

"Son of a . . . ," he blurted, cocking his rifle as he rolled over behind the low porch. "You see him?"

"Up the street," Billy exclaimed, "by the stables!"

It was pure luck that he had happened to glance in that direction, and his lightning-fast reflexes might have saved his brother. The bushwhacker had time for one more shot before both Billy and Logan were able to bring their rifles to bear on the corral, but he stepped behind the corner post in time to keep from being hit by the slugs that tore into it.

"He's runnin'!" Billy cried when he got a glimpse of the shooter through the rails of the corral. Both men scrambled to their feet and ran across the street to take cover in the doorways of the few buildings between them and the stables, dodging the few people scurrying for safety.

Running from building to building, they made their way up the street as quickly as possible. While it had been impossible to identify their assailant in the short time Billy had to see him, there was little doubt who he was. They had to assume that Jake's two friends were in on the attempt and would have to be dealt with as well.

When they reached the hotel, which was the last building before the stables, they stopped to decide how to proceed.

"Front or back?" Billy asked, for they figured the three had probably taken cover in the stables.

"I'll take the front," Logan said, thinking the gunmen would be expecting them to come in that way, and he preferred to take that risk. Giving Billy no time to argue, he said, "Let's look out we don't shoot each other!"

He took off at a sprint for the front door of the stables, his rifle cocked and ready to fire. Billy stepped out of the hotel doorway and ran down the alley between it and the stables.

None too anxious to go charging into the front door of the stables, Logan pulled up before the door and flattened himself against the wall. He hoped the three men had not had the opportunity to sober up. He had to assume they were still a little drunk to have taken a shot at him in broad daylight in the middle of town.

Without knowing where Billy was positioned, he eased up to the crack between the door and the frame and peeked in. In contrast to the bright sunlight outside, his eyes didn't focus at once, but just in time to jerk his head back from the crack before a chunk of the door went flying. Two more shots ripped into the door before he heard Billy's Winchester speak from the rear of the stables. Seconds after, he was surprised by the three men charging out of the stables at a gallop, lying low on their horses' necks. Straight across the street they fled, between the harness shop and dry goods store, intent upon riding behind the stores for protection.

Knowing that he had time to knock at least one of the assassins out of the saddle, Logan pulled his rifle to his shoulder and took aim, but he did not pull the trigger. As he had rested the front sight on the departing rider, a woman with a small child suddenly appeared in the frame, causing him to hesitate. Terrified by the three horses suddenly charging toward her, she ran, pulling the child, across the alley, barely escaping a trampling under their hooves. At first alarmed that he had almost endangered the woman and her child, his next emotion was anger for the missed opportunity to dispose of one of the assailants who had sought to murder him. He was still standing there when Billy ran out of the stable.

"You all right?" Billy asked, relieved to see Logan standing there apparently unharmed. "I heard them shootin' at you, and they were already on their horses by the time I crawled in a back window. I got off a couple of shots, but I don't think I hit anybody. I didn't have time to get in a good spot to shoot. I was worried about you, 'cause I didn't think I heard you shoot."

"I didn't," Logan said, then explained the circumstances that prevented him from taking a shot. "By the time the woman got out of the way, they were behind the buildings and gone." He was about to further express his regrets when he and Billy were joined by the owner of the stables. "Damn," Logan said in surprise, "where'd you come from?"

"I was holed up in the tack room," the man said as he stood staring toward the end of the street. "That right there is why I ask for payment in advance. Those fellers got away from here in one big hurry."

"I reckon," Logan replied.

"Well, I reckon that's that," Billy said. "I expect that's the last we'll see of them." There was no thought on either man's part to go after the three dry gulchers. Their horses were at the far end of the street.

"I think you're right," Logan said. "At least neither of us got shot, so I reckon we'll just be glad we were lucky." He thought of the anger he had felt when he had to pass up an easy shot, but after thinking about it, he decided it was just as well. He had never shot a man. Maybe it was better that he still hadn't. "Let's go get the horses. We've got a few things to pick up at the store if we're gonna have anything to eat for the next week."

Now that the danger was over, Billy returned to character. "Since Morrison's payin' for supper, we'd best eat enough to take care of the first couple of days."

"Maybe so," Logan said. "And one other thing. Next time, don't smile at a woman when she's with another feller."

"I'll try," Billy replied with a grin, "but it's a natural reaction."

Chapter 2

It seemed a good bet that the three drifters were gone for good from Fort Pierre. Logan and Billy ate their fill at supper while answering all the questions regarding the shooting incident.

"I hope I ain't made a mistake hirin' you boys on," Matt Morrison said in jest. "You might have a natural habit of drawin' trouble."

"Just as long as you keep your shootin' parties private," Percy chimed in, "it'll give the rest of us somethin' to watch. It gets kinda dull just herdin' horses."

"I'll throw a sack over Billy's head," Logan joked. "That oughta help."

"I know how you feel, Billy," Percy said. "I've always had the same trouble with women." His comment brought a laugh, especially from Red. Percy had not been gifted with a handsome package to present to the world. Thin as a knife blade, with an oversized hawk nose and ears too large for his small head—it was a blessing that he had been compensated with a healthy sense of humor.

"Helluva thing, though," Morrison said. "Come into town for the first time and somebody takes a shot atcha."

Logan shrugged. "Well, it wouldn't have happened if I hadn't stuck my nose into that little spat that fellow was havin' with the woman." He paused to give it a thought. "But if I hadn't, Billy would have, so I reckon there was no way to avoid it."

The suppertime conversation went on for quite some time with the two brothers feeling right at home with their new companions. Afterward, they said good night and retired to the stables to sleep with their horses, feeling no need to spend the money for a hotel room.

At sunup the next morning they were saddled up and waiting for the others by the corral, which pleased Morrison, although he made no comment to that effect. When all were ready, he opened the corral gate and began the drive to Sturgis, leaving the little settlement of Fort Pierre still rousing itself from sleep.

They drove the herd of horses west, following an old buffalo trail long used by the Indians. Morrison told them that up until a year before, they had been warned not to use this, or several other trails, since they cut right across the Great Sioux Reservation. But in 'seventy-seven, the government opened the Black Hills to settlement and provided the funds for three wagon roads from the east.

"Most of the traffic is headed to Deadwood, up in the hills, since the gold strike. The Injuns don't like it too much, but they ain't able to do much about it since they got whipped by the army after Little Big Horn."

"So you don't expect any trouble from the Indians?" Logan asked.

"No, not no more," Morrison said. "Couple of years ago, though, I mighta needed twice as many men to make this drive."

Long before the first day was over, Morrison decided that Oscar Bradley's recommendation had been valid. He was well pleased with both of the Cross brothers' skill as wranglers, soon realizing that they knew how horses think.

As far as Logan and Billy were concerned, pushing a herd of horses was a relatively simple matter, much more so than herding cattle. Horses were basically animals of prey, so they gravitated to the herd where there was safety in numbers, and their natural reaction to danger was flight. There was a lot less tendency to wander off from the herd as strays, as cattle were prone to do. Horses also needed to graze every so often during a drive. Even so, Logan wondered why Morrison figured to take seven or eight days to travel one hundred and fifty miles. This was especially puzzling when he told them that he wanted to push the herd almost forty-five miles the first day in order to reach Plum Creek, the first good water.

"It's liable to be a long day," Logan said to Billy. That turned out to be the case, as they kept the horses moving most of the day over a wide, rolling prairie with only a weak stream here and there. At dark, when they finally reached Plum Creek, Morrison told them that he planned to stay there the next day to let the horses drink and graze. "Sounds like a good idea," Logan said. "I know Pepper will appreciate it." Logan was a sizable man, and halfway through the day's drive he had transferred his saddle to a sorrel to give Pepper a rest.

As Morrison had predicted, there was no sign of trouble on that first long day, and none on the following days as well. By the time they reached the Cheyenne River and followed it west, the two brothers had come to know their companions pretty well, and decided they could see themselves working for Morrison permanently if there was an offer. They drove the herd of horses onto the Lazy-M Ranch, just short of the foothills east of the dark, mysterious mountains on the horizon before them. It was easy to see how the Black Hills got their name. From a distance, they stood out in stark contrast to the prairie around them. Morrison explained that their dark color came from the ponderosa pines that covered almost all of the slopes.

Riding past scattered groups of cattle as they approached the ranch house, they saw a couple of Morrison's crew at a distance. They pulled up to wave when they spotted the herd of horses thundering onto the flat approach to the creek.

Matt Morrison had not wasted any money on an elegant ranch house, a testament to the fact that there were no wife and daughters to pacify. A bachelor all his life, he had built the house with logs snaked from the tree-covered hills close by. More attention was paid to the construction of the barn, and to a lesser degree, the bunkhouse. Red had told them that there had been a woman who cooked for him at one time, but he let her go, since he ate most of his meals with the men at the bunkhouse.

After the horses were turned out to graze by the creek, Morrison told the Cross brothers to follow him to the house where he would settle up with them.

"Well, boys," Morrison began. "You fellers did a right good job for me, and I'm gonna pay you for eight days, like we agreed on, even though it didn't take us that long."

He went into another room where he had an iron safe, leaving Logan and Billy to look at each other in speculation of perhaps a permanent job offer. In a short time, Morrison returned and counted out their pay.

When that was done, he said, "I ain't hirin' right now. I've got a full crew of good cowhands. But I expect I'll be needin' some extra help in the fall, so if you boys are still around and lookin' for work, come see me."

Without showing his disappointment, Logan replied, "We'll do that. Thank you very much. We ain't sure we'll be here, but we might."

"Fine. You're good men, and you know your business, so I'm sure I'll probably have a place for you. Now, if you're in a hurry to spend that money, the town of Sturgis is that way." He pointed to the northwest. "It's a right lively little town. When I first brought my cattle in here, they called it Scooptown. That's because all the folks workin' for the army at Fort Meade used to go there to scoop up the money the army was payin'. That warn't no name for a town, so when more folks moved in, and it looked like it was gonna stick, they called it Sturgis for some officer in the army. If you ain't in a hurry to go into town, why don't you stay here long enough to get some supper with us before you take off?"

Billy spoke up right away. "I'll never turn down an offer for supper."

"Hell, there ain't no need to hurry off," Morrison said. "Stay tonight and leave in the mornin'. I'm sure there's room in the bunkhouse."

"'Preciate it," Logan said. "We'll take you up on that."

"I'll see you down there for supper, then," Morrison said, and walked to the door with them.

Very much at home in a bunkhouse, Logan and Billy sat outside after supper to swap yarns with Morrison's ranch hands. Having worked for Oscar Bradley ever since they were boys, they found it a strange feeling to be without a job in the middle of summer. There were some suggestions from the other men for ranches they might try out toward Bear Butte.

Logan, having always been the more practical of the two brothers, found this an obvious plan of action. But he had to contend with Billy's natural sense of adventure, so they were not in complete agreement on what they should do at this point. For the first time since they had started working, they found themselves free of obligations, and with a little money set aside at that. "We could afford to drift for a while and take the opportunity to see something besides the rear end of a cow," Billy insisted. "Considering the spot we landed in, why don't we go on and follow the crowd of folks pouring into Deadwood? It'd be like going to the circus."

Logan had to laugh. "Yeah, I expect it would," he allowed, "just like a circus."

Unlike his adventurous brother, he was more interested in finding permanent employment with one of the ranches raising beef to feed the miners and the army.

"Hell," Billy went on, "I'd like to try my hand at pannin' for gold. We might strike it rich, like some of those other folks—give up this business of punchin' cows." He looked at Logan expectantly. "That'ud be something, wouldn't it? Just sittin' around countin' our money."

Logan shook his head, bewildered. Sometimes he felt like a father to his younger brother. It had been his lot, he supposed, since their father died when both boys were not yet in their teens. Their mother followed soon after, for some reason Logan never understood. Maybe she just wasn't up to raising two rambunctious boys on her own. If he was in fact playing the role of father, however, he wasn't a very firm one, because he found it difficult to discourage Billy's fantasies.

"Whaddaya say?" Billy pressed. "Let's just go up there and see what it's all about."

"All right," Logan said, finally caving in, "if you ain't gonna be able to stand it unless you see for yourself."

"Hot damn!" Billy exclaimed excitedly. "I knew you couldn't pass up the opportunity."

When they expressed their intentions to Red and Percy, Percy tried to talk them out of it. "I don't know how much money you boys have got, but I'll guarantee you it won't last long in Deadwood. You'd be better off if you can find work at one of the bigger ranches up toward Belle Fourche. That's a little north of the hills. Most of the folks movin' into Deadwood and Lead, and those other towns now, are just figurin' on makin' a livin' offa the miners. They ain't diggin' for gold."

"I expect you're right," Logan said. "But some fellows have always gotta go see the elephant." He nodded toward Billy, who met his gesture with a satisfied grin. "So I reckon that's what we're gonna do."

"Well, I wish you fellers luck," Percy said. "I kinda hope we'll see you back here in the fall."

Although this was their first time in the Black Hills, they had no trouble finding the way to Deadwood

Gulch. The road was clearly marked by the ruts of the many wagon and mule trains that had plodded along through the passes. Especially hard on the trail were the bull trains—heavy wagons—pulled by ten or twelve yoke of oxen. Logan and Billy encountered many spots in the road that were so deep in gumbo mud that they were almost impassable for a farm wagon. On horseback, leading the one packhorse they had bought from Morrison, the trail was of no concern to them.

Their first glimpse of Deadwood Gulch was from the top of a steep hill. A winding road led down into the lower end of the gulch, which appeared to be one solid line of tents and shacks of various sizes and shapes. The gulch was filled with people, horses, mules, oxen, and wagons. From the hilltop, it reminded Logan of a bed of maggots unearthed by the pawing of a horse's hoof. "Well, there's your circus," he said sarcastically.

"Looks like they ain't gonna run short of people," Billy commented in return.

Assuming they had found Deadwood, they rode down the road to the bottom and walked their horses along the crowded street. It seemed that every other building was a saloon, but in between there were stores of all kinds. The gulch itself was a continuous string of placer mining claims. There didn't appear to be a lineal foot that wasn't claimed. They pulled up before a store that displayed a sign that proclaimed WHITEY'S—EATS. "Let's see if we can buy a cup of coffee and something to eat, and maybe some information," Logan suggested.

There were a few customers seated on stools along a long shelflike table attached to the wall, so Logan and Billy took a seat. The proprietor, a thin, bald man, wearing a dirty white apron, called out to them from behind a counter that separated the dining area from the cook stove, "Whaddleya have, fellers?"

"Whaddaya got?" Billy shot back.

"Stew beef and beans, or beans and stew beef. Take your pick." The wide grin on his face told them that he was joking with them.

"Have you got some coffee to go with it?" Logan asked.

"I sure do," he replied. "You fellers ain't ever been in here before, have you? I just cook up a couple of things every day, and not the same things, neither. Today, I've got stew beef and beans, and bacon and potatoes. And you can have biscuits with either one. It ain't as fancy as the hotel dining room, but it's just as fillin' and a helluva lot cheaper."

"Sounds like what we're lookin' for," Billy said with a chuckle. "I'll go with the beef and beans." Logan ordered the same.

The man served up two plates and placed them on the counter. Then he poured two cups of coffee from a large gray pot sitting on the stove and stood there waiting. When they walked over to get their dinner, he said, "That'll be two bucks apiece."

"Damn," Billy replied, "I thought you said it was cheaper than the hotel."

The man laughed. "I can see you boys ain't ever et in the hotel."

"That's a fact," Billy said. "We just rode into town about fifteen minutes ago."

"I figured as much. My name's Whitey, least that's what ever'body calls me. After you look around a little bit, you'll see my prices are pretty good."

Logan couldn't help recalling Percy's prediction that their money wouldn't last very long in Deadwood. He took a tentative sip of the coffee, then shrugged. "I've had worse," he declared as he picked up his plate. Before turning to follow Billy back to the table, he asked, "This is Deadwood, right?"

"No," Whitey answered. "This is Montana City. You're in Deadwood Gulch, all right, but there's four different towns in the gulch. Deadwood's on the other side of Elizabeth Town toward the upper end of the gulch. You lookin' for somebody or some place in particular?"

"Nope," Logan said, "just lookin'." He walked back to join Billy.

"It ain't bad grub," Billy said when Logan sat down next to him. "But if everything is as expensive as this, I expect we'll need to go huntin'. I'll bet there's a lot of deer back in these hills."

"I wouldn't be surprised," Logan said. "I figured we'd be up in the hills to make camp anyway. Damned if I wanna spend all my money in a hotel."

"You're right about that," Billy said. "Besides, we need to find us a good spot on a little creek somewhere and see if we can turn up a little gold, like the rest of these miners."

"Right," Logan said, still skeptical. "Just look around you at all the fancy rich gentlemen."

Billy didn't bother to glance at the rough assortment of men hunched over Whitey's cooking. If either of them had turned to take a hard look at the shaggy-bearded man at the end of the long shelf, he might have paused to wonder if he had seen him somewhere before. But Tom Lacey was certain he had seen the two brothers before, and he knew where, so he decided it best to stay crouched over his dinner and turn his back toward them lest they recall.

Logan had convinced his brother that it would be a

good idea to try to learn a little bit about panning for gold before they wasted their time sifting through the sand and gravel of a streambed.

"We don't even know which streams are likely prospects," he said. "We do know that there ain't nothing left in this gulch. Our best bet is to do like the prospectors workin' some of the streams comin' down from these mountains. So I think we'd do well to scout around in the mountains and see who's doin' what. Maybe that'll give us an idea of where to look and what kind of tools we'll need. Whaddaya think? That'd be better than thrashin' around like a couple of lunatics, wouldn't it?"

"I expect you're right," Billy agreed. "We'll look the country over and find us a good stream." As usual, Billy was cheerfully optimistic about their chances to strike it rich.

When they got up to leave, Whitey stopped them before they reached the door. "I couldn't help hearin' what you boys were talkin' about," he said. "You didn't ask for my advice, but I'm offerin' it anyway. You look like decent young men. Brothers, ain'cha?"

"That's right," Billy replied. "How'd you know that?"

"I could just tell," Whitey said. "But here's what I wanna tell you. The only folks makin' any money in the gulch right now are the miners who staked out the first claims and the business folks like me that are sellin' 'em what they need. You're workin' on the right idea, though, sluicin' the streams coming down some of these mountains. If you ain't got somewhere else in mind, I'll tell you this. There's been a couple of small strikes up Switchback Creek. I heard some fellers talkin' about it the other day. You might take a look up that way."

Logan studied the little man's face and decided that he was sincere in his advice. "Well, sir, we appreciate the tip. How would a fellow go about findin' Switch-back Creek?"

"Well, that is a problem," Whitey said, "seein' as how you boys ain't ever been here before." He scratched under his chin thoughtfully as he realized there was really no way he could give them directions. "It's about five or six miles west of the gulch here, runs down offa that tallest mountain over toward Spearfish Canyon. It's really more a stream than a crick. That's about the best I can tell you, I reckon." He threw his hands up, as if wondering why he even mentioned it.

"'Preciate it," Logan said again, wondering the same thing.

Outside, Billy laughed and said, "That was helpful as hell, wasn't it? Somewhere between here and Spearfish Canyon there's a mountain with no name that stands taller than the ones around it. Why, we oughta be able to find that blindfolded. Then all we gotta do is find which little ol' stream runnin' off it is Switchback Creek."

Logan laughed with him. "Hell, he was just tryin' to be helpful." He put his foot in the stirrup and climbed onto Pepper. "We need to get up out of this gulch anyway, and find us a place to camp. We might as well head west, like he said, and see what we find."

Holding the packhorse's lead rope, he started out toward a road snaking up the ridge west of the town. Billy stepped up into the saddle, wheeled the buckskin around, and loped after him.

Behind them, Tom Lacey stood just inside the door of Whitey's, watching them depart.

I swear, he thought. *Ain't Jake gonna be tickled to hear about this?*

He remained where he was, watching the two riders as they made their way through the busy street, until they had ridden about fifty yards from the diner. Only then did he step outside, untie his horse from the rail, and follow, being careful to keep a safe distance, so as not to be accidentally seen by the two brothers. He had no cause to worry because they never looked back, intent upon dodging a couple of mule trains blocking the street. He pulled up when he saw them take the narrow trail leading up toward the ridge, afraid that they might notice if he followed. He waited there until they disappeared over the top of the hill before proceeding up after them.

Upon reaching the crest, he spotted them still following the trail toward the mountains to the west. That was as far as he decided to go, anxious now to get back to the Lucky Dollar Saloon to tell Jake whom he had seen.

Big Jake Morgan sat with Everett Pierce near the back of the Lucky Dollar, a half-empty bottle of whiskey on the table between them. He was in a foul mood, because of his poor luck in a poker game that had concluded a short time before. It didn't help that he was already impatient for the arrival of his brother. Quincy and the rest of the boys were supposed to meet him sometime within a day or two, and Jake wasn't good at waiting. Quincy was his older brother, and there was no question that he called all the shots.

Quincy, he thought. *Things are going to be mighty different when he gets here. We're going to eat high on the hog then.*

His brother was scheduled to be released from the Wyoming Territorial Prison on the first of the month.

He sent word to Jake that he was going to get the old gang back together again. Most of them were already on their way to Laramie, to be on hand when he walked out a free man, after serving five years for an armed robbery. The thought made Jake laugh. He'd lost count of how many men Quincy had killed, but all they could charge him with was a bank holdup. The plan was to meet in Montana City sometime around the end of the month. Already, the last day of the month had passed with no sign of Quincy, and Jake was getting more and more antsy. His thoughts were interrupted when Everett said, "Yonder he comes."

Jake scowled when he saw Tom Lacey walk in the door of the saloon, and he wondered what Quincy would think of the two men he had picked up at Fort Pierre.

Lacey looked around the crowded barroom until he spied his two partners, then made his way directly toward them. "What are you grinnin' about?" Everett asked when he pulled out a chair and sat down. "I thought you was gonna go get somethin' to eat."

"I did," Lacey said, looking pleased with himself.

"I wish to hell I'd gone with you," Jake said. "I'da saved myself a lot of money."

"Didn't do no good in that poker game you and Everett was in, I expect," Lacey said, anxious to tell him what he had seen, but taking his time to savor the eruption that was sure to follow.

"Everett won a little money, but I didn't catch a decent card the whole game," Jake complained.

Lacey was unable to wipe the smile from his face as he proceeded to tell his news. "Well, I saw somethin' at Whitey's that might tickle you a little bit." He paused, waiting for Jake to respond.

After a few moments, Jake demanded impatiently, "Well, what, damn it?"

Anticipating the reaction he was sure to see, Lacey, still grinning, replied, "Remember that feller you had a little go-round with back at Fort Pierre, in O'Malley's Saloon?" He got the reaction he expected. The big man's eyes narrowed and he snorted angrily through his bruised and broken nose. "Yeah, you remember him," Lacey went on. "Well, I just saw him and that feller he was with—I think he's his brother—eatin' dinner at Whitey's place."

Jake almost came out of his chair. "Where? Is he still at Whitey's?"

"Nope," Lacey answered. "He left Whitey's and took that trail up beside the harness shop. I followed the two of 'em up the ridge to see which way they was headin'. Then I hightailed it back here. Figured you'd wanna know."

"That son of a bitch," Jake growled as he got up and kicked the chair out of his way. He paused then when the thought occurred to him. "Why the hell didn't you shoot the son of a bitch when you had the chance?"

Lacey shrugged. "I thought about it—I sure did—but I figured that was a score you wanted to settle yourself."

"I don't give a damn who shoots him," Jake declared, still on the verge of exploding. "I just want him dead. Him and his brother, too. He comes ridin' in here right under my nose, and you let him get away?"

"I know where he's headin'," Lacey was quick to explain. "He ain't goin' far. I could hear most of what they was talkin' to Whitey about, and it sounds to me like they was just gonna look for a place to camp up in the hills."

"You shoulda shot both of 'em while you had the

chance," Jake insisted. "There ain't no tellin' where they are now."

"Hell," Lacey pleaded, "I couldn't just gun 'em down right there in Whitey's. I'd be settin' in that little smokehouse they call a jail right now. Besides, I saw where they was headin'. We can find 'em."

"We're wastin' time," Jake said. "Quincy will be here in a day or two. I want this done before he gets here, so we're gonna go huntin' right now. Come on, it'll be dark in a couple of hours." He headed for the door.

"Hot damn," Everett exclaimed, winking at Lacey, "that sure beats hangin' around here."

He and Lacey were reluctant to complain about waiting around for the rest of the Morgan Gang, owing to Jake's violent temper, which had been honed to a sharper edge by the beating he had taken in Fort Pierre. Joining up with Jake was an opportunity for the two small-time claim jumpers to ride with a gang of stage robbers as successful as Quincy Morgan's.

Outside, Jake continued to fret over the time it was taking to get mounted and under way. When they got to the top of the ridge, he pulled up to let Lacey come up beside him.

"All right, where'd they go from here?"

Lacey assured him that Logan and Billy had continued to follow the trail across the ridge, evidently planning to follow it between the two mountains directly ahead of them.

Chapter 3

"It looks like somebody was tryin' to find a little gold here," Billy said as he walked the buckskin across the stream. "I reckon they didn't have much luck." It was obvious that the claim had been deserted for a good while.

"It's a good spot to make camp," Logan replied, "nice little stream to water the horses and a fair amount of grass on the other side." He dismounted and stood peering up the course of the stream. "Looks like there might be a waterfall higher up this mountain. I'll bet there's deer around here, too. Maybe not while there were folks here pannin' for gold, but this camp's been dead for at least a month. Deer might be comin' around again."

"Well, I wish one of 'em would come around right now," Billy said. "But I expect we'll be eatin' some more of that bacon we've been livin' on."

Logan laughed. "Don't tell me you've already forgotten that fancy dinin' room you had dinner in today."

He was actually partial to camping in this mountain country instead of taking a room in the fanciest of hotel rooms. Maybe it was just his nature. Or perhaps he was simply accustomed to sleeping out under the stars from the many years he had spent driving cattle.

And these Black Hills were so different from other mountain ranges. They seemed to be in sharp contrast to the stark rocky peaks of Wyoming. Even so, giant granite towers, rising from the slopes, were not an unusual sight. These mountains seemed to be more gently formed, and covered with trees, mostly pines, but occasionally intertwined with maple and some trees he could not identify.

At the moment, he was happy that he and Billy had decided to see the Black Hills. If it contented his younger brother to hunt for gold, then he was happy to give him the opportunity. It would also give him a chance to get to know these mysterious mountains while Billy fantasized about finding a fortune. He glanced at his brother, who was down on one knee beside the stream, peering into the clear water. He couldn't help laughing. "You see any gold on the bottom of that stream?"

"I'm not sure I'd know it if I did see some," Billy replied, knowing Logan was japing.

"Whaddaya say we pull the saddles offa these horses and get a fire started while we can still see?" Logan suggested. "Come to think of it, I'd like to climb up toward the top of this mountain to see if there is a waterfall a little higher up before it gets too dark. I ain't ever seen a waterfall that didn't attract a lot of game. You interested?"

"Not really," Billy said. "I'm more interested in gettin' the fire started and boilin' some coffee. You go on and I'll have some bacon for you to eat when you get back."

"Don't be surprised if I come back with something to cook besides bacon," Logan replied as he took his saddle off Pepper. He pulled his rifle from the saddle scabbard, turned to give his brother a grin, then started up through the trees beside the stream.

Billy turned his head to watch his brother until he disappeared in the fading light filtering through the pines. He was pleased that he had persuaded Logan to come to the Black Hills if only to give him the opportunity to explore them. That was the kind of thing that brought Logan pleasure.

The climb up the mountain took longer than Logan had anticipated. There was a waterfall, as he had suspected, although not as large as he had hoped. Still, it was a fascinating sight, even in the fading light.

Curious then to see the source of the water, he went around the falls and climbed up closer to the top of the mountain, where he discovered a small lake. As the sun sank swiftly in the distance, he told himself he'd better mind his step descending back to the camp, for soon it might be very dark. He took just a few moments longer to look around him at the smaller peaks.

It was then that he heard the shots.

Far below him, they echoed among the rocks and trees, reverberating across the mountain slope. He was not certain how many, for they were too close together to tell. He felt his blood go cold as he was suddenly gripped by a numbing fear. He had to get to Billy! A sickening feeling of panic overcame him as he made his way back down the mountain, lurching and stumbling in his hurry.

Indians? Outlaws? He could only wonder.

The trip back down turned treacherous in the growing darkness and he crashed down upon his knees, only to get up and press on, ignoring the cuts and bruises he sustained from the rocky slope. The only thing that mattered was to get to Billy—as quickly as possible.

Because of the darkness, which now cloaked the forest in a heavy shroud, he was forced to make his way more carefully. When finally he approached the camp, he stopped to look around him before charging in recklessly. The fire was still burning, forming a rosy globe of light beside the stream, but there was no sign of Billy or anyone else. Then he realized that the horses were gone. The camp was deserted. He ran then, convinced that whoever had been there were now gone.

"Billy!" he called out as he neared the fire, but there was no answer. "Oh God, no!" he cried when he saw the body sprawled facedown at the edge of the firelight. "Oh God, no!"

Unmindful of anyone waiting in ambush, he rushed to his brother's side, praying that it was not Billy. He knew that it was, however, before he turned the body over to see the cold lifeless face, staring but not seeing. He had been shot three times in the back, which were probably the killing blows, and there were other bullet wounds in his legs and arms, which told Logan that he was used for target practice after he was dead. It appeared that he had been taken by surprise, and never had a chance to defend himself.

Devastated, Logan pulled the cold body up and hugged it close to him. Then unable to contain his grief, he cried out to God above.

"Why Billy? He never hurt anybody!" He rocked

the body gently as a father would a child, large tears rolling down his sun-bronzed face. "I should never have left you here alone," he wailed. "I should have stayed to make sure nothing like this could happen. I'm sorry, Billy. I'm so sorry."

He sat there near the edge of the stream for a long time, gently rocking his brother's body, before finally telling himself there were things to be done.

He had to dig a grave, but he had no tools to work with. Everything was gone. The people who had murdered his brother had taken the horses, saddles, packs, everything they owned. He was left with only his rifle and the cartridges that were loaded in the magazine— and his skinning knife, which would normally have been in its case on his cartridge belt. He had taken the belt off before he climbed up the mountain, but on second thought, he had drawn the knife out and stuck it in his belt. He had been joking about finding game at the waterfall but decided to take the knife in case he did. Determined to bury Billy, he resolved to dig the grave with the knife, since that and his hands were all he had.

He dug the grave, although it took most of the night. He had looked for the best spot to dig, where the dirt looked as yielding as he could find. Then he toiled away through the long, dark hours, his mind filled with Billy's life ever since their parents had died. Billy had told him not long ago that his big brother had always been there for him.

Well, he wasn't there for you on this night, Logan thought.

As the hours passed, and the work grew harder, his mind dwelled more on avenging his brother's death, and he soon swore an oath before God that he would not rest until he had killed the man or men who had murdered Billy. When finally he had dug the grave as deep as he thought he could with his knife and hands, he stood up to stretch his weary back.

The first light of dawn began to filter through the pine limbs, and he apologized once again. "It ain't as deep as I'd like, Billy, but at least it'll cover you up."

He laid his brother in the shallow grave as gently as he could. "I'm sorry I ain't got a blanket or something to cover you with," he said as he pulled the loose dirt over the body. Reluctant to pile dirt over Billy's face, he put his brother's hat over his face before covering it.

When he had piled all the dirt he had over the grave, he started carrying rocks, as big as he could lift, from the streambed. These he placed on top of the grave to keep predators from disturbing it. Finished, he sat down, exhausted, as the morning sun played shadows across his face.

He didn't know how long he had been asleep when he suddenly opened his eyes, awakened by the sun now high in the sky. He crawled over to the pool of water and took a long drink. His thoughts turned to his quest to find the people responsible for Billy's death. In the morning light, it was now possible to see the many tracks that told the story of what had happened there. After studying the campsite carefully, he could not be sure how many had attacked his brother, but he was sure there was more than one man. And while he had allowed for the possibility that they were Indians, he now discarded that idea, because all the horses were shod, and there were boot prints around the fire. He looked around the edges of the camp, but the killers had left nothing. He continued scouting the perimeter of the camp until he found what he was looking for, tracks of the horses where they had left the camp. He set out at once following the tracks.

The trail was not hard to follow. Logan figured there were at least six horses, and three of them were his and Billy's, leaving three the number of assailants. There could be four, he couldn't be sure, but at least three. He followed the tracks down the course of the stream until it reached the road he and Billy had taken from Montana City. A careful study of the hoofprints told him that the murderers had turned back toward the town. This was what he had hoped for. Had they turned the other way, it would have been a great deal harder to track them, especially if they had been intent upon disappearing in the mountains. He wasn't sure how long it would take him to get to Montana City on foot, but he hoped he could make it before dark.

As he followed the road at a steady pace, his mind was filled with thoughts of his brother and what his last moments must have been like. And he could not help continuing to blame himself for not taking care of him. There was nothing he could do to bring him back, but he swore to avenge him, even though there was no way doing that could balance the scales for the taking of one so carefree and optimistic.

"Bring that coffeepot over here," Jake yelled at Lyle Weaver, the bartender at the Lucky Dollar Saloon. He waited for Lyle to get to the table before continuing. "As much money as we're spendin' in here, I oughta get better service."

"Hell, you are gettin' good service," Lyle shot back, accustomed to verbal abuse from the likes of Jake Morgan. "You ain't seen me servin' coffee to nobody else, have you?"

"Don't get smart-mouth with me," Jake said, "or I'll take my money somewhere else to spend." He was feeling right pleased with himself, after last night's little adventure. He and his boys had extra money in their pockets, and he planned to live high on the hog until his brother, Quincy, showed up.

In addition to the money found in the saddlebags, he had sold the three horses, along with the saddles, to the owner of the stable that morning. He cut Everett and Lacey in for a share, but it still left him with plenty of extra money.

Aside from that, he was enjoying the accomplishment of having settled the score with the jasper who broke his nose. The one who had actually inflicted the damage was not in the camp when he struck, but he had killed his brother and taken everything in the camp. He decided that that was satisfaction enough for his broken nose. He might have looked around that mountain a little longer for the other one, but he had evidently been hiding, and was likely running.

He's gonna have a helluva time of it, though, he thought, smiling, *since I got everything he owns.*

Everett Pierce watched while Lyle filled all three cups, and waited until he left before he commented, "You sure look like you're feelin' mighty perky this mornin', Jake." He turned to Lacey and asked, "Don't he, Tom?"

"Hell, why not?" Lacey replied. "Little extra money in your pocket'll do that every time. Ain't that right, Jake?"

"That's a fact," Jake said. "And you can get used to it, 'cause when Quincy and the rest of the boys get here, you'll see what it's like to do some real business. They've got one of those heavy reinforced stagecoaches full of gold leaving this gulch every week or so. And they're all hollerin', 'Here I am, Mr. Morgan, come and get it.'"

His remark brought chuckles from his two partners. "I'm feelin' lucky," Everett said. "I think I'll see if I can scare up a card game this afternoon. I've still got some winnin's from that game the other night, so I might as well play on the other feller's money."

"I'm up for a game," Lacey decided. "What about you, Jake? It's about time for that gambler you and Everett played with last time to show up, ain't it?"

"You don't have to worry about him," Jake said. "Just get out the cards and shuffle 'em. He'll show up before you can cut 'em."

Jake's comment was close to being accurate, because the professional gambler known as Harris showed up soon after the three gunmen started playing cards. The game went on for most of the afternoon. A second bottle of whiskey was ordered at about the same time a tired but determined man carrying a rifle walked up to the corral at the stables, down at the end of the street.

Seeing his master, Pepper came to the rail at once. Logan reached over and stroked the gray gelding on his face. In a few minutes, Billy's buckskin ambled over and stood beside Pepper. Relieved to find the horses, Logan knew that it would not likely be a simple thing to reclaim them. It was a matter now of finding everything else that was stolen along with the horses. He gave the buckskin a few seconds of attention, then started toward the stable door.

"Something I can help you with, mister?" Walt Bowen asked as he walked out to meet him.

"Yes, sir," Logan replied. "I came to pick up my horses."

"Your horses?" Walt responded. "I don't recall boardin' any horses for you."

"Well, I didn't ask you to, but you've got three of my horses in your corral, that gray, the buckskin, and that sorrel standin' near 'em. Whoever brought 'em in here last night stole 'em from my campsite, so I'll take 'em offa your hands now."

"Now, hold on here a minute, feller," Walt protested. "Those horses belong to me now. I don't know if the fellers I bought 'em from stole 'em or not, but I paid good money for those horses, and everything that came with 'em."

So he bought everything, lock, stock, and barrel, Logan thought. He had not expected to find his saddles and all his other possessions in one place. It was convenient, but it created a helluva problem. "Who'd you buy 'em from?" Logan asked, his tone soft and without emotion.

"Well, I don't know as how I oughta tell you that," Walt said. He didn't like the position he was in. This rangy fellow facing him looked deadly serious, but he knew for a fact that the man he had bought the horses from was a wanted gunman in Kansas. He suddenly found himself between two choices, neither of which was desirable.

"I don't think you understand the situation here," Logan said calmly. "The man you bought my horses, and all my gear from, murdered my brother last night. I understand how you feel about spendin' your money, but the fact of the matter is it's my stuff and I aim to have it back. I'm not in a good mood right now and I don't have a lot of patience. I'd rather not kill you, but if you stand in my way, I will. Do we understand each other?"

"But what about my money?" Walt protested. "I gave four hundred dollars for all that—" That was as far as he got before Logan cranked a cartridge into the chamber of the Winchester. "We do!" Walt blurted. "We understand each other."

"Good," Logan said. "Now, let's go get the rest of my things. In the tack room?"

"That's right," Walt said, feeling it would be suicide to resist the man. There was little doubt in his mind that Logan would shoot him. Inwardly, he cursed himself for being a fool. He knew those horses, saddles, and everything with them had to have been stolen. But the price was too good to pass up. Now he was going to be out the money he had spent.

As if reading his thoughts, Logan said, "If you tell me who you bought everything from, and where I can find him, I'll try to help you get some of your money back. Right now we need to hurry it up." He followed Walt to the tack room.

In a corner of the small room, he saw the saddles, saddlebags, blankets, gun belts, handguns, tools, cooking utensils, and everything else that had been taken. He couldn't help wondering what the real price had been for all of his and Billy's lifetime accumulation of property, but he suspected it was less than four hundred. He motioned toward the saddles.

"If you look on the underside of those saddle fenders, you'll see the initials *LC* on one of 'em, and *BC* on the other one. They stand for Logan Cross and Billy Cross." Walt didn't bother to look. He was pretty sure the initials would be there. Logan pulled his knife from his belt and tossed it at Walt's feet. "This is the knife that fits in the empty sheath on the gun belt hangin' on that saddle horn."

"Mister," Walt said, defeated, "you don't have to prove nothin' else. I believe you. I just wish to hell I hadn't been the one got skunked." He reached for the saddle horn nearest him and picked the saddle up. "I'll help you saddle up." He hesitated. "You said you might help me get some of my money back. Did you mean that?"

"I did," Logan said, "if you can tell me who murdered my brother and where I can find him."

"Well, I ain't got no way of knowin' who killed your brother, but there were three fellers that brought the horses here and sold everything to me. The one that done all the talkin' was called Jake, and I expect you'll find them at the Lucky Dollar about now."

Logan paused in the process of strapping his gun belt on. "Jake, huh?" he wondered aloud. His mind went back to Fort Pierre and the barroom fight. There were three of them, and he remembered telling two of them to take Jake out of there and go sober up. It was obvious now, the reason for the attack. This Jake had been out to get him but took Billy's life when he was not there. Logan felt the fire rising in his veins again.

He turned at once toward the door, then paused and looked back at Walt. "Put that saddle on the gray, and the packsaddle on the buckskin. I'll leave you that sorrel and the other saddle for your trouble. I'll be back as soon as I've settled with the three men who killed my brother."

"They'll be ready," Walt said.

"And I'll see how much of your money I can find."

"I'd sure appreciate it," Walt said. He stood there for a few moments after the somber stranger strode out the tack room door, wondering if he would actually get any of his money back.

At least I got a pretty good saddle and a sound horse, he thought, in an attempt to console himself. One thing was certain, he had not been dumb enough to try to prevent the man from claiming his possessions. Just the look of him told Walt that would have been foolish.

"Looks like this is my lucky day," Jake gloated as he swept another pot of cash over toward him.

"It sure looks like it," Lacey said. "Between you and Harris, there ain't been much left for Everett and me." He tossed another losing hand down. "Maybe we need a new deck of cards."

"I don't see nothin' wrong with this one," Jake said with a chuckle.

"Deal me out," Lacey said. "I gotta go to the outhouse." He pushed his chair back and stood up. "Maybe I can get rid of some of this poor luck I'm havin'."

"Hurry up," Jake said, "I ain't through with you yet."

A few moments after Lacey went out the back door, a tall, menacing figure walked through the front door of the Lucky Dollar. He paused to search the crowded saloon, which was busy as usual, no matter the hour. In a moment, he spotted the man he sought. There was no question of mistaken identity—Logan could still see the results of their fight when his right hand had rearranged his nose. He was seated at a table with two others. The one to Jake's left was recognizable as one of the two men with him in the saloon at Fort Pierre. The man across the table from Jake, wearing a frock coat, was a stranger. Logan would have preferred to find all three, for he was certain that they all had shot

Billy judging from the number of bullet holes in his brother's body. The opportunity was now, however, so he could not waste it. He walked directly toward the table, cocking the Winchester on the way.

At the distinct sound of a rifle being cocked, Jake glanced up to spot the man walking deliberately toward him. Across from him, the gambler, Harris, was startled by the sudden blanching of Jake's face. Before he had time to turn around to seek the cause of it, the first sharp crack of the rifle exploded, and Jake gasped in horror as the slug slammed into his chest.

Trying to get up out of the chair, he went over backward to land on the floor. Absorbed in his cards until that moment, Everett looked up to discover the fury that had descended upon them too late to draw his pistol. Logan's next shot turned Everett's lights out with a bullet in his forehead. Then he turned around swiftly to crank a final shot into Jake, as the dying man struggled to pull the .44 from his holster.

The double execution took place in mere seconds. The noisy room fell immediately silent and the patrons drew away from the table like a receding tide. An open space was created, with the grim avenger standing over two bodies, and a frightened gambler crouched under the table. Logan turned to survey the stunned spectators, stopping when his gaze settled upon the bartender, who was slowly reaching under the bar. Logan's look was enough to convince the bartender to forsake any thoughts toward pulling the shotgun out.

Terrified moments before, Harris decided that he was not a target of the gunman's rage. So he cautiously reached from under the table with one hand and felt blindly around for the cash still on top. For his efforts, he received a solid rap on his knuckles from Logan's rifle barrel. "That money goes with me," Logan stated soberly. "Get out from under there and rake all that money into this hat." He pulled his hat off and set it on the table.

While the gambler did as instructed, Logan turned his attention back to the crowd of astonished patrons. "These men murdered my brother in cold blood, so they got what was comin'. There was one more with them. If I find him, I will kill him, too. I don't have any intention of hurtin' anybody else, unless they stand in my way. The money I'm takin' doesn't belong to them. They stole it."

Keeping a cautious eye on the people, he quickly checked the pockets of Jake and Everett to relieve them of any money they had on them. He took his hat from Harris and dipped his head quickly to clap it on without spilling the cash. "Now, I'll ask you folks over here to clear me a path to the door." They moved at once to obey, and he walked toward the front door.

Halfway convinced that he was not about to be shot, Harris called after him, "Hey, how about me? Some of that money on the table was mine."

Logan was in no mood to delay his departure, and had little sympathy for the gambler. "That's the price you paid for playin' with outlaws," he called back.

As he passed by the end of the bar, Lyle leaned toward him and said, "You'd best not delay. Somebody's liable to run for the marshal."

"Much obliged," Logan said, and went out the door.

Back in the kitchen, Tom Lacey stood trembling, his pistol still in his hand. He had it in his mind to shoot, but he couldn't get a clear shot, because of the crowded saloon and the men standing between him and the target. He had brought his pistol up to aim when a couple of the patrons parted enough to give him a glimpse of the man with the rifle. But it was during the moments when Logan was scanning the crowd for possible trouble. And Lacey lost his nerve when it appeared that Logan was staring right at him. By the time he realized that he wasn't, it was too late. The opening was gone.

He had to admit to himself that he was glad that he didn't try to stop the man. He was better off to stay out of it and count himself lucky that he had had to go to the outhouse. He slid his pistol back into his holster and went back out the kitchen door. He didn't forget the fact that the man had walked out of the saloon with a considerable amount of money, however. It was difficult to let him ride away with it.

Walt Bowen had remained outside his stable, beside the corral, waiting for the grim stranger's return, not totally convinced that he would, for he had seen the nature of the three men Logan was seeking out. It had occurred to him that there was a good chance that he might not lose the horses and gear he had bought from the outlaws after all, so he stood, staring up the street toward the Lucky Dollar. The gray and the buckskin were saddled and packed as he had been instructed to do, but if the lone stalker was unsuccessful, they were his property to keep.

Even though he was anticipating them, he jumped, startled, when he heard the gunshots from the saloon, and he strained to stare harder at the door. In a couple of minutes, he saw a handful of people backing out of the doorway to get out of the way of the man who had obviously done what he had gone there to do.

"Yep, he did it," Walt murmured to himself softly as Logan strode purposefully toward the stables.

Not willing to take much time in the process, but with the intention of standing by his word, Logan walked directly by Walt and into the tack room. He dumped his hat on the bench there and quickly counted the money. Walt stood silently by. The total of all the money raked off the table, plus what he found on Jake and Everett, added up to a tidy sum. He had a rough idea how much money he and Billy had had with them, so he subtracted that, plus what he considered a fair price for the sorrel packhorse. When he was finished, he told Walt, "There's a hundred and fifty dollars cash there on the table. You have the sorrel and saddle I gave you already, and the horses they rode in on, so I figure you didn't get hurt too bad."

"I 'preciate you tryin' to be fair about it," Walt said. "I take it you settled with all three of 'em."

"Two of 'em," Logan replied while walking back to the horses. "One of 'em wasn't there."

"What about him?" Walt asked anxiously. "What if he shows up here, claimin' the horses?"

"Then I reckon you're gonna have to deal with that yourself," Logan said.

Knowing there was nothing he could do to help Walt, he stepped up into the saddle and turned Pepper's head toward the trail up the western side of the gulch. He considered himself fortunate that the marshal had not come looking for him yet, and he didn't plan to waste any more time.

He was disappointed not to have settled with all three of the men who had attacked Billy, but he was satisfied that the one responsible was dead, and he had no plans to seek the third man out.

Chapter 4

Logan reined his horse to a stop when he came to a clear stream running through a narrow canyon, formed by two high mountains. The somber man took no notice of the beauty of the green canyon floor, nor the dark pine forests that covered the slopes.

He supposed that he was now a wanted man in Dakota Territory, regardless of the wrong or right of his recent acts of vengeance. He couldn't say that he really cared at the moment, and the only plan he had in mind was to lose himself in these mountains in case the marshal of Montana City was set on coming after him. He didn't think there was really much chance of that, even though the bartender at the Lucky Dollar had advised him to run. Montana City didn't look as though it could afford much of a marshal.

Even so, he preferred to run than to take the chance of an encounter with the law, for no matter the situation, he could not justify a gun battle with a sheriff or marshal. In his mind, he had done no wrong, and he had no intention to surrender to the law. His brother was gone, and he missed him. But now that he had no family, he had to go forward from this tragedy. It was the hand he had been dealt.

Cramps in his stomach reminded him that it had been almost two days since he last ate. He was not hungry, but he told himself that he had to come back from the pit of sorrow that had captured his mind, and he needed food to keep his strength.

As if nature herself extended her hand to him, a young doe bounded across the stream a dozen yards in front of him, then stopped stone-still. It seemed she was presenting him a target, for she still did not move when he slowly drew his rifle from the saddle sling and carefully laid the front sight on a spot just behind the deer's front leg. He squeezed the trigger until the Winchester suddenly spoke, and the doe leaped once before crashing to the ground.

Deciding that was as good a place as any to make his camp, he built a fire and unsaddled Pepper. He still felt a stab of sorrow when he removed the packsaddle from the buckskin, *Billy's horse*, and wondered if it would not have been better to keep the sorrel instead. He shook his head, then busied himself with the skinning and butchering of the deer, remembering now and again that he was preparing his food using the same knife with which he had dug Billy's grave.

After he placed some strips of the fresh venison over the fire, the aroma of the roasting meat awakened his forgotten desire to eat.

"I reckon I'll have to see the Black Hills for both of us, Billy," he said aloud. "After that, I reckon I'll head over toward Belle Fourche like Percy suggested—see if I can get on with a cattle outfit up there."

He figured he'd be better off making his way to the western part of the hills, away from Deadwood Gulch, so as to put a little distance between him and Montana City. He was still of the opinion that the marshal of that town wouldn't make much of an effort to search for him, after he felt sure Logan was gone from his town. As for the days to come, he had no reason to expect any additional trouble, now that the situation with Jake Morgan was settled. It was a dangerous assumption.

A whinny from Pepper caught his attention, causing him to look toward the horses. Their ears were flickering rapidly and both horses whinnied then, telling him he might have company. He reached for his rifle just at the moment a slug tore into the ashes of his fire, followed almost at once by the report of the sniper's rifle. Logan's reaction was instantaneous and he rolled over and over until reaching the protection of the stream bank. Another shot ripped into the dirt above his head.

His first thought was the marshal from Montana City, but it struck him as odd that he wasn't given the option of surrendering. Maybe it wasn't the marshal. Maybe it was an Indian, or a claim jumper, thinking his camp was that of a miner, panning for gold. Whoever it was didn't seem to be interested in taking him alive, so he tried to evaluate his situation and decide what to do. It didn't look too promising. For starters, he wasn't sure where the shots were coming from. But then another round was fired at the bank above his head, and this time he saw the muzzle flash. He waited and in a few seconds, another shot came. It was from the same place.

One man, he thought, *behind that rock outcropping at the foot of the mountain to the east.*

Now that he had located the sniper, he could decide the best way to respond. Looking behind him, he observed the course of the stream as it came down the mountain. He decided his best bet was to make his way along the bank, using it for cover, until it made a sharp turn into a narrow ravine. If he was careful, he might be able to stay low enough that his assailant could not see what he was up to. Seeing no other solution that promised a greater chance of success, he crawled down into the water and set out along the stream. As he ran, hunched over as far as he could, he heard a couple more shots behind him, still shooting at the spot he had just vacated.

When he reached the place where the stream turned sharply into the ravine, he realized that he could leave it and make his way along the foot of the mountain, using the thick growth of pines for cover. As he moved along through the trees, he stopped each time he heard another shot to determine where the shooter was hiding. He was anxious to reach a place above the sniper before the man realized he was shooting at an empty stream bank. After a few moments more, he figured he had to be right over the bushwhacker, but he could not see anything through the thick pine branches between him and the large rock he had first spotted.

Then, all at once, a gentle breeze parted the boughs below him to give him a brief glimpse of his adversary. It was not enough to give him a clear shot, but it would at least give him a fifty-fifty chance. He brought the Winchester to his shoulder but hesitated.

What if it's the marshal I'm about to kill? He only considered the thought for a moment before deciding. *He isn't trying to arrest me, and murder's murder, even if it's in the name of the law.*

He realized then that he had hesitated too long, for his target started to shift to another location. Thinking he might not have a better chance, he fired, cranked in a new cartridge, and fired again. A sharp cry of pain told him that he had hit him.

Making his way down through the rocks and trees as fast as he could, he stumbled and fell, tumbling several yards before righting himself to continue. Unfortunately he reached the rock just in time to see his attacker fleeing at a gallop, lying low on his horse's neck, apparently wounded. Lawman or outlaw? There was no way to tell, but he had wounded him, and that was enough to send him running. At least Logan's horses were safe, but he decided to move his camp, just in case the shooter decided to try again.

Quincy Morgan drained the last swallow of coffee from his cup when he heard Curly Ford call out, "Yonder comes Lonnie."

Quincy looked up to see his cousin riding along the bluffs on his way back from scouting a small farm a short ride up the river. He got to his feet and wiped his mouth with the back of his hand and awaited Lonnie's report.

In a few minutes, Lonnie rode right up between the bedrolls spread close to the fire before reining his horse to a stop and stepping down from the saddle. "Damn, Lonnie," Riley Stokes complained, "why don't you just ride that horse right over us?"

"I just might," Lonnie answered him with a smirk. "You ought'n still be settin' around the fire anyway."

"What did you see?" Quincy asked, indifferent to his cousin's cocky attitude.

"Looks like two sodbuster families," Lonnie replied.

"Least, there's two cabins settin' by the river. Don't look like they been there very long. One of 'em don't look like it's finished. I didn't see no sign of cattle—a milk cow, is all."

"What about the men?" Quincy asked. "Any trouble?"

"Not enough to worry about," Lonnie said as he picked up the coffeepot from the edge of the fire and tested the weight to determine if there was any left. "Two younger men and one old man—the rest is women and children." He picked up a cup sitting on the ground near the fire and filled it with the strong liquid. "They're a pretty sorry-lookin' bunch. Don't look like there's more'n five dollars between 'em."

"What did the women look like?" Rafe Dawson asked, to no one's surprise.

"Whadda you care, Rafe?" Wormy Jacobs snorted. "Since when did it matter to you what they look like? Have you got particular all of a sudden?" His remarks drew some chuckles from the other men and a scowl from Rafe.

Quincy remained aloof from the verbal horseplay while he considered Lonnie's report. It didn't sound as though the farmers were worth the bother, and he was flush with money right now. Just as he had promised his men, the stagecoaches carrying gold out of the Black Hills were easy pickings. They had hit one that yielded them a big score on the road out of Custer, so he was thinking it not worth their while to raid these farmers. Maybe he would ride around them and let them be.

As leader of the five men riding with him, he had determined their prospects more promising in the Black Hills. That was where the gold was, he told them, and that was where they'd concentrate their activity. Lonnie had been able to round up the other men in anticipation of Quincy's release from prison, and it was his intention to pick up right where they had left off before he was captured by U.S. Marshals. If things were going the way he hoped, his brother, Jake, should be going about learning all he could concerning the gold shipments that came from the big mines located in the gulch. Those shipments were the gold that Quincy intended to strike.

Aware that Quincy was seriously mulling the prospect over, Lonnie asked, "Whaddaya think, Quincy? You wanna hit them sodbusters, or just go on around 'em?"

Lonnie studied his cousin intensely. Five years in prison would most likely change any man. So far, he seemed the same cold-blooded killer he had been, but he seemed prone to falling into deep periods of moody depression.

Overhearing Lonnie's question, Rafe said, "Hell, Quincy, we might as well see if they've got anything worth takin'. If what Lonnie says is true, it don't sound like there's much risk."

"You wanna see the women that bad?" Quincy responded after a moment. "You ain't changed much since I was in prison." He looked at the questioning faces of the others. It wasn't difficult to determine their preference. They weren't prone to passing up easy pickings, slim though they might be. So he said, "We might as well see if there's anything worth foolin' with. They might have a little bit of money hidden away somewhere."

"Now you're talkin'," Rafe said, a wide grin forming on his unshaven face.

"All right, then," Quincy said. "Let's get saddled up and go pay the sodbusters a visit."

Henry Jessop reached the end of the small plot of ground he was plowing for a spring garden and turned his mule back up the next row only to stop suddenly when he saw six riders approaching from the riverbank. He was at once concerned, for at first glance he didn't like the look of the men. Something inside him told him he and his family were in danger. He turned to call to his brother, who was on his way from the cabin.

"Harvey, we got company. Maybe you better go back to the house till I find out what they want."

If he had seen them in time, he would have taken the precaution to get back to the other end of the garden patch where he had left his shotgun. As it was, however, the only way he might make it would be to drop the plow and run for the weapon, and he feared that would only trigger a violent reaction if they did have evil intentions. Maybe he was just being overcautious, he told himself.

Harvey turned immediately to head back to the cabin. He had the same uneasy feeling that had come over Henry when he first spotted the six riders. Lucy, his two young sons, and his mother and father were all in his cabin, since his parents' cabin was not yet completed. He scolded himself for not having brought his rifle with him, but if he was quick enough, maybe he could make it to the house while Henry talked to the strangers.

To the six outlaws approaching, it was obvious why one of the farmers was hurrying back to the cabin. "Curly, head that one off," Quincy ordered.

There was no hesitation on Curly's part. He kicked his horse sharply, and the big red sorrel sprang into a full gallop. It was not much of a race between sorrel and man. Curly cut Harvey off when he was still twenty yards from the house. The horse's hooves slid to a stop in the soft dirt, freshly broken by the plow. "How do, neighbor?" Curly sang out, a smile of contempt on his face. "What's your hurry?"

At a loss for a believable reply, Harvey could only stammer over the first words that dropped out of his mouth. "I was gonna see if there was any food ready to eat."

Looking up at the huge man in the saddle, whose totally bald head was only partially covered by a weathered felt derby with a thin brim, he knew he was caught in a lie.

"Is that a fact?" Curly replied, enjoying the man's obvious fright. "Was you thinkin' 'bout invitin' us for dinner?" When Harvey could not reply, Curly said, "Ain't no need to run in the house. We just came by to say howdy."

He had no sooner said it then they heard the first gunshot, and a shocked Harvey turned to see his brother drop to the ground behind his plow. An instant later, he was slammed in the back by a bullet from Curly's pistol. Several more shots were fired to make sure the two men were finished.

Curly was the only one close to the house, so he turned to meet any attack from that quarter, backing his horse away while he trained his .44 on the cabin door. The rest of the outlaws pulled up to him, every man with a weapon aimed at the cabin, but there was no immediate response from inside the dwelling.

"Watch 'em," Stokes warned, alert to the possibility

of a sudden retaliation. "I'll go round back. We might have to burn 'em out."

"Hell, if we do that, we'll burn up whatever they got in there that's worth anything," Quincy said. "Just make sure they don't try to slip out the back. We can't leave any witnesses."

Inside the log cabin, the two horrified women clung together while the father of the two murdered brothers hurried frantically from window to window to make sure the shutters were closed and bolted. Leonard Jessop was not a young man, but he was determined to protect the women and children suddenly left in his care. Moving as quickly as he could to try to calm the terrified women, he turned to his sobbing wife.

"Mother, you and Lucy take the boys in the bedroom and close the door. You'd better take Harvey's shotgun with you." Somewhat calmer than her hysterical daughter-in-law, Myra did as she was directed, herding Lucy and the two boys ahead of her. Leonard turned his attention back to the danger outside. Peeking through a crack in the shutters, he felt his heart sink when he saw the five riders facing the cabin in a semicircle. He could see that his only hope was to convince them that it was not worth the risk to break into the cabin and expose themselves to his rifle.

Outside, Quincy and his men considered the oyster they were left to crack open. Figuring it worth a try to talk them out, he called to them, "You folks come on outta there, and we won't hurt nobody. We just wanna take a little food, and then we'll be on our way. I'm sorry 'bout your two young men, but we didn't have no choice when they ran for their guns. So open up and come on out."

"You go to hell!" Leonard shouted back. "You murderin' scum, get off this land!"

"Have it your way," Quincy returned. "I was gonna take it easy on you." He had not yet decided how he was going to attack the boarded-up cabin. Setting it on fire seemed the better option after all, but then Rafe took the initiative, anxious as he was to get to the women.

Seeing an axe embedded in a stump beside a pile of firewood, Rafe slid off his horse and declared, "I'll open 'em up." He pulled the axe up from the stump and ran to the nearest window, where he set upon the wooden shutter with a vengeance. The shutter, made from green pine, was not easy to split, but it soon gave way to Rafe's assault, and a piece a few inches wide splintered off, leaving a gap large enough to stick a rifle barrel through. The blast from the weapon that was suddenly thrust through it caught the surprised Rafe in the chest, dropping him immediately, mortally wounded. Leonard's shot was answered at once by fire from the other four, ripping holes in the shutter and the window frame around it, but causing no harm to the old man.

"Rafe, you damn fool," was Quincy's only response to the felling of one of his men. Determined to crack this nut now, he dismounted and ordered, "Find a hole to shoot through." His men scrambled to follow his orders.

Inside, Leonard heard the command and tried to reduce their number once more, hoping it might discourage their attack. Thrusting the rifle a little farther through the opening in the shutter, he sought to give himself a wider angle from which to pick a target, unaware that Curly had slipped up beside the window. With a vacant grin on his simple face, the oversized brute grabbed the rifle barrel and wrenched it from the old man's hands, slamming him hard up against the window in the process. With no fear of being shot now, Curly dropped the rifle on the ground, took hold of the broken shutter, and ripped half of it from the window.

Rallying behind Curly's assault, Lonnie ran up beside him to peer through the window. He saw the old man struggling to get to his feet and promptly shot him.

"Ain't nobody left but women and young'uns now," he sang out. "They're hid somewhere." He looked at Curly. "Tear the rest of that window out, Big'un, and I'll go in and open the door."

Happy to oblige, Curly grinned and did his bidding. When he had done so, he boosted the smaller man up so he could climb in through the window. Before dropping to the floor, Lonnie looked around the main room carefully, making sure there was no one else in the room. Then he hurried to the door and lifted the bar to let the others in.

"Come on in, boys, and we'll meet the rest of the family," he said cheerfully.

Behind the cabin, Stokes could guess what had happened, so he came out of the saddle and ran up to try the back door. Finding it still barred, he ran around to the front door, pausing only a moment when he saw Rafe lying beneath the window, choking on the steady flow of blood filling his lungs.

"Damn, Rafe," Stokes muttered before going in the door, interested more by what he might find inside the cabin than he was concerned about his comrade's condition. "What the hell happened to Rafe?" he asked when he found the others watching a closed bedroom door, their weapons cocked in anticipation of what might be waiting on the other side.

"He got hisself shot," Lonnie said.

"He don't look like he's gonna make it," Stokes said.

"He probably ain't," Lonnie replied, "but there ain't nothin' we can do about it."

Stokes paused to consider that, then shrugged and asked, "What are you waitin' for? Ain't you gonna open that door?"

"We been waitin' for you," Wormy Jacobs said. "Figured you'd wanna be the first one to stick your nose in there to see if they've got a gun."

"Maybe we oughta just slide you under the door," Stokes came back, in sarcastic reference to Wormy's scrawny build, which was the inspiration behind his nickname. "Then you can tell us if they're waitin' to blow a hole in the first one comin' through the door."

Impatient with the caution on the part of his men, Quincy nodded to Curly. "Kick the damn door open and be ready to shoot. We can't hang around here all mornin'." He knew the simpleminded brute would not hesitate to follow his orders. Curly grinned in reply and stepped up before the door, bracing himself to deliver a powerful kick. "Cover him!" Quincy directed the others. Not at all confident that the oversized halfwit would think to do so on his own, Quincy told him to jump out of the way as soon as he kicked the door open.

Curly nodded solemnly, as if grateful for Quincy's advice. He turned to the door to give it his full attention. When the powerful man planted his foot squarely below the latch, the results were as expected. The door flew open, triggering the blast of a shotgun in the hands of a diminutive gray-haired woman. Since the intruders had anticipated such a reaction, no one was hit by the load of buckshot. The only damage was the shattering of a picture of the family, hanging by the front door.

Before she was able to fire the other barrel, she was felled by three slugs in her breast, and the shotgun dropped from her lifeless hands to clatter noisily on the floor. Confident that there was no further danger, the outlaws rushed into the bedroom, eager to see the younger woman, all save one. Quincy casually walked in behind his murderous bunch, having no interest in a gang rape. Although he was as much without conscience as any of the men who rode with him, and he had been five years away from the company of a woman, he held himself above the shameless depravity of the others. A handsome man, with coal black hair and a neatly trimmed mustache, he was vain to the point of thinking he did not have to hold a gun on a woman to have his way with her.

"You might as well come on out from behind that bed, honey," Stokes said. Hysterical from the slaughter of her family, and terrified, knowing what was in store for her, Lucy Jessop could not move. She could only cower there on the floor between the bed and the wall, her two young sons held tightly in her arms. "Come on outta there," Stokes repeated while Wormy and Lonnie stood by, grinning with anticipation. He reached for her, but she cowered farther, trying to get under the bed, pulling the two children with her. No longer amused by the game, Stokes grabbed the edge of the bed and flipped it off her. Out of her mind with terror, Lucy started screaming until Stokes slapped her hard.

Disgusted with Stokes's carnal lust, Quincy told Lonnie to take the two children outside. Grabbing them by their collars, Lonnie dragged them away and out the door. In a few moments, two gunshots were heard. Knowing what had happened, Lucy screamed for her two boys as Stokes pulled her to her feet.

Thinking the woman too distressed to resist, he tried to embrace her. In her struggle to fight him off, her hand found the handle of his pistol, and she immediately grasped it. Unaware of what was happening until he felt the weight leave his hip, he reached for the weapon, but it was already gone. She cocked it and held it on him. Reacting to the amusing struggle that had suddenly turned deadly, the other men drew their weapons again, but held their fire when the frightened woman backed away, her hand trembling uncontrollably.

"Hand it over," Stokes said, as calmly as he could. "You'll just get yourself killed. Hand it over and I won't let 'em bother you no more."

He started walking toward her, his hand out, but she backed away until she was stopped by the wall. She paused calmly for a moment before abruptly pressing the muzzle of the pistol up under her chin and pulling the trigger.

"Damn!" Stokes exclaimed as he jumped back a step, startled by the sudden turn of events.

"I swear," Wormy muttered in disbelief. "What'd she go and do that for?"

Coming back in time to witness the desperate woman's suicide, Lonnie, always cynical, answered him, "Most likely took one look at you. Maybe you oughta go outside and tell Rafe she's ready for him now. He won't have no trouble with her a'tall."

His cousin's comment caused Quincy to remember the wounded man still lying outside. "Look around the place," he told the others. "See if there's anything worth takin'. I'll go see how bad Rafe's hurt. There might be neighbors close enough to have heard the shootin', so be quick about it."

With no further interest in the woman's body, Wormy and Lonnie started ransacking the house in search of money, ammunition, or valuables while Stokes lingered a few moments longer, still astonished by her desperate act. Finally he muttered, "Damn, lady, anything's better'n shootin' yourself. We mighta took you with us." He turned then and joined the others in the rummaging of the house.

Outside, Quincy stood watching Rafe for a few seconds as the wounded man struggled to breathe through the blood choking his throat. Several yards away lay the bodies of the two children. Quincy turned when Curly came up to join him. "I heard a shot," Curly said. "Did you shoot the woman?"

"She shot herself," Quincy said.

"I swear," Curly exclaimed. "She was a right pretty woman."

"She ain't now," Quincy replied, tired of talking about the young wife. He leaned over Rafe and asked, "You able to ride?"

"Yeah . . . yeah," Rafe gasped, his words slow and labored.

"You don't look like it," Quincy said, "and we've got a ways to go to Deadwood Gulch."

"I can ride," Rafe insisted painfully. "Don't leave me here." Quincy didn't reply right away, so Rafe rolled his eyes toward Curly. Trying to appeal to the simple-minded brute, he begged, "Don't leave me, Curly." His words became harder to spit out, choked as they were with blood from his lungs. "Get me on my horse and I'll stay on him."

Indifferent to suffering, human or animal, the big man spoke frankly. "Whatever Quincy says."

"I won't slow you down," Rafe insisted, speaking with even greater effort than before. Quincy didn't reply, his thoughts interrupted by a call from Lonnie inside.

"Quincy, we found their hidin' place! Little pocket of money hid under a floorboard—it ain't much. Wormy's countin' it now."

Forgetting Rafe for the moment, Quincy and Curly went back inside to see for themselves.

"Is that about it?" Quincy asked, standing in the middle of the front room, looking around him at the destructive evidence of their searching. Anything that might be useful was piled in the middle of the floor. Quincy walked over to quickly sort through it before giving the order to load it on the horses. "Wormy, split that money up five ways," he said.

"You mean six ways," Wormy replied.

"I mean five," Quincy said. "Rafe ain't gonna be able to go with us."

"We gonna burn it?" Lonnie asked, referring to the house.

"No," Quincy answered. "To hell with it. We won't take the time. There might be other farms not too far from here, and somebody would see the smoke."

They shuffled out of the cabin, carrying the loot they had gathered to be loaded on their horses. "Might as well pull that saddle off and use Rafe's horse for a pack-horse," Lonnie suggested, indifferent to the wounded man lying beside the front window. Like the other men, he felt no compassion for Rafe. He had just had a piece of bad luck.

"That's a better-lookin' saddle than mine," Wormy said. "I think I'll trade with him." He went at once to pull the saddle off Rafe's sorrel, in case one of the others might have the same idea.

"I'll take the saddlebags," Quincy said, "and we'll split any money he's got left on him."

Helpless to prevent the plunder of his possessions, Rafe pleaded weakly for compassion on the part of his partners. "Don't leave me, fellers," he choked out pitifully, gasping painfully when Lonnie unbuckled his gun belt and pulled it out from under him. "You can split my share of the money. Just take me with you."

Quincy walked over to stand close beside him. "You ain't gonna make it much longer, Rafe, so there ain't no use in you even tryin'. It's just a downright pure piece of bad luck, but that's the way the cards were dealt. We'll make it easy on you if you want to end your sufferin' right now. Or we'll leave you like you are, if you druther—maybe leave you your pistol, too. Whatever you say."

"Oh God, Quincy," Rafe begged, "don't leave me. I'll pull through."

"You're foolin' yourself," Quincy said. "It don't make no sense to carry you with us. You'd just die before we got gone good, so which way you want it, now or later?"

When Rafe closed his eyes in despair, failing to answer, Quincy said, "Put his gun belt down beside him where he can reach it, Lonnie." He bent closely over the wounded man and whispered, "We'll be goin' now. Here's your .44 right beside you if you need it. No hard feelin's." He stood up. "Let's go, boys."

While the other men moved to their horses, Quincy walked around behind the forsaken man. He drew his .44, held the muzzle close to the back of Rafe's head, and pulled the trigger. "Makes no sense to leave a damn good .44 Colt to lay out here and rust," he said, and picked up Rafe's pistol again. "Let's get goin'. We got about a three-day ride ahead of us. Jake'll think we ain't comin'." He was looking forward to seeing his brother again.

Big Jake, he thought, *a bigger hell-raiser was never born.*

The solid core of the Morgan Gang would be intact again with Jake, cousin Lonnie, and himself back on the road again. Just like old times.

It was an unusually warm day for late summer when the Morgan Gang rode into Montana City. Five strong, they walked their horses down the middle of the street, as an invading army might. Quincy took only a moment to see which saloon seemed to be the biggest. This was where Jake would most likely be waiting for him. He looked at Lonnie and motioned. Lonnie understood and immediately turned his horse toward the Lucky Dollar, the others following. Quincy held back a moment to take in the busy scene, a smile of satisfaction on his face.

All these people, he thought, *all working to find the ore that I'll be happy to take off their hands.* He nudged his horse up to the hitching rail beside Lonnie's and dismounted.

"This time of day," Lonnie said, "I wouldn't be surprised if we don't find ol' Jake tossin' back a drink or two."

"You might be right," Quincy replied, already smiling when he formed the picture in his mind.

The five dangerous-looking men did not walk into the saloon unnoticed. Their ominous appearance was enough to cause a momentary hush in the noisy barroom, a reaction that pleased Quincy. He nodded toward an empty table toward the back of the large room, and his men swaggered over to claim it. There were two miners seated at the table next to it, and Quincy stopped before it. Curly stepped up to stand beside him.

"We're gonna need this table, neighbor," Quincy said.

The two miners looked up at him, and the grinning brute of a man beside him. "We're about finished up here, ain't we, Jim?" one of them sputtered nervously.

"You bet," Jim replied. "We was just fixin' to go."

"I thought you were," Quincy said. "Pull it over here, Curly, and make one big table." He then stood there and looked around the crowded room, looking for Jake, even though he knew the gang's entrance could hardly have gone unnoticed if Jake was there.

Thinking the same as Quincy, Lonnie wondered aloud, "Reckon Jake's drinkin' in some other saloon?" He didn't wait for an answer. "This one's the biggest in town, and Jake always picks the biggest." He laughed. "Maybe he's upstairs plowin' some corn."

"Maybe," Quincy said. There were several women working their trade downstairs. "I reckon we'll find him before long."

Overhearing their conversation, Wormy Jacobs said, "Hell yeah, he'll find us soon enough. While we're waitin', let's get us somethin' to drink."

Already wondering if he could expect some trouble from the five strangers, Lyle Weaver watched nervously as Wormy and Riley Stokes came over to the bar to order a bottle. Maybe, he thought, it might be a good idea to send somebody to tell the marshal that a dangerous-looking bunch had just hit town, since they sure as hell didn't look like miners. On second thought, he didn't think there was much Henry Thompson could do against a pack of wolves like these men. He almost breathed a sigh of relief when Riley put money on the bar and said to Wormy, "Somebody else can spring for the next one."

"We're gonna need some glasses," Wormy said to Lyle, and the bartender said he would bring them over to the table.

As he placed five glasses in the middle of the two tables, Lyle avoided direct eye contact with any of the fearsome-looking men, glancing up at Lonnie only when he spoke.

"We're lookin' for somebody," Lonnie said, "think maybe he mighta been in here a time or two." He nodded toward Curly. "He's a big feller, almost as big as Curly there. Name's Jake. You seen him?"

Lyle knew at once who they were referring to. There was no chance at all that he would not remember the execution of Jake Morgan right there in his saloon, and the grim avenger who had done the deed. Judging by the look of them, he had no doubt that these men were of the same ilk as Jake. He preferred not to be the bearer of bad news, however, figuring they might punish the messenger, so he evaded the question. "Sorry, fellers. We get an awful lot of folks in here. He mighta been in, but I can't say as how I remember him apart from everybody else."

"Maybe he's been hangin' out at that other saloon at the end of the street," Lonnie allowed when Lyle returned to the bar. "He'da remembered Jake."

"This place is more to Jake's likin'," Quincy said. "Mine, too. Riley, run on up the street and take a look in that other place. Ask 'em if they've seen Jake. Hell, he's supposed to have been here awhile."

Stokes tossed his shot of whiskey down and got up

from the table. "I don't think Jake's hit town yet," he said. "Hell, place this size, he'da most likely have took over the whole town by now."

Stokes was gone for no more than about twenty minutes before he returned with a report similar to the one they had gotten in the Lucky Dollar. "Feller up there said he ain't seen nobody, neither. You reckon somethin' happened to Jake?"

Quincy only gave his question a moment's consideration before answering, "Jake? Nah, nothin' ever happens to Jake. He'll likely show up tonight or tomorrow. Ain't that right, Lonnie?"

"Most likely found him a whore or somethin'," Lonnie said.

"We'll get a couple of rooms in that hotel and look for Jake tomorrow," Quincy said. Thanks to a lucrative Cheyenne-to-Deadwood stage holdup, they could afford to stay in the hotel. After a few more drinks, Quincy sent Lonnie to the hotel to secure the rooms, but Lonnie soon returned with the news that there were no rooms available. Some were even rented to two different customers, one sleeping by day, the other by night.

"By Ned, we'll go in there and clear a couple of rooms out," Wormy declared.

"Hold on," Quincy said. "That's not a very good idea. I don't want the whole damn town down on us. We might need a place to operate out of, and this one might do us just fine. We'll camp outside town a ways and wait for Jake to show up. Then we'll decide what to do."

That effectively ended any talk of taking over the town.

Chapter 5

Quincy Morgan sat close to the fire, drinking a cup of coffee. A couple of his men were already asleep, having rolled up in their blankets in an effort to recover from too much whiskey at the Lucky Dollar. Lonnie came over to sit with him after making sure the horses were all right.

"Any of that coffee left?" he asked.

"There's a little bit left in the pot," Quincy said. "We poured a gracious plenty of it down Wormy's throat. I swear, that man just can't handle his whiskey."

Lonnie laughed and started to make a comment but was stopped by a call from the darkness of the creek. "Hello the camp! All right if I come in?"

Both Quincy and Lonnie scrambled away from the firelight, drawing their pistols. "Who the hell . . . ," Quincy started as he sought cover behind a tree. Nobody ever wanted to come into his camp except maybe a marshal's posse. Recovered from the surprise, he called out, "Who the hell are you, and how many's with you?"

"I'm a friend of Jake's," Tom Lacey answered. "I'm alone. Are you his brother?"

The exchange between the two had alerted everyone in the camp by then, except Wormy, who was dead to the world. "Maybe, maybe not," Quincy replied. "What's your business?"

"I came lookin' for you," Lacey said. "I got somethin' to tell you about Jake, if I can come in."

"All right," Quincy said. "But, friend, you'd better not be up to any funny business, less you wanna get yourself shot."

"I'm comin' in," Lacey replied.

With drawn weapons, the four conscious members of the gang watched the lone man, with a bandage wrapped around his arm, walk into the firelight, leading his horse. When it appeared that he was alone, as he had claimed, they drew in closer to the fire again. "You say you're a friend of Jake's?" Lonnie asked. "Where is Jake?"

"Jake's dead," Lacey blurted. "Murdered while he was settin' at the poker table, playin' cards."

The shocking declaration effectively staggered Quincy and Lonnie. "What?" Quincy blurted. "Who?"

While Quincy was fairly stunned for the moment, Lonnie demanded answers. "Who shot him, and who the hell are you?"

"My name's Tom Lacey. Another feller, name of Everett Pierce, was at the table with Jake when this feller walked in and blasted away without so much as a howdy-do. He killed Everett, too. I wasn't there. If I hadda been, things mighta been different. Me and Everett was supposed to join up with you fellers."

Quincy was livid, so filled with rage that he couldn't speak for several minutes, so Lonnie continued to question Lacey. "Is the man who shot Jake dead?" When Lacey answered with a shake of his head, Lonnie charged, "Well, why the hell not?"

"I went after him," Lacey said. "That's how I got this." He raised his bandaged arm to show him. "But he was able to give me the slip. I was bleedin' pretty bad, so I had to go up to Elizabeth Town to the doctor."

"His name!" Quincy suddenly demanded, finally able to speak again. "What is the bastard's name?" His face still a fiery red, he glared directly into Lacey's eyes, causing the frightened man to cower.

"Logan Cross," Lacey exclaimed, "his name's Logan Cross."

"Where is he?" Quincy roared. "Where can I find him?"

"I don't know for sure," Lacey answered. "He's a drifter, ain't stayin' nowhere in Montana City that I know of. He's gone up in the mountains somewhere over toward Spearfish Canyon, I think." It was obvious that his answer didn't completely satisfy the infuriated man. "Leastways, I can take you to the spot where I lost him after he shot me. Might be you can track him from there."

Realizing the devastating effect Lacey's news had cast upon Quincy, Lonnie sought to steady his cousin. "This is mighty sad news to hear, mighty sad. And we're gonna go get this son of a bitch. There ain't no doubt about that, but there ain't nothin' we can do about it tonight. Come mornin', this feller . . ." He paused to look at Lacey. "What did you say your name was?"

"Lacey," he replied, "Tom Lacey. Me and Everett was ridin' with Jake."

"Yeah," Lonnie continued. "Lacey here is gonna show us where he lost the bastard, and we'll track him down. He's a dead man for sure, but we'll have to wait till mornin' to get started so we can see where we're goin'."

He nodded solemnly as he locked his eyes on Quincy's, searching for signs that his volatile cousin was thinking clearly. He was well aware of Quincy's history of insane rage when something big happened to trigger it—something like his brother getting murdered—and he doubted that tendency had been lessened after five years in prison. In a few minutes' time, Quincy's eyes began to lose the glazed appearance, and Lonnie felt reassured that he had recovered enough to think rationally again.

"Right," Quincy said calmly. "We'll start out early in the mornin' and see if we can get on his trail." Seeming to be in control again, he turned to Lacey. "You say Jake picked you up to ride with us?"

"That's right," Lacey said, still marveling at the apparent transformation from a raging demon to a reasonable man. He couldn't help wondering how often he went into these fits of rage. He'd never seen anyone that angry before. Jake never said anything about his brother's tendency to do so. One thing that was impressed upon his mind, however, was the inadvisability of riling the man. He glanced at the other two men standing near him, watching with blank expressions that gave him no indication of their having witnessed their boss's violent temper before.

"Well, if Jake thought you were okay, then I reckon I do, too," Quincy said, his voice still calm. "This is my cousin, Lonnie. That's Curly Ford, Riley Stokes, and

the one passed out cold over there is Wormy Jacobs."
Curly and Stokes both nodded.

"I 'preciate it," Lacey said. "I've been waitin' for you fellers to show up. Jake told me what I'd be expected to do, and I'm ready for it. I'm your man."

"Well, if you ain't, we'll find out quick enough," Stokes said, causing the others to laugh. "Reckon you can unsaddle your horse and find you a place to bed down. It's your turn to fetch some wood for the fire."

"I ain't surprised," Lacey said, and left to tend his horse.

"He looks all right," Lonnie said to Quincy when Lacey was out of earshot. "I'll keep a close eye on him. I'm thinkin' that little bullet wound in his arm don't look like enough to stop a man from goin' after Jake's killer."

"We'll see," Quincy said. "I want him with us, anyway. He knows what Logan Cross looks like, and I don't."

The man Quincy Morgan was now obsessed with was following an old game trail that led along a low ridge, leading to a gulch between two of the mountains before him. He had no destination. He was simply tracing a trail that looked as if it might lead him to another deer.

The incident of the day before, he figured, was just a chance encounter with a cowardly back-shooter, lying in wait for a convenient target to kill and rob. If he was a typical bushwhacker, he was most likely discouraged from making a second attempt. With that behind him, he made an effort to enjoy the feel of the country around him and the abundant signs of game near the many streams that ran down from tree-covered mountains into valleys lush with grass and wildflowers.

It was not easy, though, for thoughts of Billy kept returning to haunt him. He was sure that Billy would have liked the feel of these hills and mountains. The Black Hills were in such contrast to the hundreds of miles of prairie all around them. It was little wonder that the Indians thought this place, *pahasapa*, was the center of their universe and sacred to them. Too bad these mountains were rich with gold, he thought, for gold trumped everything as far as the white man was concerned.

His meandering mind almost caused him to miss a smaller game trail that forked off from the one he had been following. Thinking it looked more promising, he guided Pepper onto it to see where it might lead him. The path wound around a pine-clad slope, climbing as it snaked its way through the thick forest. Then he suddenly came upon a rushing stream that spilled over a cliff, some seventy feet above him to crash down upon the rocks to form a deep trench that carried the water to the meadow below.

At first, he didn't notice the small tent, back under the limbs of a pine, for there had been boughs from the trees set about it to hide it from the casual eye. He reined Pepper to a stop while he took a more careful look before proceeding farther. There were no animals about that he could see. A closer look revealed what looked like a small sluice box, all but hidden behind a large boulder. It was a mining claim, but it looked to be deserted, so he urged Pepper forward and rode down to the stream. He dismounted and let his horses drink from the clear rushing water. Kneeling beside them, he filled his canteen with the cool mountain water, then placed it to his lips and took a long refreshing drink. It was then that he heard the metallic sound unmistakable as the cocking of a rifle. Having little choice, he froze with his canteen in his hand and nothing else.

"Hold on," he said. "I'm not lookin' for anything but a drink of water. I thought the camp was deserted."

Still on his knees, facing the stream, his hands raised in the air, he waited for what seemed a long time with no response from the person aiming a rifle at him. Then a figure slowly came into his field of vision, taking one careful step at a time, the rifle never wavering from the bead it had taken upon him. His assailant, a rather dumpy-looking person wearing baggy clothes, knee-high boots, and a slouchy, narrow-brimmed hat, pulled down low over his ears, said not a word but continued to aim the rifle at him. With the passing of several more long moments of silence, Logan began to get impatient.

"Look," he finally said, "I mean you no harm. I just happened to stumble onto your camp. Put the damn rifle down and I'll be on my way." He started to get to his feet, but the miner immediately jerked the rifle up as if about to shoot. Flustered now, Logan demanded, "Well, what are you aimin' to do? Either shoot me or tell me what you want me to do."

This prompted the miner to gesture toward the trail with the rifle while uttering a single word, "Go."

Logan paused, uncertain. "What?"

"Go," the miner said, and gestured with the rifle again.

Although there was an obvious attempt to sound husky, it was not enough to convince Logan. "You're a woman," he charged, astonished. He got up then, in spite of the weapon threatening him, and looked all around him. "And all alone," he added. "What in the world are you doin' out here by yourself? Where are your menfolk?"

"I'll shoot you down if you don't get off my claim," she said, no longer trying to disguise her voice.

"No, you won't," he said matter-of-factly. "'Cause it makes no sense to shoot somebody who ain't gonna do you no harm. More'n likely you need help, and I reckon it's a good thing I happened to come along, 'cause I might be able to help. How long have you been out in these mountains all alone?" Her only answer was an expression of bewilderment.

He waited to give her time to answer. When she did not, he walked up to her and took the rifle in his hand. She released it without a struggle, apparently feeling helpless to resist him. He eased the hammer down and stood the rifle up against a rock.

"Where's your husband?" he asked.

"Dead," she said, barely above a whisper.

He studied her face carefully, trying to determine how old a woman she might be, but it was hard to tell with the hat pulled down so far over her ears, and the disheveled state of her clothes. "How long?" he finally asked.

"Don't know," she replied, "two weeks, three weeks." She seemed to be in a daze, for she stood there before him, her head downcast as if awaiting her inevitable fate.

Not quite sure what he should do, he continued to study her for a few moments more before declaring, "Lady, you don't have to be afraid of me. I mean you no harm. I'll help you if I can."

Stepping from stone to stone, he crossed over the creek and went over to the tent, looking all around him at the campsite. He saw the remains of a campfire, with a coffeepot and a pan sitting in ashes that looked to be several days old. Not far from the ashes, he saw some open packs that had probably held cooking supplies but appeared now to be empty. A quick look inside the tent turned up nothing more than blankets and bedding, and a couple of packs that he guessed held clothes. He turned back to look at her.

"How long has it been since you had something to eat?"

She answered with a blank stare and a shrug.

He looked beyond the tent and for the first time noticed what appeared to be a grave. A pick and shovel had been left lying there.

"Is that your husband?"

She nodded slowly.

"Did you bury him?"

Again she nodded. He considered that for a moment, picturing the dumpy little woman laboring to bury her husband in the rocky slope behind the tent.

It was obvious to him that he was not likely to get much more out of the woman in the state she was in. It was his guess that she had run out of food some days before. And that didn't help the state of shock she was in over the death of her husband. Maybe if he could put her mind at ease, she might be able to tell him what had happened here.

"All right," he decided. "I want you to sit down on that rock by your rifle. I'm gonna get some wood and get a fire goin'. Then I'm gonna make some coffee and roast some deer jerky. I think you'll feel better after you get something to eat." She started immediately to search for firewood. "No," he ordered. "You just set yourself down on that rock and rest. I'll get the wood." She did as he said.

He gathered some limbs from the trees close by the camp and got a fire started first thing, thinking that a fire would make her feel more comfortable. After that he unsaddled the horses and let them graze in a small grassy clearing below the camp where he noticed signs that horses had grazed there before. Maybe she would be able to tell him what had happened to the horses after he got some food and coffee in her. He wasn't certain, however, that she wasn't touched in the head and unable to communicate rationally anymore.

With the horses taken care of, he went to his packs to prepare the food. While he worked at fashioning a spit for the venison, he considered the huge problem confronting him. What was he to do with the woman?

God knows, he thought. *I reckon it was my lot to find her.* He paused to think about that. *I reckon it's a good thing somebody found her, else she was on her way to perishing.* He looked back at the woman again, wondering if it was a good idea to leave the rifle propped there right beside her. He had left it there to give her a feeling of confidence that he meant her no harm. *If she is crazy,* he thought, *she might decide to pick that rifle up again and shoot me.* He decided it wouldn't be good to move the rifle now, since she seemed subdued.

Once the coffeepot was bubbling and the aroma of roasting meat rose from the fire, he thought he detected a spark of life in her otherwise dull eyes. On a flat rock by the water's edge, he found two cups, two metal plates, and silverware. He imagined that she had washed them after eating the last of her food. She watched him anxiously as he poured coffee in one of the cups and pulled some strips of deer meat from the fire, her eyes growing larger by the moment. He could see that, in spite of what he had told her, she was not sure if he was going to share his food with her. She rose quickly to meet him when he brought it to her. Taking the coffee and meat from him, she sat down again and attacked it ferociously. He couldn't help smiling.

"It's been a long time since you've had anything, hasn't it?" Too busy eating, she didn't bother to respond. He poured a cup of coffee for himself, pulled a strip of meat from the fire, and sat down on the ground facing her.

They ate in silence until the woman spoke. "Can I have some more coffee?"

"Sure," Logan replied. "Help yourself, and pull some more of that meat off if you want it. I've got some beans in one of those packs we coulda fixed, but I thought right now it'd be quicker to just cook some meat."

She filled her cup and her plate again and sat down to eat, attacking it with the same passion she had for the first plate. She paused suddenly, looked up at him watching her, and said, "Thank you." He nodded. She returned her attention to her food. When she had eaten her fill, she got to her feet and picked up both his and her plates and took them to the stream to wash.

"How'd your husband die?" he finally asked, since it appeared that she was not going to volunteer it.

"They killed him," she answered simply.

"Who killed him?" he asked.

"I don't know," she said. "They came one night, late. We were asleep. There were two of them, and they shot Jack when he ran out of the tent to stop them. I took the rifle and crawled out the back of the tent and hid in the trees."

"My Lord, ma'am, that musta been a nightmare for you," Logan responded. "You musta been scared outta your mind."

No longer reluctant to tell him, she poured the story out. "I wanted to shoot them, but I was afraid I would miss. They didn't even know I was there, and they had already killed Jack, so I just stayed hidden. They knocked the tent down and searched everywhere to see if we had found any gold. When they didn't find any, they took our two horses, the saddles, all our food supplies, and left me with nothing."

"And that was two or three weeks ago?" Logan asked. He really didn't know what to say in response to her tragedy. "Did you ever think about tryin' to walk out of these mountains, maybe findin' a town?"

"I was afraid I'd just get lost. I'm not sure of the way we came to this claim when we left Lead. Anyway, it's our claim, and I didn't want anyone to steal it. Jack and I paid most of the money we had to buy this claim from the man who first owned it."

This didn't make much sense to Logan. Why would someone sell a mining claim if it was showing real color? It sounded to him as if maybe the woman and her husband had been bamboozled out of their money. As long as she was now willing to talk, however, he continued to question her. "You came here from Lead?" He wasn't quite sure where that was, but he had heard of it.

"Yes. My husband worked for the Homestake Mine in Lead since they opened it a year ago." It seemed she had lost her fear of him, and she continued, seeming eager to tell the story. He learned that her husband, Jack, was little more than a clerk in the Homestake office. When he was offered a mining claim from someone he trusted, he decided that he would search for his fortune, instead of spending his years working for the men who really made the money. He knew very little about panning for gold, but he worked hard and she worked alongside him. And then their dream was ended on that night when they were visited by two claim robbers.

When she had told her tale, he shook his head, amazed. "Well, ma'am . . ." He paused to ask, "What is your name?"

"Hannah," she said, "Hannah Mabry. What's yours?"

"Logan Cross. I reckon I shoulda told you that right off. But what I was fixin' to say is it don't make no sense for you to be sittin' out here on this creek by yourself, with no horse, no supplies, no nothing. You've got to go someplace where there are some people. Have you got some folks somewhere you can go to?"

"No, not really," she replied. "I've got an aunt and two cousins in Omaha, but I haven't seen any of them in years. My folks are long dead."

"How 'bout your husband's folks?"

"Both of Jack's parents are still living, but we got married against their wishes, so I don't think I'd be welcome in their home, especially now. I'm sure they'd blame me for Jack's death."

Damn, he thought, *the last thing I need right now is a stranded woman to take care of.* But he knew that he had no choice other than to see that she reached somewhere safe.

"I'll tell you what we'll do, Hannah. I'll take you out of these hills to a town where you can decide what you wanna do. I'm thinkin' the best thing is to ride west till we strike that canyon I was headed for. Then, if we follow it on out, there's supposed to be a little town called Spearfish at the mouth of the canyon. I hear there's already a lot of folks settlin' there." He wasn't sure how much help that would be for her, but he didn't know what else to do with her. Maybe, he hoped, some family might take her in. "So that's what I'm thinkin'. Whaddaya say?"

She didn't respond at once, seeming reluctant to answer him. Finally she spoke just as he started to repeat the question. "I sincerely thank you for what you're offering to do for me. I appreciate it, I do. But I think I'll stay here where my husband and I have worked so hard. If you would be so kind as to leave me some of that meat, I would appreciate that, too."

He found it hard to believe that she was in her right mind. "You wanna stay here?" he pressed. "And whaddaya gonna do when that meat runs out?"

"I have my rifle," she said. "I'll hunt for something else to eat."

"Like you did before I showed up?" The woman wasn't making sense, and he was beginning to lose his patience. Then it suddenly struck him. "You and your husband found gold in this stream, didn't you?" He didn't wait for her answer. "And those claim robbers didn't find it, and that's why you don't wanna leave here. You don't wanna leave your gold." She still did not reply, but the blanching of her complexion told him that he had guessed right. "It still doesn't make sense for you to try to stay here to guard it. You don't have any supplies. You don't have any horses to pack your dust outta here, and you must have too much to tote yourself." He saw the alarm in her eyes as she stared at him, her secret revealed. "For goodness' sake, Hannah, ain't you figured out by now that I ain't gonna do you any harm? I'm not gonna steal any of your gold, but I'll help you pack it outta here, and you can put it in the bank at Spearfish, if they've got one."

She hung her head, shamed, as a child might be, caught in a lie. "I'm sorry. I know you're an honorable man. I would have known before now, if you weren't." She knew now that she had no choice but to trust him, and if she was wrong, it might be her death sentence.

"How much have you got hid away?" he asked. "Can we carry it all on my horses?"

She nodded. "Yes. There's not that much. Jack figured it was worth about twenty thousand dollars, enough to give us our money back with a good bit left over. The color had run out, though, and we decided we must have gotten all we could find panning. We were talking about leaving just before those murderers struck our camp." She paused, a wistful look upon her face. "If we had just packed up and left when we first talked about it . . ."

"Yes'um, that's a shame," he said sincerely. "It's tough to understand sometimes when hard luck hits folks that don't seem to deserve it." He thought of Billy. "A doggone shame," he murmured. Rallying his thoughts, he said, "We'll pack up in the mornin' and head outta these mountains, see if we can't find someplace safe for you and your gold."

He tried to give her a reassuring smile, hoping to encourage her, but there was still no sign of optimism in the strained frown. He wondered just how big a town Spearfish was. It might not be an easy thing to find her a safe place, especially if folks found out she was worth her weight in gold dust. On the other hand, a woman of her apparent age, with a sack of gold dust, might have her pick of the bachelors in town. Of course, that would depend on her fortune actually being that sizable.

Judging by what he had been told, very few of the inexperienced folks panning for gold ever found any of the precious metal. And most of them that did harvested little more than grub money. He hoped for her sake she and her late husband had been among the lucky few.

Although Hannah had expressed her trust in the rugged stranger who had happened upon her camp, still she slept fitfully, springing awake at every unusual sound from the horses, or the rushing stream. The morning light was a welcome sign that all was still well. There was one more test to come, however. She had not told him—and he had not asked—where the gold dust was hidden. Breakfast was coffee and venison again, and then it was time to saddle Pepper and fashion a saddle for her on the buckskin. After all was ready, he looked at his new traveling companion and could not help grinning at her reluctance when he said, "I reckon it's time to pack up that gold."

With a look of resignation, she went to the flat rock where she had washed her dishes. She stepped very carefully into the stream, trying to keep the water, which was right up to the top of her boots, from lapping over and soaking her socks and trousers. With her sleeves pushed up over her elbows, she reached under the rock and pulled out three canvas bags, one by one, and placed them on the rock. When the third bag was safely on the flat rock, she remained there, standing in the water, expecting the fatal shot, if indeed there was one to come.

"Is that it?" he asked, pleasantly surprised for her sake. She nodded, watching him intensely. "Well, come on outta there before you get your trousers soaked. I'll tie those bags on the buckskin and they can ride with you." Having a fair notion of what she was thinking, he added, "You can keep your rifle handy in case somebody tries to steal 'em."

Chapter 6

"You take a look, Wormy," Riley Stokes said. "Looks to me like he's just followin' this old game trail."

"Oughta brought us an Injun with us," Wormy japed as he stepped down to examine the tracks on the path. He looked up at Quincy and grinned, then turned it into a frown when he met Quincy's cold gaze. This was not a joking matter to the somber outlaw. He had not had a peaceful night since learning of his brother's death. Wormy wisely turned his full attention back to the game trail. It didn't pay to rile Quincy when he was in one of those moods.

"It ain't changed none, Quincy," he said. "Tracks of two horses, and they're the only fresh ones on the trail. I don't see as how it could be anybody else 'cept the feller Lacey followed to that camp back there."

Lacey had taken them to the stream where Logan had killed the deer, the place where he had attempted to kill him before taking a bullet himself. He didn't admit to Quincy that his sole purpose in following Logan had been the prospect of taking the considerable amount of money Logan had recovered in the saloon. It was better to let Quincy think that he had gone after his brother's killer solely to avenge Jake's death.

"He don't seem to be headin' nowhere in particular," Lonnie offered. "He's just followin' this game trail. Maybe he's got himself a camp up here somewhere and that's where he's goin'."

"All right," Quincy said. "Let's get goin' before we get any farther behind." He had just wanted to make sure they were following the same set of tracks they had picked up by the stream. *Logan Cross*, he thought. The name burned constantly in his mind, and he was obsessed with the need to avenge his brother's death. Everything else could wait until he took Logan Cross's life with his own hands. His urgency was mostly due to a fear that, if Cross left the game trails and turned onto one of the well-traveled roads between the towns, his tracks might be lost.

Under way once again, they followed the game trail until late in the afternoon when suddenly there were no tracks. "What the hell?" Wormy questioned. He dismounted and walked along the path, looking for the hoofprints. After walking several yards, he looked back at the others to report, "We lost him somewhere back there. There ain't no tracks."

They turned the horses around and started backtracking, searching for the place where Logan must have left the game trail. Almost right away, Curly sang out, "Here it is! I found it!" He stood by the smaller trail that branched off to wind up through the thick belt of pine trees. "I found it, Lonnie," Curly repeated proudly when Lonnie walked back to see for himself.

"He cut off on this little trail," Lonnie called back to

Quincy. Then he told the simple giant, "You did a good job, Curly." His remark left the huge man beaming with pride.

The hunt continued, climbing up the slope until the sounds of a waterfall came to them through the thick pine boughs overhead. As a precaution, Quincy sent Wormy on ahead to take a look. After a few minutes, Wormy returned to report, "We mighta found his camp. Leastways, we found somebody's camp, but it don't look like there's nobody around."

Quincy pushed past him to see for himself. He pulled up before the remains of the campfire, dismounted, and knelt to feel the ashes. "At least two or three days ago," he said. "Whadda you think, Lonnie?"

"I expect you're right," Lonnie said after sifting through the ashes himself.

"Hey, there's a tent over here," Lacey called out. "There ain't nothin' in it."

"It don't look like he's plannin' on comin' back," Stokes said, "'cause he sure didn't leave nothin' behind, but the tent. Reckon why he didn't take it?"

"Scatter out and find which way he rode outta here," Quincy said. He could feel the panic building up in his gut with the possibility that Logan might lose them at this point. The rapidly approaching darkness began closing in around the waterfall by the time Wormy found a distinct set of hoofprints starting down the eastern slope of the mountain. "Mount up!" Quincy commanded.

"Hold on a minute, Quincy," Lonnie said. "It's gonna be plumb dark in just a little while, and it'll catch us halfway down this mountain without a trail to follow. He ain't on no game trail now, so he can cut in any direction and we wouldn't catch it. I'm as anxious to catch this son of a bitch as you are, but I'm thinkin' we'd be smart to camp right here and wait till we can see in the mornin'. Whaddaya say?"

Quincy scowled. He hated to admit that Lonnie was right. They could very easily lose Logan's trail in the dark. There was also the possibility of breaking a horse's leg in the process.

"All right," he finally agreed. "We'll wait here till mornin'." His decision was met with some relief from the others, for he had pushed them relentlessly throughout the day with little rest beyond what was required to spare the horses.

"He left his tent here," Stokes reminded them. "Maybe he *is* plannin' on comin' back. He mighta just gone off to do some more huntin'."

"I reckon that's a possibility," Quincy said, and paused to think about it. He tried to form a picture of his nemesis in his mind, but found he could not. Frustrated, he called Tom Lacey over to him. "What does this Logan Cross look like?" he asked.

Somewhat surprised, Lacey answered as best he could. "I don't know. He's just a feller like everybody else—a big feller."

"Big as Curly?" Quincy asked.

"Nah," Lacey said. "He ain't quite as big as Curly. He's just bigger'n most men, I reckon." He scratched his head, trying to recall Logan's features. He had them clearly in his mind's eye, but he couldn't describe them in words. "He rides a gray horse, one of them flea-bitten ones with spots all over it. And he's leadin' a buckskin that his brother musta rode."

This caught Quincy's interest. "He's got a brother? Where is he?"

"He's dead," Lacey said. "Jake shot him."

"Jake shot him?" Quincy responded at once. "You never said anything about Jake shootin' his brother."

Lacey shrugged apologetically. "I never thought much about it."

"So Jake shot his brother," Quincy murmured to no one in particular as his mind took hold of that revealing bit of information. The task he had set for himself suddenly took on deeper meaning, and elevated the desire to kill Logan Cross to enormous proportions. It was truly a blood feud at this point. His brother had killed Cross's brother, and Cross had killed Jake, Quincy's brother. He was suddenly aware of his heartbeat pounding in his temples and he knew that nothing would stand between him and the task that was his. He continued staring at the tent across the stream, as if seeing through it, oblivious of Lacey still standing before him.

Confused by Quincy's sudden distant stare, Lacey gaped openly until he felt a tap on his shoulder. He looked around to see Lonnie standing there. Without a word, Lonnie motioned with his head for Lacey to walk away. This was the second time Lacey had witnessed one of Quincy's strange fits. It sufficiently brought home the warning never to draw Quincy's wrath down upon himself.

Lonnie turned back to his cousin. "We'll find him, Quincy. Don't you worry about that."

"I wish to hell I knew how far behind him we are," Quincy replied.

Lonnie didn't say so, but he wished the same, because the boys were anxious to get down to the business for which they had gotten the gang back together again.

Logan guided Pepper down a long ravine that opened out into a deep canyon that he guessed to be Spearfish

Canyon. Hannah followed on the buckskin, perched on her makeshift saddle with her gold and Logan's supplies packed around her. Even under the present circumstances, it was impossible for Logan to ignore the natural beauty of the canyon. The ponderosa and spruce pine that rose from the rocky creek looked in some places as if they were growing right out of the rocks, their roots taking hold in the tiniest crevices. Scattered along the banks of the creek, aspen and birch trees, along with some oaks, invaded the dominant pines. Logan wished Billy could have seen this beautiful canyon. Then he thought of the woman on Billy's horse behind him, the crumpled hat pulled low over her ears, and the oversized men's shirt and baggy pants stuffed in her heavy boots. It was unlikely she was enjoying the scenery, with her thoughts probably on the death of her husband. That caused him to wonder again what he would do with her, once they reached Spearfish.

I had to follow that damn game trail up the mountain, he complained to himself, then immediately felt ashamed for having thought it. The woman would most likely have perished, had he not happened along. *Maybe she can find some place in Spearfish,* he speculated. *Hell, she's carrying a small fortune in those canvas bags she's sitting on. She ought to be able to snag a husband for herself with that dowry.*

Bored with worrying about the woman, he returned his thoughts to concentrate on what his own prospects might be. There should be someone in Spearfish, he figured, who could tell him who some of the large cattle ranchers were, and how he could find them. If something there didn't work out for him, he would go back to Sturgis and work for Matt Morrison.

"Whaddaya say we stop up ahead by those rocks to rest the horses?" he called back to Hannah. "And we'll fix a little something to eat." She didn't give him an answer, and he didn't expect one. She usually did whatever he suggested without questioning.

The place he had pointed out seemed an ideal spot to make a camp. The creek was forced to rush through a narrow gorge, formed by huge boulders, creating a large pond above it. Logan discovered tracks of deer as well as raccoons and porcupines around the pond, suggesting a hunter's heaven. Were it not for Hannah, he might have decided to camp there for a couple of days.

Hannah did not wait for him to dismount before she slipped down from her horse and immediately started gathering wood for the fire. He let her, and turned his attention to the unsaddling of his horse and taking the packs off the buckskin. Using his flint and steel, she started the fire. "I'll cook the meat," she said, her first words since earlier that morning. She stood waiting for his response.

"All right," he said. "I'll make the coffee." She hesitated until he told her to go ahead and get whatever she needed out of his packs. "There ain't nothin' in those packs that I don't want you to see."

Bacon, deer jerky, and coffee—it was simple fare, but it almost seemed like a picnic in such a delightful setting. The only thing out of the ordinary was the lack of conversation between the participants. But that was the typical routine at each campsite as they followed the winding canyon's snakelike path through the towering mountains. They sighted the first rough structures of a town two long days later.

"Howdy, folks," Fred Ramsey greeted the strangers when they walked in the door of his store. "What can I help you with?"

"Howdy," Logan returned.

The sign on the front of the building advertised groceries and dry goods, so Logan had decided it a proper place to get some information. When he and Hannah rode into the small settlement, he saw a saloon, a stable, a blacksmith, two buildings with no signs, and Fred Ramsey's store.

About fifty yards from the stables at the north end of town was a large two-story house. There were also some tents between some of the buildings. It had all the appearances of a newly born town. Logan had hoped it would be a more established community, and before inquiring, he had his doubts about leaving Hannah there.

When Logan seemed hesitant to talk, Fred asked, "You folks ain't ever been to Spearfish before, have you?" It was unusual to see new settlers arrive with no more possessions than could be carried on two horses. "You lookin' to settle here, or are you passin' through?"

"So this is Spearfish?" Logan responded. "I'm glad to hear it, 'cause back yonder a ways I was beginnin' to wonder if that canyon had a mouth. Tell you the truth, though, I thought the town was a little bigger than this."

Fred chuckled. "We think we're pretty big right now, and we're still growin' pretty fast. Some of us thought this little spot in the valley would make a perfect place for a town. And I guess we were right, 'cause a little over a year ago the first store was built, and a post office, and that's all. Look at us now. So if you folks are lookin' for a place to settle, there's still some good land here, and you can get anything in Spearfish that you can get in Sturgis or Deadwood."

"We ain't lookin' for a place to settle," Logan said.

After he had told Fred the circumstances that had resulted in their traveling together, Fred shook his head in sympathy for Hannah's plight. "You poor thing," he said to her. "You've been through a bad time, haven't you?" He walked over a few feet toward the end of the counter and called out through a door leading to another room, "Martha! Come in here, honey."

About half a minute later, a short, round, pleasant-looking woman came through the stockroom door. "This is my wife," Fred said, then went on to explain to Martha. "This poor woman has just lost her husband—murdered by claim robbers—and she was lucky that this young feller happened to come along to help her."

"You poor dear," Martha exclaimed after she had heard the story. She took a longer look at Hannah. "You look like you've had a really hard time of it. What are you going to do?"

Hannah shook her head. Logan answered for her. "I reckon Hannah's lookin' for a place to stay till she can decide what she's gonna do."

"Mae Davis," Fred said right away, and looked at his wife for confirmation.

She nodded in agreement. "Fred's right. You should go talk to Mae Davis. She owns that big house at the end of the street, beyond the stable. Mae's a widow. Before he died, her husband built that big place as a rooming house and dining room. Mae's been running it by herself since Roger got thrown off a horse and landed on his head. That would be the best place for you to stay until you decide what you're gonna do." Judging by Hannah's appearance, Martha thought she might suggest something further. "Mae's only got one woman helping her cook now, a young woman named Daisy. She had another one, a girl named Violet, to help with the house." She laughed then and said, "Folks here in town say that Mae had two flowers in her kitchen till somebody came along and picked one. Violet met a young cowhand and left to get married. Moved to . . . Where'd Violet and that young fellow move to, Fred?" Fred shook his head. "Anyway, Mae might need some help since Violet left."

Logan glanced at Hannah to see how she responded to Martha's suggestion. She seemed interested, which was a good sign as far as he was concerned.

"Thank you for your help," Hannah said. "I'll go down and talk to Mrs. Davis."

The response from the heretofore silent woman surprised Martha. It fairly astonished Logan. She had not spoken until that moment. Logan thanked the Ramseys as well, and they led the horses down the short street, past the stables, to the house pointed out by Martha Ramsey.

"Howdy, folks," Mae Davis greeted them at the door. "You're a little bit early for supper. Won't be serving for another hour yet." A large-framed woman with a pleasant smile, she took a long look at the pair of strangers at her front door before deciding to ask, "Are you looking to rent a room?"

"Well, yes, ma'am," Logan answered, "maybe. What I mean is, she might be interested in rentin' a room."

"Oh," Mae responded, somewhat put off by Hannah's appearance. "You two aren't together?"

"No, ma'am," Logan replied, then went on to explain the events that led them to her door.

Much as Martha Ramsey had, Mae immediately expressed compassion for the tragic circumstances that had befallen Hannah. She was even moved to give

Hannah a vigorous hug, in spite of the woman's dingy attire.

"You poor darlin'," she cooed, motherlike. "Not only your dear husband, but everything else was lost, I expect. Well, you've come to the right place. You can stay here while you decide what to do. As a matter of fact, I need someone to help Daisy and me, if you're interested. That way you could earn your room and board while you're here. Whaddaya say? Can you cook?"

Hannah nodded, then answered, "Yes, ma'am, a little, I guess."

"All right, then," Mae said. "We'll give it a try, and see how it works out. Have you got any more clothes with you?" She shrugged. "I mean women's clothes? If you ain't, then I guess you might borrow some from Daisy. She'd be closer to your size." She laughed and winked at Logan. "Can't have you serving the folks in your knee-high boots." She continued to inspect her prospective employee for a moment more before making another suggestion. "My late husband, Roger, built me a jim-dandy washhouse out back. You might wanna try it out before you get started."

"Yes, ma'am, I would," Hannah said. "Thank you for your help, but I can pay for my room and board until you see if you really want to hire me to work for you."

Her offer took Mae by surprise. She glanced up at Logan, looking for confirmation, and he nodded. "Well, that's even better, but we'll talk about that later on." She punctuated her remark with a final nod of her head. "Now, let's get you settled in, and I'll take you back to meet Daisy. She's gonna be glad to see some help." Looking back at Logan again, she said, "Like I said, supper will be in an hour, if you wanna come back then to eat."

"I reckon," he said. "I'll help Hannah tote her things in." He stepped off the porch and went to unpack her meager belongings. Letting her take the two small bags of clothes she had brought, he carried the three sacks of gold, since they were the heaviest.

"I owe you so much," she said to him after they had taken her things inside. "I don't know if I could ever repay you for bringing me here. Maybe I can give you some of the gold dust, if you'll tell me how much." It was an awkward proposal, but she didn't know what else to say.

He smiled at her. "You don't owe me a thing, Hannah. You need to keep that dust. It's gonna pay for your future." It appeared to him that she was trying to give him an appropriate farewell, probably figuring she wouldn't see him again, once he was free of her. "I'll see you in about an hour. I need to test Mae's cookin'."

With Hannah off his hands now, Logan found his interest turning to his own prospects. Deciding he had earned a glass of beer before supper, he rode up the street to the establishment that displayed a sign proclaiming it to be the Gateway Saloon. Inside, he was greeted by the bartender, Cecil Grant. "What'll you have?" he asked.

"I think I'd like a glass of beer, if you have any," Logan replied.

"I sure do," Cecil said, and proceeded to produce a glass. He stood there for a moment watching Cross test it before he asked, "Just get into town?"

"Yep," Logan answered, and wiped his mouth with the back of his hand. "And right now I'm lookin' for work."

"Punchin' cows?" Cecil asked, making a judgment based on Logan's attire.

"Yep," Logan answered again. "Fellow I worked for over near Sturgis said there were a couple of big cattle outfits over this way. You wouldn't happen to know if they're lookin' for men, would you?"

"Well, no, I don't for a fact, but Jace Evans is the foreman for the Triple-T, and he oughta be in here later on this evening. He usually comes in every Saturday."

"Is today Saturday?" Logan replied. He had lost count of the days.

Cecil laughed. "You musta been roamin' around in the mountains for a while."

"As a matter of fact," Logan said, laughing with him, "I just came over from Deadwood Gulch and I reckon I kinda lost track of the days. Anyway, maybe I'll come back after supper and talk to this fellow Evans if he shows up."

He finished his beer and left after a few minutes of talking to Cecil about the town of Spearfish and how fast it was growing. He wondered if that would be a good thing for Hannah. He hoped so. With time still remaining before supper would be served at Mae's dining room, he decided he would leave his horses in the stable overnight. Both the gray and the buckskin would most likely enjoy a ration of grain. Then he would decide what to do tomorrow, after talking to Jace Evans.

By the time he had taken care of his horses and made arrangements with Sam Taylor, who owned the stable, to sleep there with his horses, it was time to go to supper. He was surprised to find a dozen customers already seated at a long table in the center of a large dining room. It didn't surprise him that they were all men. He found a place between two cowhands, who politely shoved over a little to give him room. "Much obliged," he said, and turned his plate and cup right side up.

Mae Davis was already working her way from the end of the table, spooning out generous helpings of beef stew. When she came to Logan's plate, she paused to speak to him. "We've already put your lady friend to work. I think she'll work out just fine with Daisy and me. I think I owe you a big thanks for bringing her here."

"I'm mighty glad to hear that," Logan said. "I was a little bit worried about her."

"Well, you can stop your worrying now. We'll take good care of her. Yes, sir, I'm mighty glad she came along."

She went on with her serving until reaching the end of the table. Then she went to the kitchen with the empty bowl. What had been a noisy room moments before became suddenly quiet as the patrons turned all their attention to their plates.

A trim young woman emerged from the kitchen carrying a large platter piled high with biscuits. *That'll be Daisy,* Logan thought, and waited for the platter to come within his reach. When it came to him, he quickly plucked one of the browner ones, then glanced up when the platter remained in front of him. Confused for a moment, then shocked when the young lady spoke, he couldn't believe his eyes. "Logan?" Hannah asked, surprised that he did not greet her.

He almost dropped his biscuit, unable to do anything but gawk at the transformation. "Hannah?" he finally blurted. "Is that you?"

"Well, of course it is," she said, astonished by his strange reception, and unaware of the extreme change he saw in her. "Who did you think it was?"

Before he could answer, someone at the end of the table spoke up. "How 'bout passin' those biscuits on down before they get cold while you two visit?"

"Sorry," she said, and continued along the table, leaving Logan practically stunned, amazed that he could have been with her for that length of time while never knowing what her costume was hiding.

He understood why she had attempted to look like a man when he first happened upon her camp. But why, he wondered, would she have continued to crush that honey blond hair up under her husband's battered old hat? He didn't know why, but he had assumed it was gray. He realized that he had never really paid that much attention to what the woman looked like. It occurred to him then that she had harbored fears beyond those of losing her gold dust, and she felt it safer to hide her shapely body under her disguise of baggy men's garments.

It took him a few minutes to recover from his surprise, but then he got used to seeing her in her natural appearance as she came back and forth from the kitchen. He regained his appetite then and attacked his supper once more. It was kind of funny in a way, he thought, the way she had fooled him. Before supper was finished, she paused to say that she had something she wanted to tell him before he left. So he sat there after he was finished eating, drinking coffee until he could hold no more.

When all but he and a couple of other diners were left, Hannah came out and sat down on the bench beside him. "Did you enjoy your supper?" she asked.

"Yeah, it was good," he answered, feeling as if talking to someone he had just met. "What was it you wanted to tell me?"

"Well," she began, "I could tell that you were worried about me after you left me here, so I wanted to set your mind at ease. I owe you so much. I realize now that you are an honorable man, and there was no need to ever fear harm by you. So that you can know I'm all right now, I want to tell you what I've decided to do. Mae told me of her plans to build on more rooms and eventually make this place a real hotel. She said she has been unable to get any further along than this small two-story house, because her money ran out."

He could see what was coming, and said, "So you're investin' your money in it."

"That's right," Hannah said, surprised. "Mae and I are gonna be partners. Daisy is a widow, too, so we're thinking about calling it the Three Widows Inn. Whaddaya think?" She beamed delightedly.

"That's right catchy," he said, thinking that he hadn't seen her smile like that before. He couldn't honestly say if the hotel was a good investment for her fortune, but he supposed that it was better than letting it sit in a bank somewhere doing nothing. Her newfound enthusiasm alone was worth it, he decided. So he said, "Well, that whole thing sounds like a dandy idea. I know you can make it work. That Mae looks like she's a real doer."

"Thank you, Logan," Hannah said sincerely, and got to her feet. She extended her hand and they shook. "I'd better get back and help my new partner in the kitchen before she decides she's made a bad bargain."

As she walked away, he couldn't help calling after her, "Just promise me you won't ever dress up in those old baggy pants and knee boots again."

She looked back at him and smiled. "I promise," she said.

He reached under the bench for his hat, put it on his head, and started for the door. A strange feeling, bordering on loneliness, seemed to have suddenly descended upon him, one he couldn't explain. For the past few days, he had wondered how he was going to get out from under the burden of this mournful woman. Now he might be forced to admit that he was going to miss her.

"If that ain't somethin'," he muttered as he headed for the stables.

Chapter 7

"That's Jace Evans over yonder," Cecil Grant said, and nodded toward a table occupied by four men, near the back of the saloon. "Jace is the one wearin' the black vest and the Montana Peak hat. That's three of his men he's settin' with."

"Much obliged," Logan said. "I'll go see if I can talk to him." The conversation at the table stopped when he walked up to stand before them. "Evenin', fellows. Pardon me for buttin' into your drinkin', but I'd like a word with Mr. Evans."

Evans gave the tall stranger a good looking-over before speaking. "What about?" he asked.

"I'm lookin' for work, and the bartender said you're the foreman at the Triple-T, so I thought I'd ask if you're lookin' to hire any new men," Logan said.

"He did, did he?" Evans replied. He looked over at the man seated across from him and said, "I didn't know Cecil was doin' the hirin' for me now." The remark brought the chuckle he expected from the other three at the table. Turning back to Logan, he said, "Have you worked around here anywhere?" Logan said that he hadn't. "What have you been doin' all summer, just driftin'?"

"Nope," Logan answered. "I helped drive a herd from Ogallala up to Fort Pierre. Then I worked for a man named Morrison, who drove a herd of horses from Fort Pierre to Sturgis on the other side of the mountain. I got caught at the end of the summer with time on my hands, so I'm lookin' for someplace to start work again. Figured you might be needin' some more help for the fall roundup."

Evans studied the rugged individual standing squarely before him, meeting his gaze eye to eye. He couldn't help being impressed by the way the man carried himself.

"For a fact, I might be hirin' some more men in about a couple of weeks from now, but I'll only be lookin' for the best cowhands this fall. You figure you're the best?"

Logan didn't hesitate to answer. "I don't know if I'm the best or not, but I'm pretty sure I can cowboy with the best and hold my own. And I won't take a man's pay unless he thinks I earned it."

"I'll tell you what," Evans said, even more impressed after Logan's answer to his question, "you show up at the Triple-T two days from today, and I'll give you a chance to back that up. All right?"

"All right," Logan answered. "How can I find the Triple-T?"

"That'll be the first test you have to pass," Evans replied to the chuckles of his companions at the table.

Logan smiled. "Fair enough," he said without hesitation, "two days from today. Much obliged." He nodded to the others at the table before turning around and walking toward the door.

Jace Evans's japing didn't really irritate Logan very much. It was not unusual for a new hire to be tested for his sense of humor as well as his work ethic. It would have been the obvious thing to just invite him to ride on back to the ranch with them, since he wanted him to show up in only two days. But Logan figured he would ask Sam Taylor how to find the Triple-T. In the meantime he had a couple of days with nothing to do.

He found Sam working in the tack room when he got back to the stable. "Reckon I'll be ridin' out to the Triple-T tomorrow," he said to him, "that is, if you can tell me where it is."

"Easy enough to find," Sam said. "Take the north road outta Spearfish. It runs right along Spearfish Creek for about three miles before it leaves the creek and branches off more to the west. The Triple-T is about four miles from where the road leaves the creek. There's a smaller creek that feeds into the Spearfish that runs right along beside the road, right through Thomas Towson's ranch. He's the owner of the Triple-T and they like to call that little branch Towson's Creek. Just follow the creek and you can't miss the ranch house."

"'Preciate it," Logan said. "I reckon I can find that easy enough."

The next day was Sunday and Logan was tempted to treat himself to breakfast at Mae's dining room to get one more look at Hannah before he started out to find the Triple-T. He decided against it, however, telling himself there was no purpose to it beyond a curiosity to see if she really looked as good as he had thought the night before.

"I reckon I'll just have breakfast with you," he told his horse, "like it was before we picked up Hannah."

He had no trouble following Sam's directions. They were as simple as he had claimed. When he came to the second creek that Sam had described, he followed it for a couple of miles before stopping to fix a little breakfast of coffee to go with some more of the deer jerky he had plenty of. The mountains were behind him now, with a smaller range of hills off toward the northeast, and nothing but an endless sea of grass before him. It was little wonder that the cattlemen had found this country, once the Indians were driven off to the reservations. In the saddle again, he guessed he was already on the Triple-T range, for he began to sight small groups of cattle here and there.

Jace Evans had told him to report on Monday, but Logan purposely rode out a day early for a couple of reasons. In the first place, he wanted to get a look at the outfit beforehand, just to get a feel for it. He had not definitely ruled out the possibility of returning to Sturgis to sign on with Matt Morrison. In the second place, he was always early for any job he agreed to do, so he planned to be there waiting when Evans came out in the morning.

He rode another couple of miles before he spotted the headquarters buildings lying low on the horizon. A sizable ranch house, a large barn with a corral, several other smaller buildings, plus a bunkhouse, all of them in good repair, which was a sign he was looking for. At first glance, it appeared to be a well-run operation. He would skirt well clear of it as he scouted out the surrounding range and picked a place to camp overnight.

A little before sundown, he settled on a spot on yet another creek where it made a turn around a clump of cottonwoods north of the ranch headquarters. He figured he was about a mile and a half from the ranch.

Monday morning, first day of the roundup, Jace Evans thought as he walked out of his room at the end of the bunkhouse. It was a little earlier than usual, still hard dark, but he wanted to let the men know that it was time to go to work to earn their pay. *Better get a good meal in your belly to get ahead of the day,* he told himself as he strode toward the cookhouse. He thought it was always best to be the first one up in the mornings. It served to demonstrate to his crew that he worked longer and harder than anyone.

On this morning, however, he stopped abruptly when halfway across the yard between the two buildings when he saw two horses tied at the corner of the cookhouse. He made out the form of a man sitting on the ground with his back against the building. When the man spotted him, he got up and stood waiting for him to approach.

"Well, I'll be damned," Jace drawled when he recognized him. "I wasn't sure you'd show up. Hell, I'd almost forgot about you."

"You said show up today," Logan said. "So here I am."

"I didn't expect you this early," Jace said.

"The day's already started and I didn't wanna be late."

Jace couldn't help laughing. "Well, you ain't late. Come on in and we'll get some breakfast." He opened the door and held it for Logan. "What did you say your name was?"

"Logan Cross."

"All right, Cross. While we eat, I'll figure out who I'm gonna send you out with."

Over a breakfast of sourdough biscuits, sowbelly, white gravy, potatoes, and steaming black coffee, Jace talked cattle with his potential hire. He quickly got an idea that Logan was a genuine cattle hand, so he made up his mind before half of the crew struggled in for breakfast.

As each man walked in, he cast a curious eye in Logan's direction, but Jace was waiting to introduce him after the whole crew got there. Even though he felt he was hiring a good man, Jace couldn't resist putting Logan through a test that had become a standard on the Triple-T.

"I've been thinkin' about it," he said, "and I expect I'll send you out with Ox today. He can show you the ropes."

Logan noticed that the comment brought forth a few grunts of amusement from the men seated close to them. He had no trouble guessing the reason when, seconds later, Ox Russell walked in.

One look at the imposing man told Logan that he was the resident tough. Every crew seemed to have one, and this one looked typical. Not especially tall, but broad of shoulders and thick through the chest, Ox wore his long black hair in two heavy braids, Indian-style, a bushy mustache his only facial hair.

"Looks like you got yourself a new partner, Ox," one of the men said, causing the others to laugh and drawing a frown on Ox's dark face. Jace chose that moment to introduce the new hire to the crew.

"This is Logan Cross," he began. "He'll be workin'

with us today, ridin' with Ox, so he can get a chance to see how things are done on the Triple-T." He turned to address the scowling Ox, who was still standing there glaring at Logan. "Ox, I want you to ride up toward the Belle Fourche to see how many of our cows have drifted up to the river. Might be more'n the two of you can handle. If there are, I'll send more of the boys up there to help you drive 'em back this way tomorrow. All right?"

"You're the boss," Ox grunted, still glaring at the new man. He remained to hover over Logan for a few moments more before finding an empty spot at the long table.

Looks like it's going to be a long day, Logan thought. *But at least the brute can talk.* He had seen the ritual before, but this would be the first time for him as a participant.

The rest of the breakfast went peacefully enough, with the usual good-natured ribbing and playful insults among the hands. Near the end, Jace told them how they would work the day, and who would go where on the extensive range the Triple-T covered. Most of the men made it a point to say howdy to Logan on their way out of the cookhouse, and a couple offered a handshake.

Before he could go to work, Logan had to find a space in the tack room of the barn to leave his pack-saddle, supplies, and other gear. This delay seemed to irritate Ox, judging by the expression on his face, even though he had to saddle his horse while Logan was in the process of stowing his gear. Ready to ride, Logan turned his buckskin out with the remuda and followed the belligerent brute out of the yard at a lope.

Ox followed a wide stream that meandered across the rolling prairie grassland, passing large and small groups of grazing cattle. Logan remained content to ride silently along behind him.

After about two hours, they reached the Belle Fourche River, and Ox turned east to follow the river's course. As Jace had probably expected, there were a large number of cattle that had found their way to the river, too many for the two of them to round up and drive back toward the ranch by themselves. Ox pulled up to look out over a narrow draw that led down to the water's edge where Logan counted about forty head of cows.

"I expect we'll need half a dozen men to bunch all these cows along this river and drive 'em back," Logan suggested. They were the first words spoken since leaving the bunkhouse.

Suspicious of new men by nature, Ox shot him a look of contempt, and Logan thought he was not going to reply for a long moment. Finally Ox said, "Maybe where you come from—I could round up these strays and drive 'em back to the ranch by myself, long as you didn't get in my way."

Logan had expected to get some japing, but that bordered on ridiculous. "Well, now, that would be somethin' I'd truly like to see. I'll sure as hell try to stay outta your way while you're doin' it."

"Are you sayin' I can't?" Ox responded.

"Why, no," Logan said. "I ain't sayin' you can't. I just said I wanna watch you do it."

"You callin' me a liar?"

"Not at all," Logan answered. "I was just hopin' I'd get to see somethin' a man don't get to see every day."

Ox hesitated, not sure if he was being baited or not. Logan's expression held no hint of a challenge, so he gave his horse a kick and started down across the draw.

"You might get to see somethin' you ain't seen, all right, before this day is over," he mumbled.

Logan exhaled a long, tired sigh. He was sure now

that what he had at first suspected was true. Ox obviously enjoyed the title of the toughest man in the crew. Logan figured that any new man who was a little bigger than average, or powerfully built, must be seen as a challenge to Ox's claim, and was consequently called out to contest it. Logan wasn't interested in the competition, so he intended to remain passive.

They continued along the river for a couple of miles to get a rough count of the strays. They weren't concerned about any cows crossing to the other side of the river, because of the animals' natural reluctance to cross any river.

When they reached a double bend in the river where a backup of the water had created a boggy area, they discovered a cow in trouble. It had moved too far out for the quicksandlike bottom and gotten stuck.

Upon spotting the cow, Logan automatically pulled the coil of rope from his saddle and snaked out a loop. He guided Pepper along the edge of the water, lassoed the stalled cow, and pulled it back to dry land. Somehow his actions displeased Ox, who figured the new man was showing off.

"You ought'n done that, without askin' me first," Ox said. "You coulda got that horse sucked down in that mess, too."

"I don't think so," Logan said. "This ain't my first time ropin' a cow."

"It's your first time ridin' with me, and I don't tolerate workin' with somebody who don't know what the hell he's doin'."

Logan glared at him for a long moment before he responded, still determined not to get into it with the quarrelsome bully. Then very calmly he spoke. "We'll tell Jace not to put me with you after this. Would that satisfy you?"

"Maybe," Ox replied, thinking that Logan was showing signs of knuckling under. Confident now that the new man seemed intent upon avoiding any confrontation with him, and his spirits seemed to lift a little. "All right, I think it's time to rest these horses, and get a bite to eat. I hope you got somethin', 'cause I don't figure on feedin' you." He stepped down and reached in his saddlebag and took out a biscuit and some sowbelly wrapped in a cloth. "It's every man for hisself," he said, and took a bite of the biscuit.

"Fair enough," Logan said. He dismounted and pulled the saddle off Pepper. Then he took his little coffeepot out of his war bag and went to the river to fill it. "We might as well have some coffee, as long as we've got to rest the horses. And I just happen to have some."

Ox said nothing as he watched Logan gather up some dead limbs for a fire. When the flame was kindled and the coffeepot was on the fire and starting to boil, Ox got up on his feet and announced, "Time to get goin'. We ain't got no time for that."

"I thought we were goin' to rest the horses," Logan said.

"They're rested enough," Ox insisted. "Dump that out and get mounted."

Well, here it is, Logan thought. *There ain't no getting around it.* He calmly checked the progress of his coffee, then looked up at Ox looming over him as he knelt beside his fire. "My horse ain't rested near enough," Logan said. "And neither is yours from the look of him, so sit your ass back down and we'll finish eatin'." He saw the look of shocked disbelief in Ox's eyes as the big man was suddenly at a loss for words. Before he could recover, Logan went on. "You can have some of this to wash that biscuit down if you've got a cup. As fast as you choked it down, I expect it's still stuck in your throat. If you ain't got a cup, you'll have to wait till I finish my coffee, and maybe I'll let you use mine."

"Why, you smart-mouth son of a bitch," Ox bellowed, "I'm fixin' to whip your ass."

"Take my word for it, Ox," Logan said calmly as he poured his coffee, "you'll enjoy a cup of this coffee a whole lot more."

Appearing frustrated with Logan's refusal to respond to his threats in the way he expected, Ox suddenly reached down and grabbed him by the collar. He released it a split second later when he got the steaming cup of hot coffee full in his face.

"Yow!" he yelped in pain, and stepped backward. Logan followed, springing up under him with a sizable piece of burning firewood in his hand.

Before Ox had time to recover, Logan bounced the stick of wood off his ear, sending the big man staggering. Stunned by the sudden reversal of roles, Ox tried to gather himself together and attempted to wipe his face clean of the fiery liquid, aware of the throbbing in the side of his head and his bleeding ear. He looked at the man standing poised like a big cat, his feet spread wide, his body in a slight crouch, waiting patiently to meet his attack. Ox realized at that moment that the man did not fear him. It caused him to hesitate. Being a simple man, however, he didn't know what else to do, so he charged, head down, like a bull, blindly.

It was what Logan hoped for, because he wasn't sure how well he would come out in a toe-to-toe fistfight with the hulking brute. He stood his ground, meeting the charge until the last second when, like a bullfighter, he quickly stepped aside and delivered a blow to the back of Ox's head strong enough to send him crashing face-first into the fire.

Roaring out in pain, Ox rolled off the fire, his head throbbing from two blows, frantically slapping at his clothes for fear they had caught fire. Totally confused now, unable to understand why things had happened as they did, he struggled to get up on one knee and gazed bleary-eyed at his adversary. Logan shook his head slowly.

"Quit while you're ahead," he advised calmly, "and we'll forget the whole thing."

Ox, uncertain, his physical dominance challenged for the first time, could only stare at his adversary for a long moment while he tried to decide what he should do. The longer he sat there, the more he became aware of his throbbing head and the stinging burning on his right ear. Finally he roared out his outrage and got up on his feet again, prepared to charge.

"Don't do it," Logan warned. "It's only gonna get worse."

He watched the frustrated monster closely. Ox was big and powerful, but he was clumsy, and this was the advantage that Logan knew was his. With his enthusiasm waning, Ox braced himself for one more attack, not knowing what else to do. The charge, like the one before it, came in a head-down bull rush. The results were much the same as the first. As before, Logan stepped deftly aside and this time planted his foot on Ox's backside as the bull passed by him. Ox's momentum, aided by Logan's boot, was the principal cause of yet another crash to the ground. Bewildered and frustrated, the big man rolled over and remained sitting on the ground for a moment unsure of another attempt. He started to get up, but Logan stopped him.

"Just sit right there and think about it," he said. "There ain't no reason for you to try to make an enemy outta me. I got nothin' against you, and I ain't done nothin' to make you wanna fight me. As far as I'm concerned, this never happened. Now I'm gonna see if I can put my fire back together and we'll have that cup of coffee before we go back to work. Is that all right with you?"

Dumbstruck and confused, Ox had to think about it for a few moments. For the first time in his adult life, he felt small and defeated. He gazed vacantly at the seemingly agreeable face of his reluctant adversary. Finally the simple brute said, "I wouldn't mind a cup of coffee."

In a short while, the two combatants sat drinking coffee and chewing on some smoked venison that Logan supplied from his saddlebags. Ox was not quite sure how the circumstances had changed. He knew he had been bested, but he no longer had any desire to fight the new hire.

Afterward, they continued riding along the Belle Fourche until meeting two of the men working the river in the opposite direction. With the scouting of the northern section of their range completed, their job for the day was completed. The actual roundup would probably start the next day.

The burned bruise on Ox's right ear did not go unnoticed, nor the black smudge across the back of his collar. One of the two men, Jim Bledsoe, was prompted to ask, "What the hell happened to you, Ox?"

Before Ox could answer, Logan responded for him. "He tripped and fell right in the fire we built for some coffee."

Ox shot a quick glance of appreciation in Logan's

direction before saying, "Yeah, I reckon my feet are gettin' too big to go where I put 'em." And though Logan wasn't aware of it at the moment, with that comment, he had made a firm friend on the Triple-T.

The same version of Ox's accident was retold back at the bunkhouse that night. But it was puzzling to the other men that Ox had for some reason accepted Logan without challenging him to prove himself physically. Ox was, after all, a simple man, and sometimes hard to explain. Jace Evans, on the other hand, held a suspicion that his new hire had a hell of a lot more to do with Ox's acceptance than would ever be told.

The next morning signaled the actual start of the roundup and Jace sent his men out in groups of three, riding out to the farther reaches of the range to begin the process of finding the strays and driving them back to the Triple-T. This meant returning to the Belle Fourche to pick up those cows that had strayed that far. Logan was sent out with Jim Bledsoe and Bob Whitley. They drew enough supplies and extra horses to sustain them for at least four days, since they would not be able to return to the ranch every night.

Peace of mind returned to Logan when he was back in the business of tending cattle. It was a business that he knew well, so it was a pleasure to be back doing it. Both Bledsoe and Whitley were good men to work with, so in no time at all, he felt that he had found a home. His only worry at this point was whether or not he would be cut loose when winter set in. Being the latest hire, he might be the first to be let go to ride the grub line with cowhands from other spreads who were out of work for the winter.

I'll worry about that when the time comes, he told himself.

Chapter 8

"Looks like a town up ahead," Lonnie Morgan called back over his shoulder.

"Spearfish," Quincy responded, making the same assumption Logan had. "I figured that's where he was headed. Couldn'ta been nowhere else."

They lost the tracks they had been following two days before, but they had continued to ride out the canyon to its mouth. Leaving the mountains behind now, they were glad to see the buildings of Spearfish.

"I hope to hell there's a saloon there," Riley Stokes moaned. "If I don't get a drink of whiskey pretty soon, I'm gonna wither up and die."

Lonnie laughed, ready for a drink himself. "Anytime there's two buildin's standin', one of 'em's a saloon. And I see half a dozen or more already." He reined his horse back until Quincy pulled up beside him. "How 'bout you, cousin? A drink right now would be pretty good, wouldn't it?"

He was worried about Quincy and the fact that he

had been in one of his dark moods for the past two days since they lost the trail from Deadwood Gulch. Quincy didn't answer, so deep in thought was he. He sensed that the man who shot Jake was close now.

"There it is," Stokes called out. "I see the sign— Gateway Saloon." He started for it, but Quincy yelled for him to stop. Stokes pulled up immediately. "Ain't we gonna get a drink?" he asked, disappointed.

Out of his somber reverie now, Quincy said, "Sure, we're gonna get a drink. I want one as bad as you do. But I wanna do the talkin' when we go in that saloon. I don't want the rest of you mouthin' off. You got that straight?"

"Sure, Quincy," Stokes said. "You'll do the talkin'."

They proceeded to the saloon, dismounted, and tied their horses at the rail. Waiting for Quincy to lead the way, they looked up and down the short street to get an idea of the place they had landed. Then following him, they entered the Gateway Saloon.

"Afternoon," Cecil Grant greeted the six strangers. He couldn't help noticing the way they scanned the room before advancing to the bar. "Welcome to the Gateway," he said. "You're the second bunch of folks that rode into town this week."

"The second bunch, huh?" Quincy grunted. "Gimme a bottle of whiskey for my men. Then maybe you can give me some information." He watched Cecil as he got a bottle and six glasses. "You got a sheriff in this town?"

"Well, no, we ain't," Cecil said. "Up to now, we ain't really needed one." The question made him a little uncomfortable when he looked at the six men standing at his bar.

Quincy sensed Cecil's concern. He fashioned a smile for him and said, "Don't let the look of my men worry you. I'm a U.S. Marshal and these are my posse men. We've been ridin' hard for the past week, lookin' for a killer that murdered a man in Montana City. Figured you mighta seen him. I'm pretty sure he passed this way. His name's Logan Cross." He placed money on the bar for the whiskey. "What about it? You see a stranger come through here by that name in the past week?"

"No, can't say as I have," Cecil replied, a little more comfortable now that he thought the strangers were actually lawmen. "We had a man and a woman pass through here a few days ago, but I ain't seen a man like you're lookin' for." He knew now that the lady's name was Hannah but couldn't recall if the man had given his name or not when he was in the saloon. He would have been truly surprised if that man was the murdering outlaw the marshal was looking for, however.

"A man and a woman," Quincy repeated, thinking back on the campsites they had found where they thought they found evidence of someone else with Cross. "What did the man look like?" he asked.

"I don't know," Cecil answered. "Average-lookin' fellow, I guess, pretty big." He nodded toward Curly. "Not as big as him."

That didn't give Quincy any more help than Lacey's description had. Then he remembered something else Lacey had told him. "What kinda horse was he ridin'?"

"Lemme think a minute," Cecil said. "If I recollect right, I think he was ridin' a gray horse, one of them with spots all over it."

That was enough to excite Quincy. "Is he still in town?"

"Oh no, he didn't hang around long." He picked up

a glass from the counter and began wiping it with a rag. "The lady that was with him stayed here, though."

From the look of excitement in Quincy's face, it occurred to Cecil that it would have been just as well had he not told him that. "That lady wasn't the kind of woman to be ridin' with an outlaw," he said. "No, sir, she's an upstandin' woman, settlin' down here in Spearfish. And like I said, that fellow she was with didn't look like an outlaw."

Quincy smiled. "Well, now, outlaws come in all kinds of sizes and shapes, don't they? She might not a' knowed she was ridin' with an outlaw. Where is the woman? And remember, you're talkin' to a U.S. Marshal, so don't play no games with me."

"Oh, no, sir," Cecil replied quickly. "I wouldn't do that. I've got no reason to help an outlaw. Her name's Hannah and she's stayin' at that two-story house down past the stable. A really nice lady, who's just lost her husband—she's gonna help Mae Davis run the dinin' room."

Quincy's smile grew wider. "Well, thank you, sir. You've most likely helped bring a wanted man to justice. We'll ride on down to that dinin' room, maybe take supper there." He turned toward the others. "Whaddaya think, boys? It'd be kinda nice to eat some supper under a roof, fixed by a woman cook, wouldn't it?"

His question was met with grinning nods and grunts of approval. "That's just what we need, all right," Lonnie said, encouraged to see his cousin seeming to come out of the black mood that had possessed him over the last two days.

"What time do they start servin' supper?" Quincy asked. When Cecil answered that they served supper at five o'clock, Quincy said, "About thirty minutes from now. That'll give us time to have a few drinks."

"Looks like we're gonna have a good crowd for supper tonight," Mae Davis commented to Hannah and Daisy when she looked out her front window and saw the group of six men stepping up on the porch. "Rough-lookin' bunch. I've never seen any of them before. You might better throw some more potatoes in that stew, Daisy." She walked over and opened the door for them.

Always confident in his ability to charm the ladies, Quincy wasted no time before endeavoring to impress Mae. Though not normally gullible when it came to most things, she was not totally immune to extra attention from a man as handsome as Quincy Morgan.

"Good evenin', ma'am," he began with a generous smile for her. "Fellow back at the saloon told us this was the place to get a good supper. He didn't tell us it was run by such an attractive lady, though."

Mae blushed, unaccustomed as she was to such compliments. "Why, shut your mouth," she said, unable to think of anything more eloquent. "You must be tryin' to lower the price."

She looked beyond Quincy then at the rugged collection of unkempt men behind him, most of them with amused grins on their faces. Her gaze lingered a moment on Curly, stopped by the blank stare the huge man fixed upon her. "You fellows lookin' for supper, I reckon," she managed in an effort not to show her concern.

"Why, yes, ma'am," Quincy replied. "We'd enjoy tryin' some of your cookin'. It's been a while since me and the boys have had a chance to try some home cookin'. We've been in the saddle for quite a spell." He paused then, as if just remembering. "Excuse my manners, ma'am. I'm U.S. Marshal Quincy Smith. These men are my posse men. We've been trailin' a dangerous man ever since Deadwood Gulch. He's wanted for murder."

That explained the roughshod-looking men with him to some degree, Mae decided, thinking they looked little more than outlaws themselves.

"Do you think he's in Spearfish?" she asked, immediately disturbed.

"I don't know," Quincy said, confident she did not question the charade. "We think he came here with a lady who's helpin' you here in the dinin' room—lady name of Hannah. I'd sure like to talk to her if she's here."

"Hannah's here," Mae said, worried by the prospect that Hannah might have knowingly had any connection with a wanted outlaw, although Logan hardly looked the part. "I'll get her for you. You fellows sit down at the table. We'll be bringin' the food out in a minute or two."

"Thank you kindly, ma'am," Quincy said as Mae left the room. When she had gone, he turned to face his amused partners. "It wouldn't hurt if you jackasses quit grinnin' like a bunch of hyenas. You're supposed to act like lawmen now."

Lonnie gave him an even bigger grin. "I swear, cousin, you're just as slick as ever. They didn't take none of that outta you in that prison."

"I kinda like bein' a lawman," Curly said.

"Just behave yourself," Quincy said. "Don't act like you do around those whores in the saloons. These women are like the women in your family."

"I hope they ain't like that ol' bitch that tried to raise me," Wormy said. His remark caused the others to cackle, and brought a swift rebuke from Quincy.

In a few moments, Mae returned with a worried Hannah in tow. Having already seated himself with his men, Quincy made a show of politely getting to his feet again to meet her. "I'm Hannah Mabry," she said. "Did you want to see me?"

"Yes, ma'am," Quincy said. "I wanna ask you about the man you rode into town with."

"Logan Cross," she replied. "I came to town with Logan Cross. If it hadn't been for him, I might not have made it out of the mountains."

"How well do you know him?" Quincy continued, hoping that she hadn't known him well enough to defend him.

"Well, not very well," she said. "All I can tell you is that he came along when I really needed help, and he was nothing but a gentleman. I can't imagine him as an outlaw. What did he do?"

"He murdered a man in Deadwood Gulch," Quincy said. "I guess she didn't tell you." He nodded toward Mae.

"Two men," Tom Lacey interjected, thinking of his old partner Everett Pierce. His comment brought a deep frown of irritation from Quincy, causing Lacey to hang his head and take a step back.

Hannah blanched, obviously shocked by what she had just heard. She looked at Mae, searching for some explanation. "Murder," she finally gasped, finding it impossible to believe. "There must be some mistake."

"No, ma'am," Quincy said, "no mistake. There were too many folks that saw it. He walked right in a saloon and shot a man settin' at a table playin' cards. Now, what I wanna ask you is, do you know where he went when he left here?"

"Why, no," Hannah said, still stunned by what she had just heard. "I don't know where he was planning to go. I just can't believe Logan would do such a thing. He just didn't seem like that kind of man at all." She turned to Mae. "You talked to him. He was just a cowhand planning to sign on with one of the ranchers."

"That's right," Mae said. "I remember now. He did say he was gonna try to get hired by one of the ranches."

Quincy was fighting inwardly to control his emotions, for he felt he was getting closer and closer to finding the man who haunted his waking moments. He glanced at his cousin to find Lonnie staring at him as if concerned that he might explode into one of his rages at any moment. It reminded Quincy to remain calm. Things were going too smoothly with the U.S. Marshal farce to spoil it with a fit of anger. After a moment, he asked, "Which outfit did he go to see? Did he tell you?"

Mae answered, "There are three big ones not far from here. I never heard him mention any of them." She turned to Hannah. "Did you?" Hannah shook her head. Turning to Quincy again, Mae suggested, "Try Sam Taylor over at the stable. He mighta told him where he was goin'."

"That's a good idea, Marshal," Lonnie commented quickly, encouraging Quincy to continue the charade. "Maybe we oughta go see him after we eat supper."

"Yeah," Quincy said absently, anxious to give chase right away. "Yeah, we better eat first."

"Well, amen to that," Stokes exclaimed, and received a warning look from Lonnie for speaking.

Quincy sat down again and the women went to the

kitchen to prepare to serve the food. Lonnie slid over close to him. "We might be onto a sweet setup here for a while, if we don't do somethin' stupid," he said. "These folks ain't questionin' anythin' we've said so far. Hell, they ain't even asked to see a badge. Whaddaya say we hang around here for a spell, as long as the town is buyin' it?"

Quincy frowned. "We're goin' after that son of a bitch. My mind ain't gonna rest till I put a bullet in his head, so don't talk to me about layin' around this town."

"I ain't sayin' that, Quincy," Lonnie replied quickly. "Sure, we're gonna run the bastard to ground. Ain't no doubt about that. What I'm sayin' is we can work outta Spearfish while we're lookin' on all the ranches around here. Hell, in a little while, we could own this town. Who's gonna stop us? They ain't got no sheriff. They ain't got no telegraph. There ain't no way they can say you ain't a marshal. I'm just sayin' think about that. Course we're gonna get Logan Cross before we do anythin' else."

Quincy paused to give it some thought. What Lonnie said might be a lucrative arrangement at that. The extreme isolation of the place made it ideal to operate out of for a gang of outlaws. He might even consider appointing himself sheriff. There was no one to stop him. There was one additional attraction that had entered his mind, the young woman named Hannah.

"Could be somethin' in what you say, cousin," he said. "We'll take a look at the other folks in town to see if there's anybody that might get in the way." He gave Lonnie a wink and said, "Just in case some of 'em might have to have an accident." Lonnie grinned and nodded. It looked as if the old Quincy was back in business. Their conversation was cut short then by the women with the bowls.

With the arrival of each regular customer, Mae made it a point to introduce the marshal, in case anyone was alarmed by the roughness of the men with the handsome lawman. As Quincy had ordered, the rest of his men kept their mouths shut, opening them only to insert food, while he acknowledged the introductions. All in all, it went well, as far as Mae and Hannah could determine. Plus, there was the bonus of six new customers for supper.

Before they left, Quincy approached Mae to inquire about renting some rooms. "I'm thinkin' we'll be operatin' out of Spearfish while we're coverin' this part of the country," he said. "Maybe you've got some rooms to let."

"We've only got two rooms available," Mae said. "We're planning to build onto the house in the spring, but right now two's all we have."

"That'll do," Quincy said. "We don't need no more than two."

"Good," Mae said with a smile. "Thank you very much, sir. I'll make sure they've got clean sheets."

"Mighty fine," Quincy said. "Me and my cousin, Lonnie here, can take one of 'em and my other four men can bunk up in the other one. They've got their bedrolls and they can swap off usin' the bed."

He laughed to himself, wondering if his men had ever slept on clean sheets.

Much as Cecil Grant and Mae Davis had, Sam Taylor experienced an uneasy feeling when the six hard-looking riders pulled up at his stable.

"Can I help you gentlemen?" he asked.

As before, Quincy identified himself as a U.S. Marshal, and his men as posse men. This came as some relief to Sam, although he was still not comfortable with the appearance of the marshal's posse men. Justifiably surprised when informed of the posse's purpose in Spearfish, he confessed that he had been completely taken in by the fugitive killer.

"Seemed like a helluva nice feller," he said, "just lookin' for honest work."

"Did he say where he was headin'?" Quincy asked.

"Matter of fact, he did," Sam volunteered. "He asked me how to find the Triple-T Ranch, said Jace Evans gave him a job."

Straining to keep the evidence of excitement out of his face, Quincy asked, "Can you tell me how to get to the Triple-T?" He cast a sideways glance at Lonnie.

"Why, I reckon if I could tell him, I can sure 'nuff tell you," Sam replied. "He's a big feller, but it looks like you've got plenty of good help," he commented as he looked Curly up and down.

When they found out that the Triple-T headquarters was approximately seven miles from Spearfish, it caused Quincy and Lonnie to consider the advisability of starting out right away. It was already getting along toward evening, but seven miles wasn't that far, provided they had no trouble following Sam's directions. Quincy liked the idea of arriving after dark, and the prospect of catching Logan by surprise while he was lying around in the bunkhouse. It seemed too good to pass up, so he told his men to mount up. The horses were rested, so they might as well go.

They found that Sam Taylor's directions were as easy to follow as he had claimed. Having found Towson's

Creek, they followed it until spotting the lights of lanterns in the bunkhouse and ranch house of the Triple-T.

"You reckon we'd best split up and some of us get around behind that barn, in case he sees us comin' and tries to make a run for it?" Wormy asked.

"Ain't no need for that," Quincy said. "He don't know we're trailin' him. We'll just ride right on in like a marshal and his posse."

"Quincy's right," Lonnie said. "Ain't no way he could even know about us." He looked at Lacey. "Ain't that right, Lacey?"

"That's a fact," Lacey replied. "He just knew about Jake and me and Everett."

"He ain't lookin' for anybody comin' after him," Quincy said. "So when we ride in there, Lacey, I want you right beside me to point him out just as soon as you spot him."

"What do we do when Lacey spots him?" Curly asked.

"You be ready to shoot in case any of the other men try to put up a fight," Quincy said, "'cause I intend to shoot him down, just like he did to Jake."

"Maybe we oughta arrest him and carry him off someplace to shoot him," Lonnie said, "since we're supposed to be the law."

"Yeah, we could hang him," Wormy said, seeing the possibility for some entertainment. "We could even give him a trial first. You could be the judge, Quincy. Curly there could be his lawyer, so you'd know you couldn't lose." Curly grinned at the thought, too simple to realize he had been insulted.

Though it was said in jest, the idea had some appeal to Quincy, but he said, "I'm gonna shoot him down as soon as I see him, just like he gave it to Jake."

* * *

Owner Tom Towson was down at the bunkhouse drinking a cup of coffee with his foreman, as he often did during the roundup season. A couple of the other men had sat down outside with them, taking their leisure after a hard day's work. They weren't expecting visitors this time of night, but some whinnying of the horses in the corral and the barking of the dog signaled company. Not particularly alarmed, but curious about who could be calling, Towson stood up and walked a little way away from the fire so he could see better. In a few seconds, he saw them, six riders, slow-walking their horses toward the fire outside the bunkhouse. "Who is it, Tom?" Jace Evans asked, and came up to stand beside him.

"Don't know," Towson said. "I don't recognize any of them."

"Evenin'," Quincy called out. "Mind if I step down?"

"Depends," Towson answered. "What's your business?"

"I'm U.S. Marshal Quincy Smith," Quincy said, using the same name he had given the people in Spearfish. "Me and my posse are trailin' a man wanted for murder. We got word that he might be workin' for you. Can I step down?"

"Sure," Towson said. "You and your men step down and come on up to the fire. You're traveling awful late, ain't you?"

"Thank you," Quincy said, and dismounted. "It is a little late in the evenin', but this man's dangerous, so when we got a strong sniff of his trail, we didn't wanna waste no time gettin' after him." He motioned for Lacey to step up beside him.

Looking quickly at the men now standing behind Towson, Lacey said, "He ain't here."

"I think somebody gave you the wrong word," Towson said. "I know my men. Most of them have been riding for me for a long time. We haven't hired but one new man this year, and I don't think he's the man you're looking for."

"Is his name Logan Cross?" Quincy asked. He saw the immediate shock in all their faces.

"Logan?" Jace Evans exclaimed. "Are you sure you've got the right man?"

"That's the man, all right," Quincy said. "A whole saloon full of people saw him murder Jake Morgan in cold blood."

"Fact of the matter is, he killed two men," Lacey interjected again, thinking of Everett Pierce.

"That's a fact," Quincy said with another frown for Lacey. Everett's death was never important to him, so he seldom bothered to remember.

"My God!" Jace blurted. "If what you're sayin' is true, I ain't ever misjudged a man more in my life. Are you absolutely sure he's the man they saw?"

"There ain't no doubt about it," Quincy assured him. "And I'm afraid we're wastin' time standin' here talkin' about it. Where is he?"

"He's out with the rest of the men, roundin' up cattle. They won't be back in till day after tomorrow, I don't expect," Jace said. He turned to Jim Bledsoe behind him, who seemed just as surprised as he. "Where is Logan, Jim?"

"He's with Bob and that bunch at the line camp, over by Jackrabbit Creek," Bledsoe answered.

"How far is that?" Quincy asked, not at all pleased with the way things were going.

"That's about eight miles east of here," Jace said. "It'd be pretty hard to find, especially at night. Best thing for you to do would be to wait till mornin'. I can tell you a whole lot better how to get there if you can see where you're goin'."

"It'd be a whole lot quicker if you send a man to show us the way," Quincy said. "And you'd be helpin' the law bring a killer to justice," he added when Jace seemed hesitant.

"Logan Cross murdered a man," Jace murmured in disbelief. "I swear, I'd like to hear what Logan has to say about it." He shook his head slowly, still not responding to Quincy's request for a guide. After a long moment, he looked at Towson and asked, "Whadda you think, Tom?"

Towson exhaled a long breath and shook his head. "I reckon it's the right thing to do. We sure stand for law and order, so send somebody to take them to the line shack."

"All right," Jace said. "Jim, you can take 'em over there in the mornin'. Pack up some supplies and you can stay with Bob and take Logan's place. The rest of the boys can handle things back here at the ranch."

"I reckon you and your men can camp here tonight," Towson said to Quincy. "You can sleep in the bunkhouse if you want to, since most of the men ain't here."

"That's mighty neighborly of you, sir," Quincy said. "But we're used to campin' on the run, so we'll just make us a camp right by the creek down there."

"Suit yourself," Towson said, still finding the entire turn of events hard to believe. "Where are you based? We ain't ever seen hide nor hair of a federal marshal around here."

Quincy tried to think quickly. "Fort Meade," he said. "I ride outta Fort Meade."

"Well, I never knew there was a marshal's office

over there," Towson said. He shrugged indifferently. "Like I said, you're welcome to use our bunkhouse, if you change your mind, and you can eat breakfast with us in the morning before you get started."

"Much obliged. We'll take you up on the breakfast." Quincy climbed back into the saddle again and led his sullen followers toward the creek.

After they left, Jace and the others stayed by the fire a little longer, discussing the surprising turn of events.

"You think you can know a man, just by the way he talks," Jace said. "But damn, I reckon you can't ever tell what's goin' on inside his head."

"He was a damn good cowhand," Towson said. "I hate to lose him."

For some reason, he wasn't really sleepy, so Logan rolled out of his blanket and moved quietly out of the shack that served as a line camp, being careful not to wake Bob Whitley and Lou Cheatam. He stood just outside the door of the shack for a few minutes and studied the moon hanging like a lantern over the faraway hills. Judging by the size of it, it would be full in a couple of days.

After another minute or so, he walked over closer to the creek bank to see if there were any nighttime critters working the dark water. He had wondered how it got the name Jackrabbit Creek, and Lou had told him that he was sure it was because of how crooked it was. It had so many sharp bends and cutbacks that it resembled a rabbit's hind leg in places. The thought brought a smile to Logan's face.

He decided that he was in a better place as far as his mind was concerned. He hadn't really gotten over Billy's loss. He supposed he never would, because he felt he had failed to protect his younger brother. But his mind was more at ease since he had the good fortune to sign on with the Triple-T. There was a simple peace about herding cattle. The hours were long, and sometimes hard, depending on the weather. But overall, it was an occupation that called for little more than common sense.

A low whinny from one of the horses in the small corral next to the shack snared his attention. A few seconds later, a couple of the other horses spoke.

They hear something, he thought. *Maybe a wolf or a coyote is snooping around.*

He hesitated awhile longer to see if he could find out what they had heard. Then it came to him, the sound of the soft beat of a horse's hooves on the bank of the creek. He remained there at the corner of the corral to see who the midnight visitor might be. It didn't occur to him that, as a precaution, maybe he should go back in the shack to get his rifle.

Only seconds passed before he saw the dark outline of a horse and rider approaching. It was a sizable man in the saddle. That much was obvious, but he couldn't identify him until he splashed across the creek and pulled up before the corral.

"Ox?" Logan exclaimed, surprised. "What are you doin' out here in the middle of the night?"

The big man dismounted. "Logan?" he responded. "I came to find you."

"In the middle of the night?" Logan replied. "What for?"

"They came lookin' for you, back at the ranch, and they're comin' out here in the mornin' to get you. You've got to hightail it away from here."

"Who?" Logan asked. "Who's comin' to get me?"

"A U.S. Marshal!" Ox blurted excitedly. "Outta Fort Meade, and he's got five men with him, come to arrest you." He hesitated before saying, "For murder, he said, for killin' two men in Deadwood Gulch."

The news struck Logan like a blow in his chest. A marshal? He had not really thought that the local sheriff would bother to pursue him once he was out of the Black Hills, but evidently somebody had called in the U.S. Marshal Service and they had sent a posse after him. It was time for a tough decision, to turn himself in and rely on the judge and jury to decide whether he was justified in killing the man who murdered Billy— or to run.

"You've got to get outta here!" Ox repeated, when Logan seemed to be hesitating.

"You're right," Logan decided then, conceding to his natural instincts to survive. He had no way of knowing if he would get a fair trial or not. In fact, he wasn't sure he could rely on a posse to take him back for trial. They might deem it a lot less trouble just to hang him and be done with him. That settled, he brought his thoughts back to the way he had been warned. He did not fail to see the irony in the fact that it was Ox who had taken it upon himself to ride out to warn him—the only man in the crew on the Triple-T whom Logan had had trouble with. "You mighta risked your neck, ridin' out here to tell me," he said to him.

"Didn't nobody see me slip out," Ox said. "Them fellers went down near the creek and made camp. I didn't tell none of our boys I was goin', either. I'll slip back in before mornin'."

"You're a good friend," Logan said to the simple giant. "I 'preciate what you've done for me. I just wanna make sure they don't find out you rode out here to tell me.

You'd best swap for a fresh horse to go back on." He started to return to the shack to get his things, but paused and turned back to Ox. "I reckon I owe you the truth of the matter. They're right. I did kill two men in Montana City, and I shot 'em because they murdered my brother. My brother woulda done the same for me, if the situation had been turned around."

Ox made no judgments. In his mind, Logan was an honest man, a man who had gotten the best of him when Ox forced him to fight, and then made no mention of it to anyone else. Ox appreciated that. His reputation as a fighter was all he had, and Logan could easily have taken it from him.

"I reckon if you shot 'em, they was needin' to be shot," he said.

"Thanks for that," Logan said. "And thanks for givin' me a head start. I reckon I'd best get my gear together and get on my way."

"I expect so," Ox said, and followed him to the corral.

Logan pulled his saddle off the top rail of the corral and called Pepper. The obedient horse came at once and stood patiently while Logan saddled him. "I've got my other horse back at the ranch," he said to Ox. "You know, that buckskin. I truly hate to leave that horse behind. That was my brother Billy's horse. Maybe I'll get back there one day to get him."

"I'll look after him for you," Ox volunteered.

By this time, their conversation, although hushed, had awakened the two men still inside the shack. "What the hell's goin' on, Logan?" Bob Whitley asked, coming out the door. Then, seeing Ox, he asked, "Where'd you come from?" Before he could get an answer, Lou Cheatam staggered out, still half-asleep.

Busy checking his saddlebags and tying down the

gear he had with him, Logan answered Bob's questions. "I reckon I'm gonna have to turn slacker on you boys. Looks like my past has caught up with me, and I've gotta make tracks."

"What the hell are you talkin' about?" Lou asked. "Where are you goin'?"

"I don't know, to tell you the truth," Logan said, and went inside to get his bedroll and war bag with his cooking utensils. When he came back, he said, "And I most likely wouldn't tell you if I did. That way, you wouldn't have to decide whether to lie for me or not."

Still in the dark, Bob turned to Ox, who was also busy changing his saddle over to a fresh horse to make the ride back to the ranch that night. "What's he talkin' about, Ox?"

Ox told them the story while Logan finished his preparations to depart. When he had finished, both Bob and Lou stood dumbfounded, scarcely believing that the man they had been driving cows with for the past several days was the same man who was wanted for murdering two men.

"Damn, Logan, I swear . . . ," Lou muttered, unable to think of what to say.

"They killed his brother, them two men," Ox reminded them, still trying to justify Logan's actions.

"I reckon you're right," Bob allowed. "What'll we tell that posse when it shows up here tomorrow?"

"We'll tell 'em we ain't seen you," Lou suggested.

"I 'preciate it, fellows, but accordin' to what Ox says, they know I'm out here with you boys. I just want you to tell 'em the truth. Tell 'em which way I went when I leave here. That way you won't get crossed up in any lies. They might have a tracker with 'em anyway. I don't plan on leavin' much of a trail for them to follow." He stepped up into the saddle. "I'd 'preciate it if you'd tell Jace I'm right sorry about this, and I thank him for givin' me the job." All three responded, saying that they surely would. He looked at Ox then, standing by his stirrup, reached down to shake his hand, and said, "You're a good man, my friend. Maybe I'll see you again." He turned Pepper's head toward the low hills to the east and gave him a nudge with his heels. "Good luck with the cattle."

"I swear . . . ," Lou uttered again, as the three Triple-T riders stood watching until he disappeared into the night.

"Well, I've got a piece of ridin' to do, if I'm gonna get back to the ranch before daybreak," Ox said, and stepped up into the saddle.

"Well, I ain't waitin' around this shack in the mornin', waitin' for that posse to show up," Bob declared. "We've got cattle to find, and it'll be that posse's job to track us down."

"By God . . . ," Lou agreed.

Chapter 9

"How much farther is this damn line camp?" Quincy asked, pulling up beside Jim Bledsoe.

"We're just about there," Jim said. He pointed toward a dark line of trees on the otherwise treeless plain. "That's Jackrabbit Creek. The camp's just on the other side of it."

Quincy squinted to see in the glare of the sun, feeling his heartbeat quicken with anticipation. He beckoned for Lonnie to come up beside him. Then he reined back to let Bledsoe go on ahead. "It's on the other side of that creek you can see up ahead," he said to Lonnie.

"Right," Lonnie replied. "How you wanna do this? You wanna make out like we're arrestin' him?"

"I ain't wastin' the time," Quincy said. "Get Lacey up here. I want him to sing out as soon as he sees him, and then I wanna fill that son of a bitch so full of lead he won't float in that damn creek."

"What about those other fellers at that camp?"

Lonnie asked. "We got a good deal goin' here with this posse thing. It wouldn't hurt to ride it a little further. Maybe we oughta arrest Cross, and wait till we're away from here to kill him."

"Maybe," Quincy allowed, although he was not certain he could restrain himself once he caught sight of the man who killed Jake. "We'll wait and see what he does when we get there. If he starts to run, shoot him down."

"What about the rest of them?" Lonnie asked again.

Impatient with his cousin's concerns about the Triple-T hands, Quincy barked, "Damn it, we'll kill the whole damn bunch, if they cause any trouble. Then you won't have to worry about anybody talkin'."

Lonnie shrugged and said nothing more. He would have preferred milking the ruse of being lawmen as long as they were able to get away with it. But he knew there was no use pressing Quincy further.

"Hell, we'll tell 'em Cross shot 'em after we got here," Quincy said.

"They ain't here," Jim Bledsoe announced unnecessarily as the so-called posse approached the line shack by the creek. The corral was empty, which told him that the extra horses had been turned out to graze and the men were already searching the outer boundary for stray cattle. It didn't surprise him. The sun was already peeking over the horizon. Bledsoe looked at Quincy, waiting to see what he wanted to do now. He was hoping that his services were no longer needed, and he would be free to catch up with Logan and the others on his own. If he could shake loose from this posse, he might have a little time to warn Logan.

"Well, this here's the line shack," he said to Quincy. "No tellin' where the boys might be workin', but they'll most likely be back here tonight." It was obvious by the dark frown on the *marshal's* face that Quincy was not happy with the situation. "I reckon you don't need me no more, so I'll go on back to work," Jim said.

"The hell you will," Quincy fired back at once. "You'll stay right here with us. You know this range, so you know where the damn cows like to bunch up. You're gonna show us where they'll likely be."

Jim took one look at the menacing frown on Quincy's face, then quickly glanced at the threatening leers of his posse riders. He saw no mercy in those faces, and no healthy way for him to object. So he quickly decided he had no sensible option.

"Why, sure," he said. "I can do that—always wanna help the law any way I can." *I don't know if you're in the right or wrong, Logan,* he thought, *but there ain't much I can do for you now.*

He figured there was no sense in trying to lead the posse astray, so he started out to the east, knowing that to be the direction Logan and the others would most likely be working in.

Quincy pulled up beside him. "What did you say your name was?" he asked.

"Jim," Bledsoe answered.

"Well, Jim, I reckon I oughta tell you that I'm gonna catch up with Logan Cross just as sure as that sun is risin' up over that mesa yonder. So you might be thinkin' about leadin' me on a wild-goose chase, but I promise you, if we don't find him pretty soon, I'm gonna be mighty unhappy with you. You understand?"

"Oh, yes, sir, I understand," Jim quickly assured him. "I know better than to get in the way of a lawman doin' his duty."

"Good," Quincy said. He looked back at Lonnie and winked.

It took over an hour, enough time for Bledsoe to start worrying, but finally they spotted a herd of about forty cattle coming up out of a grassy draw. Two riders could be seen coming up behind the cows, still a good distance away. "Get them rifles ready!" Quincy called back over his shoulder and drew his from his saddle scabbard. "Lonnie, you and Stokes move out a ways to the left. Wormy and Lacey can fan out to the right. I wanna close in around 'em, in case he starts to run right off."

Although some distance away as yet, the two drovers were easily recognized by Bledsoe. "He ain't here," he yelled to Quincy. When Quincy appeared not to understand, Jim repeated it. "I don't see Logan Cross. That's Lou Cheatam and Bob Whitley drivin' those cows."

"Well, where the hell is he?" Quincy demanded, frantically scanning the prairie behind the two coming toward them, his finger resting lightly on the trigger of his Spencer carbine. He kicked his horse hard and galloped around the herd to come up before the startled drovers. "Logan Cross!" he yelled at them. "Where is Logan Cross?"

Both men pulled up at once as the rest of Quincy's men galloped up behind him. "He's gone," Bob Whitley answered.

"Gone where?" Quincy roared.

"Don't know," Lou said. "He took off last night. Didn't say where he was goin', and didn't say why. Me and Bob was wonderin' the same thing. He just said he had to go." He looked at Bledsoe then, trying to appear clueless. "Left me and Bob shorthanded. I hope you can stay out here to help us."

"Jace told me to stay with you boys, since the marshal here was plannin' to arrest Logan," Bledsoe said. "They're wantin' Logan for shootin' some fellers."

"You don't say," Bob replied. "Well, I never woulda thought that."

"Where did he go?" Quincy demanded, seething with anger now, and not at all convinced that Jim and Bob were as innocent as they attempted to appear. His hand automatically cocked the carbine, causing his men to do the same. It had the intended effect on the three Triple-T hands.

"Swear to God, Marshal," Bob blurted. "He took off in the middle of the night. Said he had to go, but he wouldn't say where he was headin, or why. Ain't that right, Lou?" Lou nodded vigorously to confirm it.

It was easy to see the frustration settle upon Quincy as he gripped the carbine in his hands so tightly it appeared that he might break the weapon in two. Worried that his anger might blow up at any minute, Lonnie moved up close to him.

"We'll find him," he assured him again. "Might have to do a little trackin', but he can't have got too far."

Quincy stared at him with eyes glazed with anger. "I want him dead," he said. "He killed my brother. I want him dead."

"I know, Quincy," Lonnie said softly, looking around to make sure the Triple-T hands could not hear their conversation. "I want him dead, too, just as much as you do. Jake was my cousin. We got to be careful these fellers don't hear us talkin'. What we gotta do now is go back to that line shack and see if we can pick up his trail. Then we'll stay on his trail till we track him down. His luck's gonna run out before long."

Gradually Quincy seemed to regain control of his emotions, much to Lonnie's relief. It wouldn't do for the rest of the men to know how bad Quincy's crazy spells were getting. Some of them might start thinking about deserting, and Lonnie was convinced that they would be needed when Quincy was done avenging Jake. Then the gang could get back to the business of robbing stagecoaches. Satisfied that his cousin was under control again, Lonnie spoke loud enough for the others to hear. "Quincy said we're goin' back to that shack and pick up Cross's trail. We'll rest up the horses and fix us somethin' to eat when we get there."

Lacey looked at Wormy and mumbled, "When are we gonna stop chasin' our tails and get back to what we're supposed to be doin'?"

Overhearing, Lonnie snapped, "What did you say, Lacey? You got somethin' on your mind? Let all of us hear it."

"Nothin', Lonnie," Lacey replied quickly. "I was just sayin' I was anxious to get on Cross's trail. It mighta sounded like I was sayin' somethin' different."

"You ain't rode with Quincy and me as long as Wormy and Curly and Stokes have, so you ain't got no right to complain about anythin'."

"I ain't complainin', Lonnie. I swear."

"All right," Quincy commanded, completely recovered now, "we're goin' back to that shack." He pointed to Lou and Bob. "One of you fellers is goin' back with us to show me which way Cross went from there. Which one of you wants to do it?" When neither volunteered right away, Quincy said, "Jim here can take your place with the cattle." When there was still no volunteer, he said, "All right, you can do it." He nodded toward Lou Cheatam.

"I really oughta stay with the cattle," Lou started, but got no further when Curly drove his horse over to almost lean on Lou's. "I reckon Jim can help drive 'em on down to the creek, though," Lou decided with the grinning brute sitting a head taller in the saddle than he.

"Let's get goin'," Lonnie said. "We're gonna have to rest these horses before we start out from that shack."

He glanced at Quincy to make sure his cousin understood that.

At roughly the same time Quincy Morgan's gang of outlaws rested their horses in preparation for continuing their search, the man they hunted was resting the flea-bitten gray gelding he rode. Sitting on his saddle blanket beside a slow-moving stream, Logan fed a few more sticks to the fire he had built to make his coffee. He looked for a long moment at the powerful horse grazing on the short grass beside the stream. It had been a long night for Pepper, with only a couple of stops for rest, but Logan had deemed it important to make the most of the head start given him by his unlikely friend. He wondered if Ox had been able to get back to the ranch before daylight and avoid being discovered by the marshal. Since he had no way of knowing, it was the reason he had pushed Pepper all through the night.

Surely, he thought, *I must have a full day's lead on them.*

When he had ridden away from the line shack, he had headed east without a clear notion as to where he was going. After a few miles, he decided it might be too easy to track him if he continued on this rolling prairie. So he had turned back to the south, with the intention of returning to the Black Hills to get lost in the mountainous terrain they provided.

Sitting here now in the clear morning light, he looked

across a wide-open prairie to gaze at Bear Butte, standing alone on an empty plain. He estimated that it was at least two or three miles distant, yet he could see it plainly. And if there had been a man on a horse anywhere between where he sat and the butte, he could have seen him, too. The thought justified his decision to swing back to seek the protection afforded under the eaves of the pine-clad mountains and the isolation of their hidden gulches and ravines.

On first thought, it might seem an unwise decision to return to the vicinity where he had killed Jake Morgan and the man with him, but the Black Hills were the closest place to lose himself. He could find a spot to hole up there while he decided it was safe enough to head for distant territory. That seemed a better choice than an endless race across a hundred miles of prairie with a marshal's posse in pursuit. A second reason to return to the Hills might be that the marshal and his posse would not figure for him to return to the vicinity where he had committed the crime.

He had attempted to sleep a little while he rested Pepper, but in spite of being awake all night, he found that he could not. There were too many thoughts swirling around in his mind to permit him to relax. He thought about the attitude of the men he had worked with on the Triple-T. It had been for such a short time, and yet their reaction upon hearing he was wanted for killing two men was to help him escape.

But the most surprising had been the actions of Ox. He would never have imagined that his simple act after their confrontation would generate such a sense of loyalty on the part of the big man. One thing that troubled him greatly was having to leave the buckskin that Billy rode, and he promised himself that, if at all possible, he would return to get it. He couldn't help smiling when he remembered Ox telling him he would take care of the horse until he came for him.

I hope he remembered to tell Jace I was sorry I had to run out on him after he was kind enough to give me a job, he thought.

He had never quit a job before, and that was important to him. At least he had not been around long enough to get a payday. That relieved his sense of responsibility a little.

"All this thinkin' hurts my head," he told Pepper, although the lack of sleep was more likely the cause of his headache. "I expect we're both rested enough to get goin' again." He drained the last swallow of coffee in his cup and swished the cup a couple of times in the stream before returning it to his saddlebags. "Time to saddle up, boy." The patient gelding stood waiting while Logan approached with the saddle.

He entered the dark mountains well east of Deadwood, following one winding valley after another as he worked his way to the southern part of the Hills. With no shortage of camping sites by the many rushing streams, he sought to find a place where there was no evidence that others had camped there before.

On most of the larger streams that gushed from the heights above him, he found old campsites where hopeful miners had either struck it or not. They brought back thoughts of Billy, and when the two of them had first explored the Black Hills. There were also recollections of Hannah Mabry, and he pictured her as he had last seen her, a handsome young woman, instead of the dumpy forlorn-looking widow in baggy men's clothes he had traveled with. He wondered how the partnership between Hannah and Mae was progressing. He did not know a great deal about Daisy, since he had not had the opportunity to meet her.

The Three Widows Inn, he thought as he sat beside his campfire after another day following old game trails. *I wish I could have supper there tonight.*

He gazed at the strip of roasted venison he was eating and shrugged. At least there was plenty of game in these mountains. He wasn't worried about going hungry as long as he had plenty of cartridges for his rifle. When he had first returned to the mountains, he was very reluctant to fire his rifle, even though he had become very low on food. As the following days found him deeper and deeper in the mountains, he became less concerned, for he felt confident that he had covered his trail adequately. He decided it was very unlikely the posse could track him.

Now his concern was finding a more permanent camp that he could prepare for winter while there was still plenty of time. For the leaves of the birch and aspen had not yet begun to change. He found what he considered the perfect spot a day later in a narrow canyon with steep mountain walls reaching almost straight up to form a broad granite face. High up, a rushing waterfall spilled over the face to create two smaller streams below. It was above the granite face where Logan made his camp, halfway up the slope where a small meadow lay hidden behind a thick wall of pines. It would provide some grazing for Pepper, and not a likely spot for someone to stumble upon. If a prospective miner was searching for a place to pan for gold, he would most likely build his sluice box below the granite wall, Logan reasoned.

He immediately set about preparing it for winter. He would need shelter for himself and his horse, so he began by bending some of the younger pines over to be tied together to form a framework on which he could weave smaller branches to construct his roof. He had never been called upon to construct such a dwelling before, but as it progressed, he felt it might be adequate. When he finished his, he set to work on one for Pepper. The work took him three full days, and the final product was not pretty, but he was satisfied that it was the best he could do. Only the coming of winter would determine his work successful or not. He decided it was time now to concentrate on adding to his supply of meat.

While Logan was now busy hunting in the mountains, the man who sought to kill him had come to a dead stop on another trail that had yielded nothing. Thanks to Wormy's skill as a tracker, they had been able to follow Logan right up to the point where he had entered the foothills of the mountains.

"Damn," Quincy cursed, knowing that had he continued on toward Fort Pierre, they would have had a chance of overtaking him. "Look hard," he said to Wormy, who had dismounted to verify what he already knew.

"He rode into this creek, all right," Wormy said. "There ain't no doubt about that, and I can't track him in water." They had no way of knowing if the trail they had picked up was, in fact, that of Logan Cross's, but they intended to follow it, wherever it led them.

"The only thing we can do," Lonnie said, "is scout both sides of this creek and see if we can find where he came out of it." So with no other option available for them, they split up and rode up the banks of the creek.

The farther up into the hills they rode, the harder it

became to follow the creek. Because of the outcrop-
pings of rocks they encountered, some extending well
out into the water, they were often forced to ride around
them. Consequently they could not be absolutely sure
they had not missed Logan's exit from the creek somewhere along the line. As the day progressed, Quincy
became more and more frustrated. The waning enthusiasm for the chase he was seeing in his men as darkness drew near only increased that frustration and
triggered his wrath.

"Damn it!" he roared out in anger. "He wouldn'ta
rode up this creek this far. We missed it somewhere
back there. Some of you ain't keepin' a sharp eye on
that creek bank." He cast an accusing glare in Wormy's
direction on the opposite side of the creek.

"If there'da been tracks, I'da seen 'em," Wormy said
in his defense. "Maybe that damn gray horse he's
ridin' sprouted some wings."

The remark didn't strike Quincy as humorous. "You
think this whole thing is funny?" he railed. "This son
of a bitch shot my brother down in cold blood, and you
think it's funny?"

"Ah, hell no, Quincy," Wormy pleaded immediately.
"I don't think it's funny. I didn't mean it that way atall."

"Wormy didn't mean nothin', Quincy," Lonnie said,
seeing that his cousin was about to work up another fit
of anger. He was the only one who could settle Quincy
down when he became blinded by his rage. And Lonnie
worried that they might lose Wormy if Quincy didn't
calm down. "It's gonna be dark under these trees in just
a little while, and we sure as hell can't do much trackin'
in the dark. So let's just go back to that little clearin' we
passed a few minutes ago and make camp. We'll be able
to see better in the mornin'. Whaddaya say?"

Quincy continued to glare at Wormy for a few seconds before turning toward Lonnie. After a few more moments, he seemed to get a grip on his emotions. "I reckon you're right," he finally replied. "We'll make camp and hit it hard in the mornin'."

"Hold on!" Wormy suddenly blurted, and pointed to a single hoofprint at the base of a flat rock shelf. "By God, he didn't get all of his horse's feet on this damn rock. Lookee there!" He stood up and looked down the slope toward the valley below, pointing triumphantly now. "I bet he's down in that valley. Maybe he's got a camp down there."

Catching Wormy's excitement, Quincy exclaimed, "Let's get down there! It's him! I know damn well it's gotta be him!"

"Let's take it slow and easy," Lonnie said, hoping they had finally had some luck. "We need to be careful he don't see us comin' and take off again." He picked a spot about two-thirds of the way down the mountain. "See that ridge there? We oughta be able to get a good look at anybody who's in that narrow valley." He looked at Quincy, who was tense and eager to descend the slope. "Why don't you and Lacey and I go on down by ourselves, and leave the rest of the boys here? We don't wanna take a chance on him hearin' us."

Quincy was not sure he was in favor of that plan, since he was inclined to charge down the slope firing away. But he knew that Logan might be flushed from his hiding place before he got down there. "I want that first shot," he reminded Lonnie. "I don't want anybody cheatin' me out of my right to kill that son of a bitch."

"All right, cousin," Lonnie said. "We ain't gonna do nothin' but find out for sure where he is, so you can take the shot."

* * *

The narrow little valley he had found was abounding in deer sign, so much so that he decided to camp there instead of returning to his base camp. Hunting had been so good that he sorely missed his extra horse to pack all the meat out. In the meantime, Pepper was just going to have to carry the whole load. The big gray had so far shown no signs of revolt.

"One of these days, I'll get back to pick up the buckskin to give you a little help," he said to the patient horse.

He interrupted the chore of butchering the young doe that he had recently killed to gather wood for a fire. There was plenty of wood on the banks of the narrow stream that dissected the valley, so he gathered up an armload and carried it back to a level spot by the water.

"I reckon I oughta take that saddle off you, since we're gonna stay here tonight," he said to Pepper, and turned toward the horse. He heard the snap of the bullet as it passed within inches of his leg. The sound of the rifle echoed in the narrow valley moments after. Logan dropped the firewood and sprinted to his horse as the ridge above him erupted into a hail of gunshots, raining around him as he ran. Leaping into the saddle, he galloped away down the stream with no time to think of the danger of his horse tumbling on the rocky streambed.

Not until he had rounded a granite column that protruded into the stream could he be sure he was protected from the rifle fire on the ridge. He knew that he had best push Pepper hard to increase the distance between him and his assailants. The posse had to negotiate the descent down the steep slope, and that was going to take a little time. So he held the big horse to a lope for half a mile until reaching the fork of a second stream that flowed down from a neighboring mountain. Slowing Pepper to a walk, he guided him up the middle of that stream. Confident that he now had a decent lead on his pursuers, he kept his horse in the water until he found a place to come out without leaving tracks.

As he watched for some rocks or pine straw, he thought about how close he had just come. If he had not turned toward his horse at that precise moment, he would have caught a bullet in his leg, which would probably have stopped him long enough for the fatal bullet to hit him. It was the posse that had been looking for him ever since he left the Triple-T. Of that he was sure. The thought that really struck him was the fact that there was no attempt to arrest him. They had fired upon sighting him in the valley, with no chance of surrender. They had no intention of taking him to be tried.

"Come on, damn it!" Quincy shouted to the men on the slope above who had been left to hold the horses. He, Lonnie, and Lacey were scrambling down the steep mountain as fast as they could, stopping every few feet to cock their weapons and fire at the fleeing man. "He moved!" Quincy yelled. "I had the son of a bitch, and he moved just when I pulled the trigger!" He was almost ill with frustration, and he tried to hurry, causing him to slide and stumble, falling to his knees. Bleeding anger from every pore, he pushed Lonnie's arm aside when his cousin tried to help him up. Cursing and flailing his arms in anguish, he fired his Spencer carbine as fast as he could, long after Logan had reached the safety of the granite column. When finally they reached the stream at the bottom of the narrow canyon, he was forced to realize that they had missed their opportunity. He turned to Lacey, who was coming down behind him.

"Was it him?" he demanded. "Was it Logan Cross?"

"Yes, sir," Lacey answered apologetically. "It was him, all right. He was a little piece off, but I could see him good enough to tell it was him."

"Goddamn!" Quincy swore, beside himself with anger. He turned to yell again at the men carefully leading the horses down to the bottom. "Come on! Bring those horses! He's gettin' away!"

"Look at that," Lacey said. "He left us a good supply of deer meat."

"Damn that deer meat!" Quincy roared.

"Right," Lacey apologized quickly. "We don't care about no deer meat. We've got to get after that son of a bitch."

As soon as the horses were down at the bottom, the outlaws climbed aboard and followed Quincy, who was heading toward the granite column at a gallop. Lonnie was right behind him, anticipating the job of calming him down. The evening light was already fading in the narrow valley. Pretty soon, they were going to have to admit it was too dark to try to follow Cross, and Quincy was going to be furious, most likely visited by another one of his fits. They followed the stream up the second mountain, scouting in the poor light for tracks leading out of the water. There were none, but Quincy kept them at it until Lonnie convinced him that they could no longer see them, even if there were tracks.

"We'll find him," Quincy vowed, "if we have to cover every inch of these damn mountains. We'll start early in the mornin'. He can't hide from me forever."

The following day, and the day after that, offered no signs of Logan Cross's trail after he left the creek. Finally, when it was certain that they had apparently missed it, they started combing the mountainside, searching for any sign of a horse and rider. Lonnie knew that the rest of the men were weary of the hopeless search, and were anxious to give it up, yet none had the nerve to test Quincy's ever-growing frustration. And then, when even Quincy was thinking of admitting defeat, Stokes and Curly caught up with the others after splitting off to check a ledge that extended out over a thick belt of tall pines.

"We found somethin'!" Stokes called out excitedly as he and Curly urged their horses up the slope. "We mighta found his camp, back in them trees below that ledge back yonder."

"I saw the smoke," Curly said proudly. "It was almost too dark to see, but I saw it."

The sighting was enough to generate newfound enthusiasm in all of them. "All right, then," Quincy said. "It's about time. Let's go have a look."

Stokes and Curly led them back to the spot on the ledge where they had seen the camp. They dismounted and moved up close to the edge. The camp was there, all right, below them where a busy stream cut its way through a thick growth of pines. It was just possible to make out the form of one man as he seemed to be tending something over the fire. Quincy could feel the pounding of his heartbeat in his temples as he realized he was about to have his second chance to gain his vengeance.

Lonnie, always the calm one, suggested that they should leave their horses where they were while they went down the slope on foot to approach the camp through the trees. Quincy nodded his approval, and they hurried back off the ledge.

When they reached the belt of trees, Quincy sent Stokes with Lonnie to circle around behind the camp to make sure Logan couldn't run that way. "I'll give you time to get where you can cut him off," he said to Lonnie. "But I'll take the first shot. Don't nobody shoot until I do, but when I do, you can all cut loose. I don't want any chance for him to get away this time."

"You're the boss," Lonnie replied, knowing how important it was for Quincy to be the one who killed Logan. He and Stokes hurried off through the trees.

Quincy, with Curly and Lacey following, worked his way carefully through the thick growth of pines until he reached a position where he could now see the man, still kneeling by the fire. The darkness was already closing in around the camp, but his target was well defined in the glow of the campfire, and well within the effective range of the Spencer carbine.

Down on one knee, Quincy raised the weapon and sighted carefully, taking care not to rush the shot. He wanted his bullet to be the one that killed Logan. He slowly squeezed the trigger, startling the darkness with the sharp crack of the Spencer. It was followed almost immediately by a barrage of shots into the already dead body. With a triumphant roar, Quincy sprang to his feet and charged down to the camp to find that the body had fallen across the fire.

"Drag the son of a bitch outta there," he commanded. "I wanna see his face."

Curly grabbed the victim's boots and dragged the bullet-riddled body off the fire amid the gleeful shouts of the hunters. Quincy bent over it and stared down into the face that stared back at him in death. "What?" he demanded, hearing someone speak behind him.

"I said that ain't him," Lacey repeated.

"What?" Quincy demanded again. "Whaddaya mean it ain't him?"

"Like I said, that ain't Logan Cross."

A total silence fell over the would-be avengers, broken a second later by a loud wail, like that of a wolf, as Quincy roared out his frustration. Looking around him then, Lonnie calmly said, "Just a minin' claim."

"Reckon did he have any luck?" Stokes wondered, unconcerned about their mistake that resulted in the death of an innocent miner. His question prompted the others, except for Quincy, to start plundering the camp in search of gold. Infuriated, Quincy remained to stare at the body.

"I found somethin'," Lonnie called out. When the others ran over to see what he'd found, they were surprised to see him standing over a frightened man who he had caught trying to crawl off through the bushes by the creek. Lonnie had pinned him down with his boot firmly placed on the terrified miner's ankle. He aimed his .44 at the man's head and cocked the hammer.

"Hold on a minute," Stokes said. "Ask him where he's got his gold hid."

Lonnie paused, thinking that a good idea. "Well," he said, "where is it?"

"We ain't found but a little bit," the doomed man muttered, barely able to speak. "You can take it all. I'll tell you where it is if you'll just let me go."

"All right," Lonnie said. "That's a deal. Where is it?"

"It's buried under that flat rock where the mules are tied up," the frightened man answered, his voice trembling with fear.

"You better not be lyin' to me," Lonnie warned him.

"No, I swear," the miner said. "Just let me go."

"All right, you can go," Lonnie said, and removed

his boot from the unfortunate man's ankle, releasing him. The horrified man got up on his hands and knees and started to crawl toward the creek. Lonnie let him crawl about ten feet before raising his .44 and shooting him in the back of his head. He turned then to Wormy, who was standing behind him. "I didn't see no mules. Where are they?"

"They're on the other side of the stream, behind those berry bushes," Lacey said, having just seen them himself. "Looks like two of 'em."

"Let's go see if that gold is there," Lonnie said.

Just as the miner had said, there were two mules tied to a rope stretched between a couple of trees about twenty yards down the stream at the foot of a steep cliff. It was so dark back in the shadows that they had been hard to see.

Eager to see how much they had gained in the murders of the two miners, they started looking around frantically for a flat rock. With no luck at first, they thought the man had lied, but then Wormy pointed toward a massive rock outcropping at the base of the cliff. A flat stone was tight up against it.

"There it is," he said. "Pretty slick, it just looks like a piece of the cliff." He went immediately to turn it over but found it was too big for him to move. "I reckon it took both of 'em to roll it over," he decided. "Somebody gimme a hand."

"I can roll that rock over by myself," Curly boasted. "I don't need no help."

"Is that so?" Wormy scoffed, unconvinced. "Well, go to it, big boy."

Regaining control of his frustration by then, Quincy joined the others as they gathered around the heavy stone to see if Curly could move it. Grinning confidently, Curly walked around the stone, deciding where he wanted to set himself to lift the backside of it. Satisfied that he had picked the position that would give him the best leverage, he spat on his hands and rubbed them together vigorously.

"Stand outta the way, Wormy. I'm fixin' to roll it right where you're standin'."

Wormy no longer doubted the big man's ability to do it, so he got well out of the way, as did the others. Curly braced himself, his feet set wide apart. Then he squatted and took a firm handhold with both of his huge hands. Lifting with his legs, he grunted with the effort he was applying against the rock. It did not move for thirty or more seconds. Then gradually it began to come away from the rock wall as he strained mightily. His efforts brought a cheer from his friends, giving him the will to continue until the massive stone surrendered to his strength. And with one mighty heave, he rolled it over to reveal a hole beneath it, but too late to see the family of rattlesnakes that dwelled there. With a shriek of horror, he jumped back, but not in time to avoid being struck by two large rattlers. The angry serpents struck again and again while he desperately tried to pull them away from his arms and legs.

There was nothing his friends could do to save him from being bitten over and over as other snakes struck as well. The only thing they could do was to shoot the snakes, so Wormy, Stokes, and Lonnie emptied their pistols into the hole, killing all but two that were still clinging to the crazed brute of a man. Lonnie grabbed one of them by the tail and yanked it off Curly, flinging it away to barely avoid getting bitten himself.

"Damn!" he swore, reacting to the close call. Since no one else stepped forward to remove the other snake, however, he grabbed the second reptile and flung it as quickly as he could. Stokes and Lacey shot them before they could escape into the rocks.

The big man sat down on the rock he had just turned over, whimpering with fear, afraid that he was going to die. He looked desperately from one face to another, pleading for some word that he was going to be all right.

All he received in return was a sympathetic shake of the head until Quincy said, "That's damn tough luck, Curly, I swear it is. The only thing you can do is lay down over there." He pointed to a little plot of grass near the stream. "And be real still, and maybe the poison won't get pumped up in your heart."

This was not very encouraging advice to the now frantic man, but he didn't know what else to do, so he got up from the rock and stumbled over to lie down in the grass. With Curly out of the way, Quincy and the others turned their attention to the hole and the snakes.

Peering down into the dark nest, Quincy decided it too difficult to see if all the snakes were dead. "Go get a stick outta that fire so we can see what we're doin'," he said.

Stokes hurried over to the campfire and pulled out one of the larger pieces of wood that had a healthy flame going. Quincy took it from him and extended it down in the hole.

"Damn," he swore softly. "There must be a dozen rattlers in there." He moved the torch around the perimeter of the hole to make sure none were moving. "They're all dead now, though."

"Anythin' else in that hole?" Lonnie asked hopefully.

"Yep, sure is," Quincy said, looked back at him, and

grinned, "a couple of canvas sacks." He looked over at Stokes on the other side of the hole. "I'll hold the light for you. Reach down in there and pull them sacks outta there, and we'll see what these two jaspers were worth." He saw no need to risk his hand down in that nest.

"That son of a bitch was smart," Wormy said, referring to the miner who had told them about the rock. "He pretty much knew we weren't gonna let him live after he told us where they hid the gold, so he didn't bother to tell us about them snakes."

"I reckon," Stokes said as he stared down in the hole. He was no more enthusiastic about reaching down there than Quincy was, but he nevertheless took the chance. He reached down in the nest, pulled one of the sacks out, then went after the other one without mishap. "They feel pretty heavy," he said. "I believe we struck it rich, boys." Everyone crowded around to have a look, leaving Curly to deal with his horrors alone.

"This is the only smart way to mine for gold," Wormy said as he peered down into an open sack. "How much you think it is, Quincy?"

"I don't know," Quincy answered. He picked up each bag to test its weight. "I'll bet those bags weigh about thirty pounds apiece. We'll have to get it weighed to find out for sure, but I can tell you it's a right healthy amount." Like the other men's, his spirits were lifted considerably from the cranky mood that had preceded this stroke of luck. For the moment, thoughts of Logan Cross were pushed from his mind in the celebration of their windfall.

Witnessing his cousin's apparent change in attitude, Lonnie sought to take advantage of it and make a suggestion he had been hesitant to propose. While Lacey whooped and hollered with Wormy as they watched

Stokes perform a clumsy version of a spirited dance, Lonnie captured Quincy's ear. "It looks to me like we're set up pretty good for the winter now. I think we're just wastin' our time roamin' around in these mountains lookin' for that son of a bitch. He's give us the switch for sure. I think you know that. So why don't we go on back to that little town, Spearfish, and pass the winter in style? Hell, we can afford it. And there ain't no lawmen lookin' for us right now." When he saw a frown begin to form on his cousin's face, he continued hurriedly. "I ain't sayin' we oughta forget about Cross. Hell no, he's got to pay for what he done. But a man like that is bound to show up sooner or later, especially if he thinks he lost us for good. One thing for sure, we could ride all over these mountains from now on and never find him. There're too many hidin' places. He'll come outta his hole sometime to go to one of the towns where he can buy supplies. That's when we'll find out where he is. We'll work all the towns till we find him. Whaddaya say?"

Quincy didn't answer right away while he considered Lonnie's proposal. His desire to kill Logan Cross had become a mental disease that knew only one cure. But maybe what Lonnie was trying to tell him made sense. Maybe it was useless to continue searching just for the sake of searching, with no reason to expect results. And while gold was not the cure for his sickness, it could ease the symptoms temporarily.

In his present state of calm, he was able to realize something that Lonnie had been concerned about, the weariness of the men with this fruitless search—and the possibility that they might decide to leave one dark night. He quickly glanced over at Curly, shivering and moaning on the ground. It was a good bet that he had already lost another man. That would leave just five of them, when they had started out as six with plans to pick up Jake and two others.

"All right," Quincy finally said. "I reckon that's the best idea right now. I'll let Logan Cross go for a while, but I ain't forgot him."

"No, sir, Quincy," Lonnie replied. "We ain't forgot Mr. Cross. We'll get him." Eager to get under way before Quincy had enough time to sink back into the dismal state of mind that had driven him, he suggested that they should leave first thing in the morning to go back to Spearfish. "We can get a better idea if Curly's gonna make it by then." With that thought in mind, he went over to see how the injured man was doing.

"I'm burnin' up, Lonnie," Curly complained pitifully. "I don't feel so good."

"Lemme take a look at those bites," Lonnie said, and pulled Curly's sleeve up to check his arm. There was already some swelling around the bite marks, and what appeared to be venom residue on Curly's skin. "Does it hurt?"

"It stings," Curly moaned. "I feel 'em all over me, stingin' ever'where they bit me, and I feel like I'm gonna throw up. I tried to get up, but my head took to spinnin' so bad I had to set down. I can't see. Ever'thin's kinda fuzzy lookin'."

"You just need a good night's rest," Lonnie said, although he was not sure Curly would make it through the night. "We're gonna start back to Spearfish in the mornin'. When we get there, you can lay up in that house where we've got some rooms. That'ud be pretty good, wouldn't it—have them three women waitin' on you?"

"That'ud be good, Lonnie," Curly said childlike, his face twisted in a painful frown.

* * *

With the arrival of morning, there was no sound of suffering from the stricken man. He did not stir when the others rolled out of their blankets to start a fire. Quincy and Lonnie stood over him for a few seconds, but seeing no signs of life, they left him while they prepared to get under way.

After the horses were saddled, including Curly's, Lonnie went over to take one last look at the huge man. He stood there for a few moments, thinking of the simple giant.

Born with the body of a bull and the brain of a gnat, he thought. He reached down and searched Curly's pockets to relieve him of his money. Then he unbuckled his gun belt. When he tugged on it to pull it out from under the massive body, Curly's eyes opened slightly, startling Lonnie. "Oh, shit!" he exclaimed, pulled his .44, and shot him in the head. The gunshot startled the others, causing them to think they were under attack. "It's all right," Lonnie called out. "He wasn't all the way dead yet."

"Well, that was a piece of bad luck," Quincy said. "Curly never was very lucky. I expect we'd best get started, if we're goin'."

"Reckon we oughta bury him?" Wormy asked.

"No, I reckon not," Quincy said, after considering the question for no more than a second. "The buzzards will take care of him when they come after those two miners. Curly ain't in no place to care one way or the other. I expect he's got other things to worry about now."

Chapter 10

Winter sent her calling card early in the form of an unexpected snow well before the birch and aspen trees had lost their autumn colors. It was the first test of Logan's winter camp. The huts he had fashioned for himself and Pepper successfully withstood the blanket of snow that coated his structure of young ponderosa pines. While he was pleased with the results, he could not be certain how well his roof would hold up under a heavy snowstorm. It would appear that the marshal's posse had given up in their search for him. Either that or they were simply looking in the wrong place.

In any event, he felt reasonably safe, as the passing days turned into weeks, with no sighting of any other human beings. He had begun to range farther and farther from his camp in search of game, and he was satisfied that he was well fixed for meat, having prepared several caches of smoked venison. There were other basic cooking supplies that he needed, since his forced departure from the Triple-T had caught him with coffee, beans, salt, and flour enough for only a few days. His craving for a cup of hot coffee was enough to make him risk a trip into a town. Of more importance, Pepper needed shoeing, so Logan decided he was going to make the trip before the weather worsened.

On one of his hunting excursions he had seen what appeared to be a trading post of sorts on a broad creek toward the eastern edge of the mountains. He could probably have bought his supplies there, but since he needed a blacksmith, he was going to have to find a town large enough to support a forge. He figured if he followed the creek out of the mountains, there was a good chance he'd find a town out in the foothills or beyond at the edge of the prairie.

His guess was accurate, for he came out of the mountains to find what seemed to be a well-established town, with several stores, a couple of saloons, what appeared to be a hotel of sorts, a stable, and luckily, a blacksmith.

He decided to take care of Pepper first, so he rode past the second saloon to the smithy beyond. A short, muscular man came from the back of the shop to greet him. "How do, neighbor? What can I do for you?"

"I'm needin' my horse shod," Logan answered.

"Don't believe I've seen you around town before," the smithy said.

"Ain't been in this town before," Logan replied.

When Logan didn't seem to be especially chatty, the smithy said, "I'm Hank Mosley. Let's take a look."

Logan stepped down and handed the reins to Mosley. "I'm Logan Cross, pleased to meet you." He studied Mosley's face carefully, looking for any sign that he recognized the name. There was none, at least that he could see. He had thought at first to use a fake name in case there were wanted posters circulating with his name on them. But he decided to give his real name to see if it caused any reaction that might indicate the smithy had heard it before. He felt a little more secure now in knowing he had not.

Mosley led Pepper back into the shop where his forge was located and preceded to inspect the horse's hooves. "You weren't lyin'," he remarked. "You need some shoes, all right. A little bit longer and you'da been ridin' an Injun pony."

"I reckon," Logan said. "I'm glad this town has a blacksmith. What's the name of it, anyway?"

"Rapid City," Mosley said. "You passin' through, or are you thinkin' about stayin' with us? I can tell by your rig that you've worked some cattle. You with one of the ranches over toward Bear Butte?"

That seemed to be as good a story as any, so he went along with it. "I'm on my way over to see Matt Morrison. I've worked for him before and he told me to come on back over to see him. You know Matt Morrison?"

"Know of him," Mosley said. "His spread's quite a little piece from here, near Sturgis, ain't it?"

"That's a fact. Well, I'm needin' some camp supplies. I'll just go pick up some things while you're shoein' my horse."

"If you're talkin' 'bout stuff to cook with, coffee and such," Mosley said, "place right across the street can take care of that, Donald Brooks."

"'Preciate it," Logan said. "I'll be right back."

He decided to test the recognition of his name once more to be doubly sure, so he gave his real name when he said howdy to Donald Brooks. Just as Mosley had done, Brooks gave no indication that he had ever heard the name before. Logan was convinced that he had nothing to fear in Rapid City. He completed his transactions with Brooks, putting most of the items in the cotton war bag that he tied behind his saddle cantle. He said good day to the store owner and headed back to the blacksmith.

As he walked across the street, avoiding the deeper ruts left by heavy wagons in the mix of snow and mud, a man came from the saloon, also walking toward the blacksmith. Reaching Mosley's shop at the same time as Logan, the man nodded and said, "Howdy." Logan responded with a howdy as well, and paused to let the man precede him.

"You're all finished and ready to ride, Marshal," Mosley called out when he saw the two men walk in. Startled, Logan froze.

"Good," the man replied. "We'll settle up, then." He reached inside his coat to pull out his wallet, exposing a marshal's badge. Logan remained frozen at the front of the shop, trapped.

"I'm about to finish shoein' your horse, too, Mr. Cross," Mosley said. There was no reaction from the marshal as he fished some bills from his wallet. Making an effort to be polite, Mosley didn't stop there. "This here is Ed Welch. He's a deputy marshal outta Cheyenne, up here lookin' for some stagecoach robbers. Ed, this is Mr. Cross. Logan, warn't it?"

"That's right," Logan managed to answer.

"Pleased to meet you, Mr. Cross," Ed Welch said, and extended his hand.

Logan accepted it, bracing himself in the event it was a trick. "Likewise," he said. Astonished that there was no name recognition, he decided to press for more information. "Lookin' for stage bandits, huh? I woulda figured you'd be looking between Deadwood and Cheyenne, instead of over here."

"And you'd be right," Welch said. "Sam Bass and his gang of road agents, in fact. They've been pretty busy lately up closer to Deadwood. I ain't had much luck findin' where they hole up, but I got a tip that they've been seen over in these parts."

"You say you're outta Cheyenne?" Logan asked. "I'da figured you'd be workin' outta Fort Meade."

"There ain't no marshals workin' outta Fort Meade. That's an army post," Welch said.

Logan merely nodded in response, his mind in disorder as he tried to sort out what he had just learned. So deep in thought was he that he was suddenly startled when Ed Welch bade him a good day and led his horse outside the shop.

Ox had told him the marshal that had come for him was out of Fort Meade. He was sure of that. Ox was not the smartest man he had ever met. Maybe the big man had gotten it wrong. Even so, this marshal said he was looking for somebody named Sam Bass.

Confused, Logan knew that he needed to think this thing through. He hurried outside after Welch, who was just stepping up in the saddle. "Say, Marshal, do you know a marshal named Quincy Smith?"

"Can't say as I do," Welch replied. He hesitated, waiting to see if Logan had anything else to ask.

"I was just wonderin'," Logan said. "I heard there was a marshal in these parts by that name."

"If there is, I don't know anything about him," Welch said, and waited for a few moments before again saying, "Good day," and rode away.

If there's no marshal in these parts, then who the hell is chasing me?

The question was staggering, considering all he had done to escape. It didn't make sense, but there was definitely a posse out to get him. He had to conclude that the gang tracking him was somehow connected to Jake Morgan, and not the law at all. Thinking back now, he realized he had made a mistake in not going after the man who had tried to bushwhack him right after he left Montana City. He had wounded him, and at the time, he thought that would be the end of any attempt at retaliation. He had figured the man was a bushwhacker who just happened upon him. But upon thinking back on it, he now thought it more likely that it was the same man as before.

So now he's got a posse coming after me, he thought, *a devil's posse.*

He knew now why there was no arrest attempted by this posse. This was a death posse. The question he needed an answer for was, where were they? Had they given up, or were they still searching?

This revelation that had occurred today put a whole new spin on the game. He would no longer be concerned about possibly killing a lawman. Now it was no different from being attacked by a pack of wolves, and maybe the best way to fight a pack of wolves was to thin them out. Angry to have been duped into believing he was on the run from the law, he decided that he was no longer running. He would reverse the roles and become the hunter instead of the prey.

He jumped when he suddenly felt a hand on his shoulder. "Whoa!" Mosely blurted, and jumped as well. "You musta been thinkin' hard about somethin'."

"Sorry," Logan said, "I was at that. What were you sayin'?"

"I was tryin' to tell you I'm done with your horse," Mosely explained.

Undecided as to what his next move should be, he rode back into the mountains and returned to his camp, where he stood looking at the shelters he had built, trying to decide whether he should go in search of his pursuers. It was just the beginning of winter, and not a good time to be traveling out in the open night after night. He was thinking not so much for himself, but of how hard it might be on Pepper. Still, he could not help being infuriated by the thought that he was being chased by a gang of outlaws, posing as lawmen. If he had known who they were, he would have taken his chances on the Triple-T, instead of fleeing to these mountains and running out on what had promised to be a decent job with Jace Evans.

By now, they had already driven the cattle to the holding pens for shipment to the East. He still had money, more than enough to carry him through the winter, but it wasn't going to last forever. And spring would find him a drifter, looking for work again. He didn't care much for the prospect. Then he reminded himself that there was still a gang of assassins searching for him.

"Damn it!" he cursed angrily. "I'd rather hunt them than have them huntin' me!"

With that thought firmly in mind, he decided to go back along the trail that he had taken to this camp, feeling it important to find out for sure what had happened to the posse. At least he might be able to determine if they had called off the hunt and withdrawn. That would be better than sitting here in this camp wondering if he was going to have company one dark night.

When morning came, he packed up a supply of smoked deer meat, coffee, and dried beans, as well as a sack of oats he planned to feed sparingly to Pepper. He took one last look at the camp he had labored so hard to build, and wondered if it would still be there should he return. Then he made his way down past the waterfall to the twin streams below and started backtracking along the trail that had led him to this spot. He found that he remembered his way clearly, recalling places where he had left one game trail to take another that looked more promising—and where he had entered streams to confuse his trackers. With only a light blanket of snow to cover the ground, it would still have been possible to pick up some sign of six horses, even after this long a time, but he found none.

On the second day, late in the afternoon, he came upon the sign he searched for. In several tight places where a game trail had led through a thicket of pines, he found broken branches. And when he dismounted and carefully brushed snow away from the path, he found hoofprints. So, he thought, they had gotten this far before they lost his trail. He stood up and looked around him. Judging by the number of broken pine boughs, it appeared that they had divided to look in different directions.

They didn't know which way I went, he thought. *So now they're just looking for sign.* There seemed to be one trail that led down the mountain under a ledge that jutted out over a grove of pines, so he followed it.

The trail led through the thickest part of the pines below the ledge. Logan's eyes were fixed on the ground ahead of Pepper, watching for any places that might cause the horse to stumble.

When he glanced up, he caught a movement in the

trees ahead, causing him to rein Pepper back hard. Mostly hidden by the trees, he saw what he thought was a deer, or maybe an elk, judging by the size. When it whinnied, he realized it was a mule. Astonished, he pushed on through the trees to find a stream and the remains of what appeared to be a camp. It was not until he stepped down from his horse that he discovered the bodies of the two miners. Apart from them, he then discovered a third body of what had to have been an extremely large man. It looked to him that all three had been dead for days, nothing left but bones and rags, though; they had not managed to escape the notice of the buzzards and coyotes.

It was easy to guess that they had had the misfortune to have been found by the posse. It impressed upon him the kind of ruthless men who sought to find him. It was up to somebody to stop these murderers, and it was beginning to look as though he was the one who was going to have to do it. For it seemed he might be the only one who knew they were not real lawmen.

His mind made up, he found their trail where it left the camp, marked only by the few branches broken as their horses pushed through a bank of small bushes. It led down the mountain. He left the three skeletons as he had found them, as well as the mule to continue to shift for itself. It followed along behind him for only a little way before deciding it preferred to remain free and trailed off to return to the stream. There was no deviation in the trail he now followed. They had obviously broken off the chase and decided to return the way they had come. He followed until darkness forced him to make camp. He continued on the next morning and throughout that day until his next camp found him in the foothills north of the mountains. The second

snow of the season fell during the night, making it difficult, but not impossible, to follow the posse through the
foothills to the prairie beyond. That was as far as it led,
however, for the snow covered any tracks that might
have been left on the open prairie.

He decided to stop and rest Pepper, build a fire, and
make some coffee while he decided what he was going
to do. He felt the frustration of knowing there was a
gang of men somewhere looking to kill him, and he
didn't know where they were. Worse yet, unless they
all came at him at once, he wouldn't know them if he
saw them individually. It was not a comfortable feeling to be unable to identify his enemy. It might be safer
to return to his camp in the mountains, but since he
had already come this far, he had a strong desire to
continue on to the Triple-T.

It was important to him to let Jace Evans and Thomas
Towson and the men of the Triple-T know that he was
not a wanted man, at least not by a U.S. Marshal. It
was also important to him that Hannah know the truth.
There was the possibility that the sheriff in Montana
City might have been looking for him after he had exe-
cuted Jake Morgan in the Lucky Dollar Saloon. But he
doubted the sheriff had any interest in coming after
him, and was probably satisfied that he had left town.

There was another reason to go to the ranch. He had
a horse there, Billy's buckskin. He intended to return
for it sometime—might as well be now. With that decision firm in his mind, he set out for the Triple-T.

"I'm not sure we're so lucky to have their business,"
Mae Davis remarked to Hannah Mabry when she saw
the marshal and his men file in the door of the dining
room for supper. "They don't seem to be short of

money, but I'm afraid they're gonna scare some of our regular customers away. They've been minding their manners so far, but I declare they look like they're liable to bust loose at any minute. If Marshal Smith wasn't here to control them, I think they might turn into the animals they look like. I know I shouldn't say it, but at least the worst-looking one of them didn't come back." She was referring to the fact that Curly had been killed in a desperate gun battle with some road agents. This was according to what they had been told by Quincy. "That was one scary-lookin' man," Mae went on.

"I agree with you," Hannah said. "I'm afraid to go into either one of those two rooms they've let. I'm glad Daisy doesn't mind cleaning them. That may have been our biggest mistake, letting them have those rooms. The marshal seems nice enough, but his men, even his cousin, Lonnie, might be better suited to sleep in Sam Taylor's stable."

Mae looked at her and grinned. "You're just taking up for Quincy because he's sweet on you."

"No such a thing," Hannah responded, but could not suppress a blush. "Don't forget I'm a recently widowed woman. The marshal's just a friendly person, that's all."

"Right," Mae replied with a bigger grin.

"Surely they won't be staying here much longer," Hannah speculated. "I mean, won't his superiors send him somewhere to catch some other outlaws, since they weren't able to find Logan?"

"He told me that he aimed to stay here till he was able to track him down," Mae said. "Said he was gonna make Spearfish his headquarters."

"I don't know how he can track Logan down if he's staying here."

"I don't, either," Mae said playfully. "You might have to go up in the mountains to get Quincy to go look for Logan up there."

"Stop it, Mae!" Hannah fussed, pretending to be angry. Then she became serious for a moment as she confessed, "I really hope that he doesn't ever catch Logan. I don't care if he did do what they claim."

"Uh-oh," Mae said, "conversation's over. Here he comes." They stood waiting while Quincy ambled over to greet them.

"Well, now, ain't this a pretty sight to see first thing in the mornin'?" Quincy teased playfully, his hair slicked back and parted, his mustache neatly trimmed. It was obvious that he was intent upon impressing the ladies. "Like two spring flowers bloomin' in the snow."

Mae couldn't help laughing. There was no doubt in her mind which one of the flowers Quincy was set on plucking. "More like a flower and a clump of sour grass," she said. "Set yourself down and we'll see about feedin' you and that bunch of hounds with you." She had to admit that the marshal was a handsome man, in a devil-may-care kind of way. She glanced at Hannah, wondering if Quincy's attempt to charm was having any effect on the young widow.

I hope to hell not, she thought. *That man doesn't look like the settling-down kind.*

Hannah smiled sweetly at him and said, "I'll go fetch the coffee for you and your men." She turned at once to return to the kitchen.

"Thank you, ma'am," Quincy was quick to reply. "I could surely use a cup of it this mornin'." He watched her until she was out of his view, then turned to favor Mae with a smile before heading toward the table prepared for him and his men.

A special section had been set up for the marshal and his posse. Mae and Daisy had pulled two tables together in the back corner of the dining room in an effort to separate them as much as possible from the other customers. The four menacing-looking posse men filed into the room like a pack of hungry hyenas, leering at the few diners already eating at the one long table in the center of the room. But they made no loud remarks as they pulled their chairs back and sat down. Quincy had made it very clear to them all that any boisterous behavior would be reserved for the saloon. Here in the rooming house they were to behave like gentlemen, or they would answer directly to him.

"Boy, ol' Quincy is turnin' it on for that young one," Wormy remarked aside to Stokes as he watched Quincy approaching. "I'll bet he'll bed that one down before long."

"He might at that," Stokes said as Quincy pulled a chair out and sat down. "Looks like you've got your brand on that pretty one," he said to Quincy. "That just leaves that older one for the rest of us, but she looks like she might buck a little." He and Wormy laughed.

"Don't forget that'un in the kitchen," Lacey said.

Neither Quincy nor Lonnie joined in the laughter. The remarks brought an immediate response from Quincy. His heavy dark eyebrows dipped in a deep frown as he laid down his rules once more.

"I told you to keep your mouths shut in this dinin' room. If you want a roll in the hay with a woman, there's a couple at the saloon that'll take you on. We've got to keep these folks here thinkin' we're respectable lawmen."

"We know that, Quincy," Stokes was quick to assure him. "We was just japin' a little bit. Hell, we'll behave like deacons in a church when we're around here."

Unless one of those women is partial to an outlaw, he said to himself. He looked at Quincy and smiled.

"We've got us a good spot here," Quincy said. "I ain't plannin' on messin' it up just because you boys are gettin' rutty. Damn it, that's what they made whores for."

His scowl was quickly replaced with a smile when Hannah and Mae came from the kitchen with food for the table. The whores at the saloon were not good enough for him, he thought as he watched Hannah placing a couple of bowls down before him.

I'm aiming to get a hell of a lot more from you than potatoes and beans, he thought. Hannah met his gaze with a smile. *Might not be as hard as I thought.*

That evening, when supper was finished and the kitchen was cleaned up, Hannah stepped out on the front porch to get a breath of the cold evening air after helping Daisy clean up around a hot kitchen stove. She had taken no more than a couple of deep breaths when she was aware of someone coming up behind her. She turned to find Quincy only a few steps away.

"Oh," she exclaimed, startled.

"I'm sorry," he said. "I didn't mean to surprise you. I was just takin' the air myself." He slipped out of his coat and placed it around her shoulders before she had a chance to protest. "You'll catch a chill for yourself out here in this cold air, a lady as dainty as you."

"Oh, why, thank you, sir," she said, not certain how she should respond. "That's very considerate of you, but I was not really that cold." She took the coat off and gave it back to him. "I was kinda enjoying the cold. I have to hurry back to help Mae and Daisy finish the cleanup anyway."

"I'm sorry you have to run off so soon," he said. "I'd surely admire visitin' with you for a while."

"Well, perhaps some other time," she said, and turned to leave.

"I hope I haven't offended you, ma'am. My intentions are purely honorable, I assure you. But you can't blame me for wantin' to know you better." He stepped quickly to the door and opened it for her. She nodded and gave him a smile before stepping inside.

Play your woman's game, he thought confidently, *and when you're done, you'll come around.*

Inside, she hoped the flush she was feeling had not been evident to him. She was not sure what she should think about the brief encounter on the porch. He was obviously interested in more than a casual conversation, and she was taken by surprise.

At once she felt ashamed of herself for being flattered that the marshal was paying her such attention. But at the same time, she could not help thinking that it was all right to enjoy his company, even if it was so soon after Jack had been killed. She loved her husband, and would always be true to his memory, but he had left her alone to go on with life as it was presented to her.

Damn it, she thought. *He is rather handsome.*

"Whoa! Look out where you're about to throw that water," Riley Stokes sang out, effectively startling the young woman with the dishpan full of dirty dishwater.

"Well, what in the world are you doing outside the kitchen door, anyway?" Daisy Welker exclaimed, still trying to keep from spilling the water on herself after she had come so close to letting it fly.

"I was just using the outhouse," Stokes said. "I

didn't think I was gonna get a bath on my way back."
He gave her a lecherous grin. "Course, if you was wantin' to give me a bath, I might consider lettin' you."

"Oh, you would, would you?" Daisy replied, well
aware of his intentions. "What are you doing coming
around to the kitchen door, anyway? Our guests use
the front door. It's closer to the privy."

"Maybe I was just hopin' I'd run into you," Stokes
said. "I saw you throwin' the dishwater out last evenin', so I figured you'd appreciate a little help. It looks
like a pretty heavy dishpan."

"Is that so? Well, I'm a pretty strong woman, so I
don't need no help."

"I figured that, too," he went on, undeterred. "I
heard tell you was a widow, and that's my specialty,
takin' care of poor women that's been without their
husband for a spell. In some parts they call me the
widow pleaser."

"Ha!" she blurted. "You're talkin' to the wrong widow.
Didn't anybody tell you that the reason I'm a widow is
because I shot that no-account I was married to?"

Stokes threw his head back and laughed. "Is that a
fact? Now I know me and you could help each other
out. Why don't I slip up to your room after a while for
a friendly visit?"

"Well, one reason I can think of is, if you were to
happen to show up at my door, you'd most likely get a
load of buckshot from the same gun I shot my husband
with," she said. "There's women up at the saloon to take
care of men like you, so why don't you go up there?"

"Men like me?" he responded, offended. "Whaddaya mean by that? I was just tryin' to be friendly.
Maybe you're just a stuck-up bitch who thinks you're

too good for fellers that work for a livin'. Well, honey, you ain't the prettiest flower in the bunch."

"I ain't the most desperate, neither," she replied, well aware that what he said was true, but not particularly worried about it. She was long past any desire to couple with a man, just for the sake of coupling. "Now, I've got work to do, so if you keep standing where you are, you're liable to get hit with some of this dishwater." She drew it back as if about to throw it.

He backed away a couple of steps. "I was just tryin' to be polite. I sure as hell ain't interested in no scrawny-lookin' woman like you. There's better-lookin' ones up at the saloon."

"Well, go to it, Romeo. Maybe you can find one drunk enough to take you on." She let the dishwater fly. He jumped aside in time to avoid it, but just barely. Some splashed on his boots.

"Why, you ornery bitch," he fumed. "I've a good mind to jerk you off that porch and whup you good."

"If you had a good mind, you woulda had better sense than to waste your time makin' a pest outta yourself." She spun on her heel and went in the door, slamming it behind her.

"Damn bitch," Stokes smoldered.

"By God, that was real smooth."

He turned to see Wormy leaning against the back corner of the building, laughing at him. "I always wanted to see one of the real smooth talkers in action," the little man teased. "I swear, that woman's liable to be chasin' after you to marry her."

"You go to hell," Stokes replied angrily.

Wormy stopped laughing and turned serious for a moment. "You'd best not let Quincy or Lonnie find out you've been sniffin' around that woman. You know what he said about behavin' ourselves around here."

"To hell with that, too," Stokes said. "It looks like it's all right for him to keep sniffin' around that other woman. He ain't got no right to tell us not to talk to them."

Deadly serious now, Wormy said, "It ain't no question about him havin' the right or not. You oughta know it don't take much to send him into one of those fits that strike him."

Stokes was fully aware of what that might result in, and he was not angry enough to risk that possibility.

"Well, he don't need to know about it. That woman's too scrawny for my taste, anyway."

Even though he could not disagree with what Wormy said, he was still irritated by the double set of rules that Quincy laid down. Besides, in spite of having been thoroughly rebuked by Daisy, he was now more determined than ever to bed her down.

Before this is over, he silently promised himself.

Chapter II

The lone rider reined his gray gelding to a stop and sat gazing at the little collection of buildings a quarter of a mile distant at the foot of the mountain behind them. Spearfish looked small and vulnerable, even more so than on the first day he had seen it. That day, it had been a welcome sight after following Spearfish Canyon to its mouth. Now there was a cloud of uncertainty hovering over him.

How would they receive him after thinking him a fugitive from the law, a murderer no less? Would they believe him when he explained the circumstances that had compelled him to kill?

He continued to sit there staring at the town, trying to decide if he should bypass it and go directly to the Triple-T as he had originally planned to do. But he felt it important to see that Hannah found out the truth, certainly as much as the crew at the Triple-T. Maybe it was more important, although he could not explain why.

Finally he justified his decision by thinking, *I haven't*

had a good meal in a while, and it's about suppertime at the
Three Widows. He nudged Pepper and continued on
toward the town.

He walked his horse slowly down the muddy street
past the dry goods store and the blacksmith. As he
passed the Gateway Saloon, a slight man wearing a
heavy woolen coat and a black hat with a flat crown
and a narrow brim stepped out the door and stood
watching him for a few moments. Past the stables,
Logan pulled Pepper up before the boardinghouse. He
smiled when he noted that there was no sign up proclaiming it to be the Three Widows Inn yet. As a man-
ner of habit, he drew his rifle from the saddle sling and
stepped down from the saddle. Casually looping Pepper's reins over the hitching rail, he walked in the
front door.

She was standing in the parlor, her back turned to
him, putting a stack of folded napkins in a cupboard
next to the dining room door. "Pardon me, miss, can a
fellow get somethin' to eat in this establishment?" he
asked.

Unhurried, she turned to face him. She appeared startled when she saw him standing there; her eyes grew
wide with shock. "Logan!" she exclaimed in distress.
"What are you doing here?" Before he could answer, she
said, "You can't be here!"

Surprised by her frantic reaction to his appearance,
he started to explain why he had come, but was stunned
himself when Tom Lacey came out of the dining room,
working away at his teeth with a toothpick. Without
hesitation, Lacey grabbed for the .44 he wore on his
hip. In the excitement of the moment, however, he
fumbled with it, getting it halfway out of his holster
before Logan reacted, cocking the Winchester and cut-

ting him down. Hannah screamed, terrified. There had been no time to think; he had simply reacted. Now he stood there, dumbfounded, not certain what to do.

In the next second, Hannah regained her senses and exclaimed, "You've got to get out of here! The marshal and his men are here!"

"I didn't . . . ," he started, still confused. "I just came to tell you—"

"Get out of here!" she screamed. "They'll kill you!"

He realized then what he had unexpectedly walked into. He had given no thought to the possibility that the men who had been stalking him could be in Spearfish. There was no time now to think about it, so he ran out the door, freed Pepper's reins, and was off at a gallop out the end of the street and onto the open prairie. Unless they made a move on him, he could not recognize any of the others in the posse apart from any ordinary citizen of the town. So it made no sense to do anything other than run.

Behind him, he left a town startled by the sudden killing of one of the marshal's men, blatantly, while most of the posse were right there in the same building. Wormy Jacobs came running from the saloon when he heard the shot, just in time to see Logan gallop out across the snowy plain. He was too far away at that point for Wormy to even attempt a shot with his pistol. He ran into the boardinghouse and found the rest of the posse gathered around Lacey, who was fading rapidly.

"I saw him when he rode by the saloon!" Wormy blurted. "I coulda blowed him right outta the saddle if I hadda knowed it was him. Damn, I wish I'da remembered what Lacey said about that horse he rides. 'Cause he was settin' up there on a flea-bitten gray horse, just big as you please. But I never thought about it." When he saw that it was Lacey who had been shot, he asked, "How bad is he hurt?"

"He's done for," Lonnie said.

"Did you say you got a good look at him?" Quincy wanted to know. When Wormy said that he had, Quincy said, "Good, then you'll know him when you see him again, right? Even if he ain't on that gray horse." He stepped back, no longer concerned with Lacey's fate, while the three women tried their best to tend to the wounded man. Hannah gave Mae a look of disbelief when Quincy showed no compassion for the loss of one of his men, especially when overhearing parts of the conversation between him and Lonnie.

"Well, who'da thought it?" Quincy said. "The man we searched for all over those mountains came right to us, and we've still got a man who can identify him. That's like a great big Christmas present, and it ain't even Christmas yet. We need to get the horses and get after him while there's a nice fresh trail in the snow."

Daisy could not help commenting, "One of your men is dying and we can't do anything to save him. You don't seem to care a helluva lot."

Realizing that she had heard what he had said, he tried to repair the damage. "You don't understand, lady. Of course I care, but this is a hard business tryin' to uphold the law. This murderin' skunk has killed two of my men, but we can't let ourselves get to grievin' about it too much, or we won't be able to do our job. The only thing we can do for Lacey now is to go after his killer and bring him to justice. I'm just sorry he had to come to do his murderin' in your house." He turned to Lonnie then and said, "Come on, boys, we've got to get our horses saddled and get after that killer. We'll be doin' it for Curly and Lacey. We owe it to both of 'em."

"Yeah," Wormy said, "poor ol' Curly, he always was kinda snakebit when the lead was flyin'." His comment caused Stokes to laugh.

Puzzled as to why the comment made Stokes laugh, Mae asked, "What about this one?" She looked to Quincy for an answer as she pressed firmly on Lacey's chest in an attempt to slow the bleeding.

"I leave him in your good hands," Quincy answered, "while we do the only thing we can to avenge him. I hope you and the other two ladies understand that we have to be tough, or the outlaws will take over this territory like they did in Oklahoma Injun Territory." They hurried out the door and ran to get their horses from the stable. "Maybe we'll get lucky this time," he said to Hannah as he went out the door.

"You try to hang on there, feller," Mae said as she tightened up on a piece of an old bedsheet she had used to bind Lacey's chest. "Get that other pillow off the settee, Daisy, and stick it under his head."

Daisy hurried to do her bidding, both women knowing that it was a useless endeavor, but trying to do everything they could to make his passing more comfortable. No matter what they did, he seemed to be suffering extreme pain. In a few minutes after his comrades had gone out the door, he opened his eyes halfway, his lips parted, and he spoke.

"Damn that son of a bitchin' skunk." Then his last breath rushed out of his lungs and he was gone.

Mae and Hannah looked at each other with puzzled expressions. "Those are mighty dignified last words, ain't they?" Mae said facetiously.

"Ha!" Daisy snorted, trying to keep from laughing.

The small crowd of spectators that had gathered after hearing the gunshot parted to let Marvin Patterson and his son, Marvin Jr., into the room. Marvin was the barber, dentist, and undertaker. He and his son picked Lacey up and carried him out the door.

"I'll go fetch a bucket of water and a mop," Daisy volunteered. "But I don't know if we'll get all that blood up before it stains those boards for good."

Now that the immediate shock was over, Hannah looked at Mae and remarked, "I still can't believe I misjudged Logan Cross that much. I mean, he was nothing like the coldhearted killer he turned out to be when he brought me here. To find out that he is so evil as to come here to murder the marshal's men, instead of running away, is just hard to believe."

"I thought you said he was surprised when Lacey walked in," Daisy said. "He might notta come here to kill anybody." She raised an eyebrow and said, "Maybe he just came here to see you."

"Well, it did look like he didn't expect him," Hannah admitted, "but he still came here where they were. Why would he come here, if not to kill them?"

"Well, if he did, he ain't too overly bright," Daisy said, "seein' as how he was goin' up against five lawmen. I think it's more likely he didn't have any idea they were here."

"I don't know what to think," Hannah replied. "But I do know that Logan came here and killed a lawman. And I'm sorely disappointed in him for that."

"I was wonderin' when he was gonna get smart enough to cut over on the road outta Spearfish," Lonnie said when the others caught up with him. Logan's trail had been easy to follow up to that point as he had raced across a clean white prairie. But now his tracks were lost in all the other tracks left by horses, oxen, and wagons that traveled the road, which eventually led to Belle Fourche. Many of the tracks were old, but there were enough new ones, going in both directions, to make him unsure which ones belonged to the gray gelding Logan rode. "That horse he's ridin' is wearin' new shoes, too. But I still can't make out which tracks are his."

"Well, it looks like he's headin' for that ranch, the Triple-T, so that's where we'll head for," Quincy said. "Keep a sharp eye out in case he decided to leave the road somewhere between here and there."

"From the looks of them tracks before he got to the road, it looks like he's ridin' the hell outta that horse," Wormy said. "Ain't no way of knowin' how far he rode before he got to Spearfish, and how tired that gray was then, so that horse might be gettin' pretty damn wore out by now. Maybe we'll catch up with him before he gets to the Triple-T."

"We might at that," Quincy allowed. "And that would be to my likin'. I'd love to deal with Mr. Logan Cross without no witnesses around."

"We're wastin' time," Lonnie said. "Let's get goin'. It ain't but about four miles from here."

Lonnie's speculations had been right on the mark. Logan had driven Pepper hard and the gelding was badly in need of rest. He did not doubt for a second that the so-called posse was hot on his heels. He gave consideration toward finding a place to ambush them, but the snowy flat plain he was riding afforded very little in the way of protected spots. So when he came to the road to Belle Fourche, he figured his best chance to lose them was to take to the road.

But instead of going on to the Triple-T, he wheeled Pepper around and took the road back to Spearfish, gambling on the chance they wouldn't expect him to reverse his flight. After riding for about a mile, he dismounted and walked to give Pepper a little rest. He remembered a long mesa just northeast of the town, and he decided he would give Pepper a longer rest there. There was still no one in sight behind him, so he figured he had been successful in losing his pursuers.

When he reached a point from which he could see the buildings of Spearfish, he stopped once again to gaze at the tiny town. It was the second time that day, and this time it was from north of the town. He looked to his left at the long, low mesa and the many gullies and ravines leading up from its base. He should find a suitable place to set up a camp on the far side of it to let Pepper rest. Beyond resting the big gray, he was undecided what to do next.

First and foremost in his mind was whether or not he should make another attempt to see Hannah and tell her why he had no choice in this war with the men set on killing him. From her reaction when he had surprised her in the parlor, she still believed the man he shot was a lawman. So this gang of outlaws was still carrying on their charade, and the whole town was evidently buying it. It boiled down to his word against theirs, and so far, every action he had been forced to take made it difficult to believe he was not the killer they were telling the town he was.

But why, he asked himself, was it so important that Hannah should know the truth? There was no real reason, and yet the fact that she did not believe his innocence continued to weigh heavily on his mind. Finally he surrendered to his emotions and made up his mind to try to see her again and tell her his side of the story. There would be no better time to do it while the outlaw posse was gone, hopefully still chasing him on the road to Belle Fourche.

When he came to a little stream running across the road, he decided it a good place to leave the road without leaving tracks, so he climbed back into the saddle to keep his boots dry. Then he turned Pepper off the road and rode up the stream toward the mesa, leaving no trail in the snow. After a couple of hundred yards, the stream led him up a narrow ravine guarded by a sparse growth of stunted pines.

This'll do, he thought, and guided the horse out of the water, dismounted, and led him toward the upper part of the ravine.

"I'd best leave the saddle on you, boy. We might not be stayin' here long." He would give the horse about an hour's rest before riding on into Spearfish. Supper at the boardinghouse would be over then, and the women would more than likely be finishing with the cleanup. It was already beginning to get dark, so that should help. He wasn't sure how, but he would try to find some way to get to Hannah when she was alone.

The hour passed painfully slowly, but at last he decided it was all right to leave. The ravine the stream had led him to seemed as good a campsite as he was likely to find. It offered some protection from the cold winds sweeping down the mountains to rush across the prairie. If all went well in town, he would most likely return here to camp for the night.

"I'd put you up in the stable if I could," he said to the gray. "But I ain't sure Sam Taylor wouldn't take a shot at me as soon as I walked in."

* * *

Hannah couldn't help wondering if she was going to have a severe attack of nerves before this day was over. She and Mae had managed to get through the supper hour without dropping any dishes, although just barely. She envied Daisy's hard-shell indifference to stressful situations. The outspoken woman claimed she had enjoyed the evening.

"It was kinda like a little vacation with that pack of coyotes gone chasin' after Logan," she had said. But Daisy had not known Logan as Hannah had.

She could still see the horrific expression on Lacey's face as Logan's bullet ripped through his chest. It made her shiver uncontrollably when she brought it to mind. She had not felt that terror since she witnessed her husband's death. Then the picture of Logan formed in her mind, as he whipped his rifle up to deliver the fatal shot. He had reacted so fast, as if no thought was required, his face expressionless as if he was acting on natural instinct. It was difficult not to assume he had done it many times before. And she had spent days and nights with the man, unsuspecting of the killer inside him. She shook her head violently, trying to rid her brain of the image as she finished her toilet. Upon opening the outhouse door, she found herself facing her nightmare. He was standing in the path, waiting.

"Oh my God, my God . . . ," she began to cry helplessly, scarcely able to believe he was there again, ghostlike in the shadows of the lone cottonwood behind the house. Maybe he was an illusion conjured by her frazzled nerves. She hoped that was what was happening to her, but then he spoke.

"Don't be afraid, Hannah. You oughta know by now

that I'm the last person that would hurt you. I'll be gone in a minute, but I wanted you to know that I ain't the man they said I am. And I wanna warn you. That bunch that says they're lawmen have been lyin' to you and everybody else in town. They're friends of the man who murdered my brother. I killed that man and another man who helped him kill Billy. So they're out to get me for that. The law ain't got nothin' to do with it. And whoever's leadin' this gang ain't no marshal, and I thought you and Mae needed to know that, 'cause there ain't no tellin' what they've got in mind after they get me." He paused to judge her reaction, realizing after he had said it that it was more confusing than he had intended it to be. "They killed my brother. That's what started the whole thing."

She was unable to say anything for a long moment, not sure she could believe him or not. He seemed sincere, but Quincy seemed equally earnest when he spoke of his duty to capture Logan. True, she thought, Quincy's posse men were a rough-looking collection of hard-living men, but she understood the necessity for such men in a marshal's posse. As Quincy had remarked to her, *"You don't go after a mad dog with a switch."*

Logan stood there waiting while she continued to despair. Finally she spoke honestly. "I'm not sure I can believe you. It might have been better if you had not come back." She paused again, still struggling with whether he was the man she first thought him to be. Then she asked, "Did you kill Curly?"

"Curly?" he responded in surprise. "No. Who's Curly?"

"One of Quincy's men," she said, "a big, simple man." When he shook his head, she said, "The marshal said he was killed when they went after you." She wanted to hear Logan's answer, even though there were two different stories concerning Curly's death.

"No," he repeated. "What I'm tryin' to make you understand is that I'm not the cold-blooded killer they've told you I am. I'm just tryin' to keep from gettin' killed. Surely you saw that the man I shot in your parlor was reaching for his gun to shoot me." She did not answer, obviously still confused. "Surely you saw that," he repeated.

"I don't know," she replied, flustered. "I guess so. Maybe he was just going to try to arrest you. I don't know."

Logan slowly shook his head in frustration. He realized that he might have made this trip into town for nothing. Hannah clearly could not let herself accept his version of the events that had led them all to this confrontation. This imposter, Quincy Smith, or whatever his real name was, had done a thorough job of selling himself and his men to her, and the rest of the town, too.

"Well," he said, defeated, "looks like I've wasted my time, but I wanted to tell you my side of it." He turned to leave but was stopped by a voice behind him.

"Just hold it right there, 'less you want a load of buckshot in your behind." He turned to see Daisy standing near the back steps, aiming a double-barreled shotgun at him. "You all right, Hannah?"

"Yes," Hannah answered.

"I'll be goin' now," Logan said. "I've said my piece."

"You just hold it right there," Daisy repeated, this time with more authority. "Maybe we oughta hold you till the marshal gets back." She cocked the hammers back to emphasize her authority.

"I reckon you'll just have to shoot me," Logan

replied calmly, and turned to walk away. "I'd rather have you shoot me in the back than one of those killers in that crooked bunch of outlaws."

Daisy held the shotgun to her shoulder for a few moments before pulling it down and carefully releasing the hammers. "Just get the hell outta here before one of Quincy's coyotes puts a bullet in your back," she called after him.

Without stopping, he threw up his hand to acknowledge her advice, then disappeared behind the smokehouse where Pepper was tied.

"Hell," Daisy admitted to Hannah, "I couldn't have shot him. I like him better'n any of that bunch of posse men." She waited until Hannah walked up the steps, and then asked, "What was he doin' here? He acts like he just wants to get himself killed."

"He wanted to tell me that Quincy is not really a marshal," Hannah said, still shaken, "that they're all just a gang of outlaws."

"Huh," Daisy snorted. "It wouldn't surprise me none atall. It's gettin' where you can't tell the chickens from the fox. Whadda you think?"

"I honestly don't know what I think," Hannah answered truthfully.

Daisy gave her a serious look, suspicious that there were some deeper, more complex thoughts troubling Hannah's mind. "Quincy's a better-lookin' man, but I reckon I like Logan better," she stated simply. "It's cold out here and I'm about to pee in my britches." She handed Hannah the shotgun. "Here, take this back in the house. I gotta go to the privy."

Logan returned to the ravine at the foot of the mesa to make his camp. He was tired and hungry, and more than a little bit downtrodden, a result of his unsuccessful attempt to persuade Hannah to reject Quincy's story.

"I don't know why I give a shit," he complained to Pepper, then went about the business of gathering enough wood to build a fire. He told himself that he would be able to decide what to do next a whole lot better with a cup of hot coffee and some jerky inside him.

A smart man would ride out of these parts and head back down to Texas, he thought. *Maybe hire on with another outfit driving longhorn cattle up to Ogallala.* He paused to consider that possibility.

"I've got to go get Billy's horse first," he said aloud. The more he thought about it, the more it made sense. "This is pretty country, but it's bad for your health," he said to Pepper when he fed him the last of the bag of oats he had bought in Rapid City. "We'll head for the Triple-T in the mornin' and pick up Billy's buckskin."

Chapter 12

"Riders comin' in," Bob Whitley announced when he walked out the barn door and looked toward Towson's Creek. He pointed them out to Jim Bledsoe, who was walking out of the barn with him. They both stopped to try to make out who might be coming to call this late in the evening. "Looks like four of 'em."

There was no reason to be concerned, but it never hurt to be cautious, so without saying another word, both men turned around, went back into the tack room, and fetched their rifles from their saddles.

With rifles in hand, they walked back out to the front of the barn to watch for their visitors, who were now within a hundred yards. "I'll go tell Jace," Bledsoe said, and went at once to the bunkhouse, where Jace Evans and some of the hands were playing cards.

In a couple of minutes, Jace, along with Bledsoe, Lou Cheatam, and Ox, came to join Bob. Within fifty yards now, Quincy yelled out, "Howdy, Triple-T. It's Marshal Smith."

"Well, I'll be damned," Jace muttered. "I wonder what he's doin' back here." He raised his voice to yell back, "Howdy, Marshal, come on in." He turned to Lou and said, "They look like they've been ridin' a spell. Go back and tell Spud to put on a new pot of coffee and see if there's anything he can scare up to feed 'em." Quincy and his men rode into the barnyard, looking every bit as weary as Jace had speculated. "What brings you boys back up this way?" he asked. "And pretty late in the day at that."

"We've been on Logan Cross's trail," Quincy said. "And it was leadin' up this way. Looked like he was headed here."

"Logan?" Jace responded, surprised. "You think he's come back here?"

Quincy and his men stepped down. "Like I said, he was comin' this way. Don't suppose he's holed up around here somewhere? Maybe he figured he'd come back home to hide out. He's still a wanted man, and we got him now for two more counts of murder." He looked around him in the darkened barnyard as if looking for Logan to appear.

"Damn," Jace swore. "You are short two men since the last time you showed up here. I still can hardly believe we're talkin' about the same man who worked here. But if he's holed up around here somewhere, I don't know it." He turned to Bledsoe. "You boys know anything about Logan?" They all shook their heads.

Aware that Ox had for some reason formed a special allegiance to Logan, he asked the simple man directly. "Ox, have you seen Logan since he ran off from the line shack?" The big man slowly shook his head, his eyes still wide with the excitement of the news.

"I'm afraid he's give you the slip again, Marshal,"

Jace said. "He ain't come back here." He could see that the marshal was not pleased to hear he had reached another dead end. "You fellers look like you're a little wore out. Why don't you unsaddle those horses and turn 'em out in the corral? Then we'll go on up to the bunkhouse and find you something to eat."

"That sounds mighty fine to me," Wormy said, without waiting for Quincy to say yea or nay. His vote was seconded by Stokes, and they started unsaddling their horses.

Only slightly perturbed by their actions, Quincy looked at Lonnie and shrugged. "Why, that's mighty neighborly of you," he said to Jace. "We could sure use some grub."

Jace waited for Quincy to take the saddle off his horse, then walked with him up to the bunkhouse. "Killed two of your men," he pondered aloud. "That's still hard for me to picture that man doin' something like that."

"He's a dangerous killer," Quincy said. "You're mighty lucky he didn't cause any trouble while he was workin' for you. I expect he was just tryin' to keep his nose clean, 'cause he knew the law was after him."

"Just goes to show you, you can't always judge a man. That's what riles me. Hell, I was really fooled by that man. I've gotta give him credit, though, he was a helluva good cowhand. It's just a shame he broke bad. Say, why don't you and your men stay here tonight? You ain't got no idea about tryin' to track him in the dark, have you?"

"That's a right good idea," Quincy said, thinking it would give him a better chance to look around the place in the daylight. He wasn't sure he'd put it beneath Jace to cover for Logan.

* * *

After spending the night in the bunkhouse as guests of the Triple-T, Quincy and his men were treated to a big breakfast of eggs and bacon and biscuits and gravy, all washed down with plenty of strong black coffee. "I swear," Wormy joked to Stokes, "I might wanna leave you three to go on after Cross, and I'll sign on with the Triple-T."

"What makes you think they'd hire a scrawny little feller like you?" Stokes asked. "You know about as much about herdin' cows as the hog they sliced that bacon off of."

"The hell I don't," Wormy protested. "I drove a sight more'n the three of you, I'll bet. Course, they was all rustled, but I drove 'em just the same. If I hadn't met up with Quincy and Lonnie, and got led astray, I mighta been set up on a ranch like ol' Towson here."

"You mighta been flyin' all around like that hawk up there, if you'da sprouted a pair of wings, too," Stokes slurred, "instead of a forked tongue."

Poised to continue the nonsensical banter, Wormy was interrupted by the arrival of Quincy and Lonnie from the ranch house, where they had supposedly gone to thank Towson for his hospitality. The actual purpose for seeking Towson early that morning was mainly to gain access to the inside of the house, alert for any signs that Logan Cross might have been hiding there.

Wormy and Stokes could tell by the familiar set of his dark eyebrows that Quincy was approaching one of his angry moods. There was no need to ask if he and Lonnie had detected anything in the house that indicated Cross had been harbored there. They stood by their horses while Quincy and Lonnie were engaged in an earnest discussion on what they should do at this point.

"He's done give us the slip again," Stokes said to Wormy under his breath. "And Quincy looks like he's about to go into one of his fits."

"Yeah, looks like it," Wormy replied in a whisper. "And Lonnie's tryin' to talk some sense into him." It was a scene they had witnessed many times before, and one that had happened with a lot more frequency ever since Logan Cross killed Jake Morgan.

Tom Towson came out the door then, pulling a heavy coat on as he walked down to the barn to join them. "I reckon I could say I'm sorry you didn't find the man you came for, Marshal," he declared. "But to tell you the truth, I'm just as glad you didn't find him on my land." He still preferred to think of Logan Cross as a bright, hardworking young man. It troubled him to think of a young man with so much potential taking the wrong path through life.

Lonnie spoke up quickly when Quincy failed to respond with his usual touch of showmanship. "Understand what you mean, sir. Me and the marshal wanna thank you for your hospitality. I expect we're ready to ride out now, get on back to Spearfish. Right, Marshal?" He locked his gaze on Quincy's eyes.

"That's right," Quincy said, after a moment's hesitation. Then, seeming to come out of it, he expounded. "Yes, sir, we appreciate the neighborly hospitality. Thank you, sir." He turned to Lonnie and ordered, "Mount up."

Jace walked over to stand next to Towson and they watched the marshal lead his men across the barnyard to strike the trail that led back to the Belle Fourche wagon track. "Kind of a strange fellow, ain't he, that marshal?" Jace asked.

"You could sure say that," Towson replied. "I'm not sure his brain's laced up real tight." He paused before concluding, "But I suppose his line of work can make a man go a little bit rattled after a while."

"Looks like they got sent off on a wild-goose chase to come back here lookin' for Logan," Jace said.

"Looks that way, all right," Towson agreed.

The mottled gray gelding stood tied beneath the cottonwood trees that grew along both sides of Towson's Creek, waiting patiently while the man Quincy Morgan sought knelt on the snow-covered bank a few feet away. There were four of them. He watched them as they rode single file up the path that led to the wagon road. When they were almost to the road, he moved quickly along the bank to a position where he could see them clearly, close enough to see the faces of those who had hunted him. They were not familiar to him. He had never seen any of the four before. But they sought to kill him, so it was time to strike back. He drew the Winchester slowly up to rest against his shoulder and rested the front sight on the back of the rearmost rider.

He paused before pulling the trigger, a moment of indecision causing him to hesitate. Could he justify what he was about to do? It was too late to question his actions, however. It was either kill or be killed, he decided, and his finger squeezed slowly around the trigger. After that, his actions were automatic without thinking consciously. The first target straightened up violently and slid sideways out of the saddle when the bullet struck between his shoulder blades. A second bullet was already on its way toward the next man in line, and Wormy Jacobs keeled over to join Riley Stokes on the snowy track.

Quincy and Lonnie were quick in their reactions. With a natural sense of survival, they bolted at a gallop, both men lying low on their horses' necks. Logan ran between the trees, trying to get a clear shot as they raced along the road toward Spearfish. When he reached the edge of the cottonwoods, he stopped and fired another shot at the fleeing outlaws, missed, and fired again. They were too far for an accurate shot, but he had at least shortened the odds again. Now there were only two against him to play this deadly game to its end. He had no idea who the remaining two were, and whether or not they were committed to taking it to a final conclusion. His first thought was to pursue them in hopes of finishing it for good, so he ran back to the trees where he had left Pepper tied and jumped into the saddle.

As he approached the road, he pulled up short when he saw the two bodies lying in his path, left by their friends to die. Aware of the possibility of being shot by a wounded man, he decided it wise to make sure they were both dead. So he dismounted and checked the first corpse. Riley Stokes was dead, so Logan moved quickly to check the second man. Wormy Jacobs grunted painfully when Logan rolled him over on his back. He was alive, but just barely. He gazed up at Logan with fearful eyes, pleading for mercy. Logan stood up and aimed his rifle at Wormy's head, but he hesitated to pull the trigger, reluctant to execute a helpless man.

"Who are you?" he demanded. "Why were you tryin' to kill me? What the hell did I ever do to you?"

"Nothin'," Wormy gasped painfully. Struggling to get his words out, he started to say more, but Logan was distracted by the sounds of horses approaching from behind him. He turned to see Jace Evans with three of the other men riding out to investigate the shooting. He turned to face them, his rifle held in both hands before him, not sure what their reaction might be upon seeing the two men on the ground.

"God A'mighty," Lou Cheatam blurted when the three pulled up at the scene of the shootings, stunned to find Logan standing over one of the bodies.

"My God, Logan," Jace exclaimed as he quickly dismounted. "Are they dead?"

"This one ain't," Logan answered simply. Astonished, and clearly not certain what he should do about it, Jace hesitated, trying to decide whether he should have his .44 in hand. When his hand hovered over the weapon, Logan said, "You ain't got no need for that. I've got no reason to harm you." He glanced quickly at Cheatam and Bledsoe, who had come with Jace, and added, "None of you." He relaxed his hold on his rifle then and let it drop down to his side, holding it in one hand. "Maybe you can ease this one's pain a little," he said, nodding toward Wormy. "There's two more of 'em gettin' away. I'm goin' after 'em."

Jace found himself in an awkward position. As far as he knew, Logan had just shot two members of a marshal's posse, and now he intended to go after the marshal. He could not simply stand by and let him murder a U.S. Marshal. Surely Logan was not in his right mind.

"I can't let you do that, Logan," he said, whipping out his pistol and aiming it at Logan's belly. "Don't even think about that rifle. If you raise it, I'll shoot you down." When Logan appeared to hesitate, Jace threatened, "I mean it. I ain't got no choice. I've got to know what's goin' on here."

"Don't do this, Jace," Logan pleaded. "You're costin' me time."

"I can't help that," Jace said, confident that he was doing the right thing. "Lou, ride over yonder and get his horse." Turning back to Logan, he said, "I'll have to ask you to let Bledsoe take that rifle from you. Don't give me any trouble, now. I don't wanna shoot you, but I swear I will, if you do."

"I'm sorry, Logan," Bledsoe said as he took the Winchester out of his hand.

"Now, the first thing we need to do is take care of this wounded man," Jace said. He hesitated, uncertain again. "Maybe we'd better tie your hands behind your back, just in case you decide to try somethin' crazy."

"You're makin' a big mistake," Logan said calmly, but he made no attempt to resist when Bledsoe tied his hands with the end of a rope coiled on his saddle, apologizing again while he did it. Logan knew that he had already lost too much time to prevent the other two outlaws from escaping.

"Okay," Jace said when Logan's hands were tied. "Watch him while I see what I can do for this man." Bledsoe balked, clearly not wanting to guard Logan, so Jace said, "All right, damn it, I'll watch Logan. You take a look at the marshal's man."

"You wanna hear what I've got to say now?" Logan asked patiently.

"Well, I reckon I surely would," Jace replied.

"In the first place, these two lyin' here ain't lawmen, posse men, or nothin' else to do with the law. They're outlaws and murderers. And that one that says he's a marshal is a damn liar. They've been huntin' me for weeks, tryin' to kill me, because I killed the man who was responsible for murderin' my brother, and the ones who helped him do it. Now you've got the truth of it, Jace, and if that little son of a bitch there don't wanna go to hell with it on his conscience, maybe he'll tell you the same thing."

Jace was stunned. Could he believe Logan? he wondered. He knelt down beside Wormy. "Watch Logan," he ordered Bledsoe. "Lou can help you," he added when Cheatam pulled up, leading Logan's horse. Turning his attention toward the wounded man, he said, "We're gonna try to do what we can to help you, you understand?"

"There ain't nothin' you can do for me," Wormy gasped painfully between coughing fits that brought up great quantities of blood from his lungs. He knew he was dying, and was only intent upon getting it over with.

"Did you hear what he said?" Jace asked. Wormy didn't answer but nodded.

"Is what he said true? Were you and your friends tryin' to kill him?"

"Hell no," Wormy gasped in pain, then reconsidered since he could clearly feel the claws of death reaching out for him. "Yeah, he's right. Quincy ain't no marshal. He's Quincy Morgan, just got out of prison." A spasm shot through his lungs, causing him to cough feebly and spit up more blood. "The feller with him is Lonnie Morgan, Quincy's cousin. That was Quincy's brother Cross killed. I'm sorry for my part in it." He stiffened with the pain of another spasm, and his body relaxed with the passing of his life.

Logan and the three Triple-T riders stood in silence for several long moments, amazed by the dying man's confession. No one knew what to say, so Logan finally spoke up. "Can somebody untie my hands now?" Bledsoe jumped to do his bidding. When he was free, Logan took his rifle back.

"I reckon I . . . all of us . . . owe you an apology," Jace said. "But, damn it, we thought that bastard was a U.S. Marshal. He sure acted like one. He had us all fooled."

"I shoulda knowed you warn't the killer they said you was," Bledsoe said. "But Jace is right. That marshal— I mean that lyin' skunk—had all of us buffaloed, just like Jace said. Hell, the whole town thought he was the law. You can't hardly blame us for goin' along with it."

"I don't," Logan said. "I thought they were the law, too, even though I found it hard to believe they were after me. I figured it had to be because I shot Jake Morgan. I didn't know he was that phony marshal's brother. I shot him because he murdered my brother, Billy. So that's the whole story, only it ain't ended yet, not as long as those last two are alive. I'll be goin' after them now."

"I knew you were in the right," Ox suddenly spoke up, having been silent to that point. "And I'm thinkin' you could use some help, so I'll go with you."

Logan was not surprised. "I know you would, and I appreciate it. But I figure this is somethin' I've got to finish by myself. I don't wanna take a chance on any of my friends gettin' killed. I've already lost my brother. So thank you just the same. I won't forget it." Ox started to protest but was stopped by a patient shake of Logan's head. They all knew that he meant what he said.

"Well," Jace concluded, "I reckon there ain't nothin' we can do for you except wish you good huntin'." He paused, then remembered something else he wanted to say. "I reckon you know there's a job waitin' for you here on the Triple-T when you finish what you've gotta do."

"Much obliged, Jace," Logan said. "I was hopin' you'd say that." He looked around him at the circle of concerned faces, all of them nodding as if confirming Jace's offer. "I reckon I'll need to take that buckskin of mine, since I don't know how long I'm gonna take, or how far I might have to go."

"I'll get him for you," Ox volunteered quickly.

Their hooves thundering upon the hard road, the two horses galloped toward Spearfish, flogged continuously by their frantic riders until they threatened to founder. Forced to pull up to let them rest, Quincy and Lonnie dismounted quickly, drawing their rifles as they did. "I don't see nobody!" Lonnie exclaimed as he peered back down the road behind them.

"These horses are spent," Quincy said, and looked around him for a spot to wait in ambush. "They were set up and waitin' for us while foolin' us with all that hospitality. Now they'll be comin' after us."

"I ain't so sure," Lonnie said. "I don't think there was but one rifle doin' all the shootin'. It was him, and now he's killed Stokes and Lacey. There ain't nobody left but you and me."

"We don't need nobody else," Quincy said. "We'll wait for the son of a bitch over there." He pointed to a low rise that the road curved sharply around. "He won't be able to see the horses behind that rise, and we'll knock his ass outta the saddle when he comes down that road."

There were really no other options available for them, since their horses were exhausted, so they led them around the bend in the road and left them behind the rise. Once the horses were taken care of, Quincy and Lonnie climbed the rise to take positions at the top. Lying flat on a bed of snow about two inches deep, they aimed their weapons down the road and waited. "Let him come on," Quincy said.

When half an hour passed with no sign of pursuit, they entertained the possibility that they might have been tricked. Lonnie rolled over and sat up to look all around behind them.

"Why ain't he comin'? There ain't no way he coulda circled around behind us."

"Hell no. He ain't had time to circle around us."

Quincy was impatient for Logan to show up, even more so than Lonnie. And as each additional minute passed with no sign of pursuit, he grew more and more suspicious that they were somehow being tricked. Finally he decided to withdraw.

"He ain't comin'. We'll be better off goin' on into town. Let's go."

"The horses ain't hardly rested enough yet," Lonnie said.

"We'll walk and lead 'em awhile longer," Quincy said. "That'll be better'n settin' here like a couple of doves on a fence."

Lonnie was not so sure Quincy knew best, but out of habit, he didn't protest. So they backed away from the top of the rise and went back for the horses. With a distance of about four miles ahead of them, they started down the road to Spearfish, figuring on walking probably around two of those miles before riding the rest of the way. As they walked, Quincy became more and more irritated by the sudden role reversal.

For so long now, he and his men had hunted one

man. And it galled him to be running from that same man. Lonnie reminded him that the crew at the Triple-T were probably standing behind Logan Cross, even though it was Cross alone who shot Wormy and Stokes. They might very well be preparing to ride into Spearfish with him, and that was the reason Cross had not come after them immediately.

If this was true, then the advantage in numbers would now lie with Cross, leaving Quincy and Lonnie outnumbered. It was something to consider.

"Somehow the Triple-T knows that you ain't a marshal," Lonnie said.

"I don't know how the hell they coulda found out unless somebody told 'em," Quincy replied. "Couldn't been nobody but Cross himself. They musta believed him, but everybody in town believes he's an outlaw, and that's what we're gonna depend on. That's why we need to get on back to Spearfish and let those folks know there's a dangerous killer headin' their way and they need to help us fight him."

"I hope to hell you're right," Lonnie said. They climbed back into their saddles then and rode on into town.

Chapter 13

Riding two weary horses, Quincy and Lonnie reined up at the stable in Spearfish. Sam Taylor came out to greet them. "Howdy, Marshal. Where's the rest of your men?"

"Well," Quincy replied, "that's a terrible thing to have to tell you. They were murdered, all of 'em, by that back-shootin' coward, Logan Cross. Me and Lonnie are lucky to be here to tell you about it. And while we're at it, I need to warn you that he might be comin' this way, so you'd be wise to be ready if he shows up here at your place."

Sam was visibly upset by the news. "Why would he wanna do me any harm?" he asked. "The little bit I've had to do with him he's always treated me just fine."

"A man like Logan Cross is hard to figure out," Quincy said. "One day he'll buy you a drink, and the next he'll put a bullet in your brain. Some killers are just like that. You just be careful and let us know if you see him in town."

"Much obliged, Marshal," Sam said, still concerned.

"Give these horses a ration of grain," Lonnie said to him as they were leaving. "They worked hard today."

They went by the saloon and gave Cecil the same story they had given Sam. They even stopped by Fred Ramsey's dry goods store to alert him to the possibility of Logan Cross's return, and the danger to everyone in his path.

"Remember what happened to one of my posse men right there in the roomin' house," Quincy said to him. "Don't mean to frighten you, ma'am," he said to Fred's wife, Martha. "Just want you folks to be careful. Let me know if you see him.

"That oughta about cover most places he might show up," Quincy said when they left the store and headed for the Three Widows Inn.

They had talked it over and decided that it was the best place for them to wait for him. Logan was soft on Hannah. He had rescued her from the mountains and brought her to live with Mae and Daisy. Maybe he had stronger ideas about the young widow; Quincy couldn't be certain about that. But it figured that he would be more careful about any gunplay with her near harm's way. Quincy was also interested in Hannah, but not in a charitable way. He would not hesitate to use her as bait if that would give him an advantage. And if she got in the way of a stray bullet, he would not grieve her loss.

"Well, I see you're back, Marshal," Mae Davis said when the two outlaws walked into the parlor. Eager to hear their report on pursuing Logan Cross, she asked, "Is it all over? Did you capture Logan?"

"No, ma'am," Quincy answered. "I'm sorry to say he slipped away from us again."

Mae was not really disappointed to hear it, and she knew that Hannah would feel the same. "You're not havin' much luck arrestin' that man, are you?" He didn't bother to answer, only scowling in response, so she continued. "Well, we'll have dinner ready in half an hour. Where's your other two men?"

"They won't be comin' to dinner," Quincy said. "They were both killed in the line of duty by that back-shootin' killer."

"Oh my!" Mae responded, horrified. "That's a terrible thing."

"Yes, ma'am," Lonnie remarked humbly, "two good men, shot in the back."

"Why can't you catch him?" Mae asked, finding it incredible that such a professional-looking group of gunmen could not capture one man. She began to think that maybe she and Hannah were both wrong about their feelings for Logan Cross.

"We'll get him," Quincy said. "I'll personally put him in the ground. Don't you worry about that."

Daisy Welker, who had paused by the dining room door to listen to the conversation, offered a comment. "Well, I reckon it don't make much sense to keep them two tables pushed together in the back corner, if there ain't but two of you left." When Mae frowned at her for her insensitive remark, Daisy responded with "Well, it don't."

"We're all sorry for the loss of your men," Mae said.

"I appreciate it, ma'am." Quincy formed a kind smile for the two women. Looking at Daisy, he held the smile a little longer while thinking, *If I catch you outside after dark, I'm going to break that sassy neck for you.* Daisy smiled back at him, as if she had read his thoughts.

"I suppose we'd best wash up a little before dinner,"

Quincy said. "And I need to get somethin' outta that other room before you clean it up."

When they had gone, Daisy walked over beside Mae and said, "Clean up that room—ha—might be easier to set it on fire, after those pigs have been sleepin' there."

"I declare, Daisy, you don't have an ounce of charity in your whole body. Those poor men died trying to uphold the law and protect helpless people like you and me."

"Ha!" Daisy snorted. "I reckon I don't count myself as one of the helpless people. And lawmen or not, if a pussy cat's got white stripes on his back, he's a skunk, no matter how he purrs."

Mae raised her eyes to the ceiling and shook her head. "I'll go tell Hannah the news about the lawmen." She went to the kitchen.

Busy rolling out biscuits to go into the oven, Hannah was as distressed as Mae had been to hear of the death of two more of the marshal's men. Also like Mae's, her distress was more for the disappointment she felt for Logan's criminal behavior, and the tragedy of a good man who had chosen the wrong path in life. She found herself hoping that the marshal would finally be successful in capturing Logan before he killed anyone else.

But why, she wondered, did Logan keep coming back when he should be running away? He should know that if he killed the marshal and his one surviving posse man, there would surely be another marshal sent to get him, maybe even a detachment of soldiers.

"Maybe he knows something about that marshal that we don't," Daisy said, startling Hannah, who had been so deep in her thoughts that she didn't hear the footsteps behind her.

"Oh," Hannah blurted. "I didn't hear you come in. Maybe who knows something we don't?"

"The fellow you were thinkin' about just then," Daisy said. "You know, the one that saved your ass from starvin' to death and brought you here safe and sound."

Immediately defensive, Hannah was quick to respond, "I'll always be grateful to Logan for what he did for me. But things are different now. How can you condone what has happened since then?"

"I don't know," Daisy answered stoically. "What does 'condone' mean?"

Not certain if Daisy was japing her or not, Hannah said, "How can you ignore the fact that he's killed all these men?"

Daisy made a face while thinking that one over. "Well," she finally answered, "that is something that I'm havin' trouble wrappin' my mind around. But if the Lord asked me which the world would be better off without, I'd still say get rid of that raunchy-lookin' bunch ridin' with the marshal and keep Logan Cross."

Hannah could only shake her head. There was no explaining Daisy's way of thinking. One thing for sure, once the perplexing woman made up her mind about something, there was no changing it, even if Logan came in and shot everyone in town.

"What is the marshal planning to do?" Hannah asked Mae. "Did he say?"

"Nope, he didn't say if he and that cousin of his were goin' to go back lookin' for Logan or not," Mae said.

"Probably just gonna sit around here and make puppy eyes at you," Daisy said. "Twirl the ends of that pretty little mustache he's so proud of and wait for you to swoon."

"Daisy!" Hannah scolded. "I don't know where you come up with that nonsense. I'll have you know I don't swoon. Now, get busy and slice off some of that ham while I finish making these biscuits."

She was well aware of Quincy's interest in her, but she was not sure she had any interest in him. She was flattered by his attention, at the same time cognizant of the fact that Mae was too old and Daisy, while as young as she, was by no means a beauty.

I shouldn't clutter my mind with such nonsense, she thought, scolding herself, and tried to turn her full concentration on the biscuit dough.

"I've been thinkin' about what we're doin'," Lonnie said as he and Quincy searched every inch of the room Wormy and Stokes had occupied, hoping that they had not been carrying all their money in their saddlebags when they were shot. "Maybe this ain't the smartest thing to do, sittin' up here in town, waitin' for that jasper to show up."

Quincy turned a canvas sack that had belonged to Wormy upside down, emptying the contents on the bed before responding to Lonnie's remark. He threw the empty bag on the floor and glared at his cousin. "We done settled that. What's the matter, Lonnie, are you gettin' scared of that son of a bitch now?"

"I reckon you know better'n that," Lonnie answered patiently. "I just don't think we oughta be takin' him so lightly. He's had a lot of good men goin' after him, and somehow the bastard's shaved us down to just you and me. I ain't sure it's luck, good for him, or bad for us. I'd just feel a lot more comfortable havin' my rifle sighted on him out in the open when he ain't lookin' to get hit."

"What are you sayin'?" Quincy demanded. "You wanna take off and run?"

"No, that ain't what I'm sayin'. I'm sayin' we ought not be holed up here in this house. We oughta ride back up the road above town and wait for the bastard to come along—find us a good spot to cut him down before he ever gets to town."

Quincy paused to think about it. It did seem like a smart thing to do, but then he thought about lying up on a snowbank, shivering in the night wind.

"There ain't no tellin' when he's gonna show up, so we might as well wait right here where there's a warm fire and hot coffee." He lifted a corner of the mattress and peered under it. "Besides, we're the law in town. We've got folks who'll tip us off when he sets foot in Spearfish. Then we'll just shoot him down, and it'll be official business." He flipped the mattress over on the floor. "You're sayin' he'll be comin' down the road to town. What if he don't take the road? We'll be settin' out there freezin' our asses off, and he'll be in here by the fire."

"Well, I reckon there's somethin' to that, all right," Lonnie said, reconsidering. "I was thinkin' that if we were able to shoot him down on the road to town, we could just tell folks that he wouldn't come peacefully, and we had to shoot him. If we just blast away at him when he comes through the door, we'll have to explain why we didn't give him a chance to give up. That might be what they would expect a marshal to do." He shrugged. "Course, if we ain't gonna try to keep them thinkin' you're a real marshal, it don't make no difference how we kill him."

"I ain't really worried about what the people of this town think. As many men as this bastard has killed, we'd be crazy not to shoot him on sight. And I think most every man in town would think the same thing."

"I s'pose you're right," Lonnie conceded.

"I know I'm right. Now let's go down and get some dinner." They both checked to make sure their pistols were loaded. "Maybe we'll have a guest show up to eat with us."

They paused at the dining room door to look the room over before entering and proceeding straight to the table in the back corner. Both men sat facing the door. Daisy could not help noticing their caution. "They look like they're expectin' trouble," she said aside to Mae.

"I hope to hell not," Mae said, "not in my dinin' room." She walked over to the table then with the coffeepot. "I expect you're wantin' coffee. You usually do." She turned two cups over and filled them.

"Where's Hannah?" Quincy asked.

"In the kitchen," Mae replied, "bakin' biscuits."

"I like her to wait on us," Quincy said, abandoning his usual charm that he customarily spread among all three of the women.

"I'll let her bring your plates out," Mae said, and returned to the kitchen, where she told Hannah and Daisy of the marshal's request.

"You know, I'd kinda like to keep an eye on these biscuits," Hannah said, mildly perturbed.

"He requested you," Mae said.

"If they would sit at the big table with everybody else, it'd be a lot easier to serve them. And with just the two of them left, maybe they wouldn't make the other customers nervous," Hannah said, looking at Mae. "Will you watch my biscuits?" She was irritated because she would have to fix a plate for them, which was more trouble than walking the different bowls along the big table.

"I'll fix a couple of plates for you," Daisy volunteered. "Then you can run out there with 'em."

"Thanks, Daisy," Hannah said, and cracked the oven door to check the progress of the biscuits. "I want these to be perfect."

"No trouble a'tall," Daisy said as she picked up two plates and went to the stove.

She piled the plates high with food, the main course of which was cowboy stew. She picked out a little sliver of bone from the pot and started to discard it, then reconsidered and dropped it in the generous serving on one of the plates.

We'll see who the lucky winner is, she thought, depending upon who got the stew with the sharp piece of bone in it. When the plates were ready, she decided the beans needed a little thickening, so she glanced over her shoulder to make sure Mae and Hannah were too occupied to notice what she was doing. Satisfied, she cleared her throat and spat on both plates. *There, that's better,* she thought, and stirred the beans thoroughly.

"Here you go, honey," she said, and held the plates out for Hannah to deliver.

"I'll bring out some fresh biscuits in just a minute of two," Hannah told them when she set their plates down before the two outlaws.

"You're lookin' as pretty as a prairie flower today," Quincy said, causing her to blush.

"Well, that's nice of you to say, but I doubt I look very fresh," she said. "I've been working in the kitchen all day."

"Maybe you oughta get outside in the cool air after dinner," he said. "I'd be proud to escort you on a little walk."

Already attacking his plate of food, Lonnie paused to cast a critical eye at his cousin, wondering if Quincy had forgotten the little problem they had. "I reckon you're forgettin' that little piece of business we've got to tend to, Marshal."

"I ain't forgot," Quincy said, annoyed by Lonnie's remark. "But I've always got time for the prettiest woman east of the Rockies."

He flashed his toothy smile at Hannah, who was undecided how she should respond to the compliment. So she smiled shyly and spun around to return to the kitchen.

"I figure you're just funnin' with that woman," Lonnie said as he stuffed another huge mouthful of stew in his mouth. "Leastways, I hope to hell you are." A moment later, he cried out in pain, "Damn!" His outcry startled everyone in the dining room. "I've been stabbed!"

In the kitchen, Daisy paused as she filled another bowl of beans for the long table. "We have a winner," she announced softly.

A wide smile of satisfaction spread across her face as Mae went out to apologize for the bone in the stew.

It was already late in the morning when the lone rider leading the buckskin horse rode slowly toward the stable at the edge of town. A light snowfall dropped softly on the street, rutted with the passing of oxen and mules. He thought about the first time he had ridden into the little settlement. It was a friendly town then, with friendly people, eager to help Hannah and him.

But so much had changed since that first visit, and he was not certain what kind of reception he might receive this time around.

He pulled up before reaching the door of the stable to consider the wisdom of this latest visit. Pepper was in dire need of grain, more so than the buckskin, which had been well taken care of by Ox. The decision to be made was whether or not to risk leaving his horses at the stable for the short time he intended to be there. He could not be sure that he would not need his horses in a hurry. He was not even sure that the two men he sought were in town. Sam should be able to tell him. He always had good relations with Sam Taylor the few times he had been to his stable. His mind made up, he decided that Sam would take care of his horses without spreading word that he was in town, so he stepped down and went in the stable.

"Oh . . . ," Sam started when he turned around and saw Logan walk in. "You kinda startled me," he said. "I didn't hear you ride up."

It was obvious that his sudden appearance had caused a considerable amount of nervousness on the part of the stable owner, so Logan sought to put him at ease. "I need to put my horses up for a little while, if it's all right with you. I might be needin' 'em in a hurry, so I'll just leave Pepper's saddle on him till I know for sure. All right?"

"Sure, Logan, anything you say," Sam replied.

"Course, I expect to pay for a full day, even if I do wanna leave in a hurry. Tell you the truth, I'm more interested in feedin' Pepper some grain. He don't do too good, feedin' on nothin' but grass."

He could tell by Sam's worried expression that he wasn't comfortable talking to him. Too much had happened since Logan first came to town, and most of it was bad. He decided to get right to the point.

"You need to know somethin', you and everybody else in town. That marshal ain't no real marshal. He's just a damn outlaw out to get me. He's got all you folks fooled into thinkin' he's out to arrest me, but it's killin' he's got in mind. He's after me because I shot his brother, but his brother had it comin'. He murdered my brother. So now you know why I've got to finish this thing between him and me. I'm not wanted by the law anywhere."

He paused to study Sam's reaction to what he had just been told. There was no visible clue that would tell him what Sam was thinking. His jaw was hanging slightly open, and his eyes seemed glazed and expressionless. Logan had expected a greater response. After a few moments when Sam failed to remark, Logan asked, "Are those two in town, Quincy and his cousin?"

"I reckon," Sam finally said. "They left their horses here."

"They still roomin' at Mae's house?" Logan asked. Sam didn't speak but nodded slowly. "All right, well, good, then," Logan said when it appeared that Sam was too stunned to speak intelligently. "I'll be on my way. Don't forget to feed Pepper some grain. Might as well give 'em both some grain." He received another slow nod in response.

He left Sam standing there holding Pepper's reins and started walking the almost fifty yards from the stable to the Three Widows. He thought about Sam as he walked. The normally talkative stable owner seemed to have been struck dumb by Logan's sudden appearance and the story he told. It was not surprising, since the town had bought Quincy Morgan's story, lock, stock, and barrel.

As he approached the boardinghouse, he became more careful. With his rifle ready, he stepped up onto the porch and stopped beside a front window to take a look at what he would be walking into. Through the sheer window curtain, he could see an empty parlor and the open door to the dining room.

Dinnertime, he figured. *Good, that's better than having to go upstairs to search for them in their rooms.*

He turned away when a last-minute patron ran up the steps and went in, anxious to get a place at the table before the choice cuts were taken. The man seemed to pay no attention to Logan standing there, so Logan followed him inside, but stopped beside the dining room door before walking in. He scanned the room. The long table in the center was about half-full, so he shifted his gaze to the table in the back corner apart from the other customers. He had had no more than a glimpse of Quincy and Lonnie Morgan as they fled down the road to Spearfish the day before, but there was no doubt in his mind who they were. While he watched, Hannah came from the kitchen and carried a platter of some kind of meat to them. Logan waited until she returned to the kitchen. It was better that there were no other diners close to the corner table, for no one else should be injured in the actions he was about to take.

There were no thoughts of fair play in Logan's mind. He had no intention of calling them out to settle it in the street. He intended to shoot both men down, just as they would have done to him, just as Jake Morgan had with Billy, and just as Logan had with Jake.

His sole purpose was not to duel, but to rid the world of some dangerous vermin.

He stepped quickly inside the door and called out, "Morgan!" He wanted them to know who shot them. The two startled outlaws pushed the table over and hit the floor. Logan raised his rifle, preparing to rip the table apart. Before he could swing his rifle around to aim it, he felt the barrel of a rifle between his shoulder blades.

"Pull that trigger and you're a dead man," a voice behind him warned. In that split second, he decided to pull the trigger anyway, even though he knew he couldn't get both of them before he went down. It was too late—a blow to the back of his head knocked him senseless.

Scrambling frantically to get up from the floor, Quincy and Lonnie came out from behind the table with guns drawn, both leveled at Logan. "Now, you son of a bitch," Quincy roared, "this is the way you gave it to Jake."

Lonnie, thinking more rationally, in spite of the near miss with death, grabbed Quincy by the shoulder. "Hold on, Marshal," he cried, thinking it wise to continue the charade. "We've finally caught him, and now we need to do the right thing for these good people of Spearfish."

"I'm fixin' to do the right thing," Quincy ranted, still intent upon putting a bullet in the dazed man's head.

"The authority vested in you as a U.S. Marshal says you have the right to sentence the prisoner to death by hangin'," Lonnie said. He had no idea if a marshal had that authority or not, but he was willing to bet that no one else in the town knew it, either. Quincy wasn't completely sold on the idea. He was passionate to spill the hated man's brains on the floor. "It'll all be legal that way," Lonnie whispered in Quincy's ear. "We can milk this town dry before we're through."

Quincy began to see the advantage in what Lonnie was pushing for. "You're right," he exclaimed grandly. "I sentence this murderer to death by hangin'." He looked at Lonnie and winked. "Sentence to be carried out as soon as we can find a rope and a tree."

"First off," Lonnie said, "we need to thank this outstandin' citizen who was smart enough to help the law." He gave Sam Taylor a big nod of recognition. "That was a helluva whompin' you put on him." Sam could only stand there shaking, still unable to believe he had actually stepped in to stop a killing. "You stood up for law and order, Mr. Taylor, and I reckon you'd be the man to get us a rope."

"Yes, sir," Sam stammered, and immediately left to get a rope.

The noisy dining room of a few minutes before was shocked into almost total silence. Standing in the door of the kitchen, Hannah and Daisy peered over Mae's shoulder in horror at the bleeding man on the floor, two pistols aimed at his head.

"Sam Taylor, you son of a bitch," Daisy murmured softly.

Quincy, now in control of his anger, and convinced that Lonnie was onto something that might pay off generously in the future, sought to implant the right picture in the minds of the shocked spectators.

"Everything's under control now. Won't none of you fine folks have to worry about this killer no more. We've been on this murderer's trail for a long time, and we'll send him to hell with the rest of his kind." He made it a point then to look at Mae. "I'm especially pleased that we were able to arrest this man without a lot of gunplay in your dinin' room, and no innocent people got hit by a stray bullet."

Still on his hands and knees, Logan felt his brain beginning to clear enough to hear his sentencing, although he still did not know who had struck him from behind. He only knew that his head felt as if it had been cracked open, and through his carelessness, he had gotten himself into this predicament.

When his head cleared enough to look up, it was to meet the scornful gaze of Lonnie Morgan. "You ain't so smart now, are you?" Lonnie asked, so only Logan could hear. "We're fixin' to stretch your neck for you and leave you hangin' till the buzzards pick your bones clean."

Logan did not reply—his senses still addled somewhat. He shifted his gaze to meet that of Quincy's. The counterfeit marshal smiled at him, basking in his triumph. A moment later, he holstered his .44 and cut off a short length of rope from the coil Sam Taylor had fetched. Then he pulled both of Logan's arms behind his back and bound his wrists securely. With their prisoner completely under control, they lifted him up to stand on his feet.

"I'm thinkin' that big cottonwood tree outside the back door is the perfect place to carry out the execution," Lonnie suggested.

Almost paralyzed by the horror that had just occurred, Hannah finally found her voice. "Must you hang him?" she beseeched. "Maybe he could go to prison instead."

Hearing her own words, she realized how pitiful her plea, but her mind was in a swirl of confusion. What the marshal said must be right, but she could not understand how Logan could be two different people—one good and one evil.

"No, ma'am," Quincy said, making a show of patient benevolence. "For what he's done, he wouldn't get no prison time. They'd hang him, so it don't make no sense to carry him all the way to Laramie when we can just get it done right here."

Unlike Hannah, Daisy had no confusing feelings regarding Logan's right or wrong. In spite of evidence to the contrary, she saw him as a good man, especially when compared to the duo of Quincy and Lonnie Morgan and the rest of the scum that had made up the posse. She was also unafraid to say what she thought.

"You're in a helluva hurry to hang a man," she spoke out. "Why don't we give the man a fair trial?"

Quincy cocked his head around to glare at her. "There ain't no judge here in Spearfish," he said.

"Well, you're actin' like you're the judge," Daisy shot back. She returned his glare without a sign of wilting under his intense frown. "Besides, we can sure have a jury and give the man his day in court."

"He don't deserve a day in court," Quincy replied impassively. He had never felt anything beyond hostility from the cynical young woman, and he was in no mood to hear anything she had to say. "This is the business of the marshal's office, and you'd best let us worry about it." He grabbed Logan by the arm and announced, "Let's get on with it!"

Fully back to his senses now, and with no intention to go peacefully to his death, Logan responded with a violent kick, driving his boot up between Quincy's legs. Caught completely by surprise, Quincy doubled up and dropped helplessly to his knees, grunting in agony.

Although caught off guard as well, Lonnie was nevertheless quick to rap Logan across the side of his head with the barrel of his pistol, staggering him.

He then turned to the spectators and demanded, "Couple of you fellers get over here and help carry this man outside." Too fearful to refuse, Sam Taylor and a few of the other men came to do his bidding. "Mind you don't let him get away," Lonnie warned as they dragged Logan toward the door. "Hold it right there," he said, stopping them before they went out. Knowing his cousin would never forgive him if he did the hanging without him, Lonnie paused to look at Quincy, who was still doubled up in incapacitating pain. "The marshal has to witness the hangin' to make it official," he offered in explanation for the delay.

With no one knowing what to do for the helpless marshal, the room grew silent again while everyone waited for someone to act. Finally Daisy walked over to Quincy and quipped, "Is there something I can do for you, Marshal? Throw some cold water on you, or something?"

"Get her away from me, or I swear I'll shoot her," Quincy growled to Lonnie.

"Daisy," Mae scolded, "get back over here!"

"All right, I'm comin'," Daisy replied. "I was just tryin' to see if I could help." She looked at Logan before she turned and said, "That's what I call puttin' your best foot forward."

"Get away from here," Lonnie ordered angrily.

They waited until Quincy was finally able to slowly rise to his feet, humiliated and still in excruciating pain but able to walk, as Lonnie ordered them to drag Logan outside. Quincy followed them, walking slowly and gingerly.

Chapter 14

"Bring that horse around back," Lonnie ordered, and the horse's owner obediently ran to the hitching post in front of the boardinghouse and came back leading it. The word of the lynching having quickly spread, he was joined by most of the other men in town, as well as a few women. These included Daisy, Hannah, and Mae, who didn't want to witness the hanging, but could not stay away.

"Lemme do that," Quincy insisted, and took the reins from Lonnie. "You throw a rope over that limb."

Lonnie took the coil of rope that Sam had brought, tied one end of it around a stick he found on the ground, and threw the stick over a suitable limb. Flipping the rope to give it slack, he worked the stick low enough to grab it. Then he untied the stick and began to fashion a hangman's noose in the rope, glancing up frequently to give Logan a mocking grin.

"Make sure you get it right, Lonnie," Quincy said. He grabbed a handful of Logan's hair and jerked his head back so he could make sure his victim knew what was coming. "I want that noose real tight," he taunted. "Then I'm gonna lead this horse out from under you nice and slow so you don't break your neck and go too quick. I want you to slide off easy so you hang there till you choke to death." He gave Logan a sharp yank of his hair for emphasis. "And I want you to think about all the trouble you've caused me while your neck is stretchin'."

"How's that?" Lonnie asked, holding the finished noose up for inspection.

"That'll do just fine," Quincy said, and watched while Lonnie slipped the noose over Logan's head and tightened it around his neck. "All right, you boys set him up there on that horse." The reluctant volunteers picked Logan up and sat him in the saddle while Quincy held the horse's reins.

At this point, one of the spectators, Fred Ramsey, the owner of the dry goods store, spoke up. "Marshal, would it be all right if he had something he wanted to say? Maybe he needs to get right with God or something."

Quincy hesitated, but when Lonnie nodded, he said, "All right, but make it quick. I don't wanna keep the devil waitin'."

Logan, now resigned to his fate, decided to speak, although it was obvious that the whole town believed Morgan's lies. "All I've got to say is, one day, and I hope it won't be long in comin', you'll all find out that this son of a bitch ain't no more a marshal than I am." He looked Quincy in the eye and said, "I'll settle with you two, if I have to come back from the grave to do it."

"All right," Quincy said, "you've had your say." He started to lead the horse out from under Logan, but paused when a group of riders suddenly rounded the back corner of the house and pulled up before them. Coming out of their saddles even before their horses were fully stopped, they pushed through the small crowd of spectators.

"Just hold it right there!" Jace Evans commanded. "There ain't gonna be no hangin' here."

"What the hell are you doin'?" Quincy demanded. "This is official business."

"The hell it is!" Jace responded. "You ain't no U.S. Marshal, Quincy *Morgan*. You've been in prison for the past five years. So cut that man down."

Realizing that his hoax was discovered, Quincy knew he was going to have to act fast, but his desire to kill Logan Cross was too strong to ignore.

"The hell I will," he said, and slapped the horse on its croup. The startled horse sprang into a gallop, leaving the man in the saddle to fall as the crowd cried out in horror. Before the slack had time to jerk out of the rope, Logan was caught around his legs, his body held up to prevent his weight from breaking his neck. Standing next to the trunk of the tree where the other end of the rope was tied, Lou Cheatam quickly drew his knife and cut it, leaving Logan safe in the powerful arms of Ox Russell.

In the confusion that followed, Hannah and Daisy ran to help Logan while Quincy and Lonnie, their guns drawn, backed away quickly, knowing they had only seconds to save their lives.

In a desperate move, Lonnie grabbed Hannah around her waist and pulled her hard up against his body. He jammed his .44 up under her chin and started backing away again.

"Get behind me, Quincy, and shoot the first son of a

bitch that makes a move." With his cousin behind him, he continued to back away toward the stable. "One little move to stop us and the lady gets her brains blowed out." He nodded toward Sam Taylor. "You've been right helpful so far, so you can get in that stable and saddle our horses, and be quick about it. And remember, you try anythin', and I'll blow her brains out. All of you better listen to what I'm sayin'. I got nothin' to lose if I have to kill her, but we'll make you this deal. We're takin' her with us, settin' right in the saddle in front of me. You don't make any move to stop us, and we'll let her go as soon as we get clear of town. We ain't done no harm to anybody in this town. Our fight was with Logan Cross, so you ain't got no reason to come after us, right? That's the deal. We'll be gone for good and nobody has to die, but you try somethin' funny and a lot of you will die. That's a promise."

"All right, you've got a deal," Jace Evans said, not willing to take a chance with Hannah's life. "But make no mistake about it, you're to clear out of this territory for good. If you show up here again, you'll be shot on sight. Is that understood?"

"Don't worry about that," Quincy responded. "There ain't nothin' in this town we wanna see again." He and Lonnie continued to back away, using Hannah as a shield, while Sam ran to the stable to saddle their horses. "We'll be keepin' an eye on all of you from the stable while we're gettin' ready to ride. Don't do nothin' stupid. It ain't worth gettin' shot over."

The shocked crowd of spectators stood helpless as the two outlaws backed into the stable. The silence that had cloaked the gathering began to give way to murmurings of anger, and soon random voices spoke out against letting the outlaws ride out unharmed. It continued to rise until Jace spoke out.

"Which one of you thinks it's worth that young woman's life to try to stop them from leaving town? We're gonna have to take them at their word. They ain't likely to wanna take a chance on harmin' her and givin' us a reason to come after them."

To remind them of his warning, Quincy appeared behind a couple of hay bales near the door, his rifle trained on the crowd. He remained there until Sam led the two saddled horses up behind him.

"Step up in that saddle," Lonnie told Hannah, and stood ready to boost her up on the horse. When she was seated in the saddle, he pulled her foot out of the stirrup so he could step up behind her. Once he was settled, with his arm tightened around her waist again, he signaled Quincy. "I'm ready," he said. "Climb on your horse and let's get the hell outta here." While Quincy mounted up, Lonnie had a parting word for Sam. "Now, suppose you walk on out in front of us, and remember what I said about tryin' anythin' funny."

Sam, still smarting from the critical role he had played in upsetting Logan Cross's confrontation with the two outlaws, thought seriously about doing something to prevent their escape. But he could think of nothing that would not endanger Hannah, so he did as he was told.

"I'm truly sorry, Hannah," he apologized as he walked by her.

"'I'm truly sorry, Hannah,'" Quincy repeated, mocking him. "Get goin'!"

At a gallop then, they bounded out of the stable and raced down the street toward the south end of town and the mountains beyond, leaving a bewildered group of citizens behind. Jace Evans took a moment to see if Logan was all right before getting his men in the saddle and ready to ride after the two outlaws and their hostage.

"We'd best not crowd 'em too close," he advised, "or they might not let her go. All I wanna do is bring the woman back. I ain't interested in tryin' to stay on their trail and endin' up ridin' into an ambush." He only had three men with him, and he wasn't willing to risk losing any of them. So he figured, *To hell with them*, as long as they kept going.

"What if they don't let Hannah go?" Daisy wanted to know.

"I reckon we'll have to worry about that if they don't," Jace replied. "But I don't think they wanna get us on their tails. They'll let her go."

Jace and the Triple-T men rode out then, leaving Ox behind, still concerned about Logan's injuries. He stood silently by, watching Mae and Daisy clean and bandage the wounds on the back and side of Logan's head. Their patient was not content to hold still for the treatment, insisting that he had to get under way after the two men who had sought to kill him.

"If you don't hold still, I'm gonna knock you in the head again," Daisy threatened him. "You're still bleedin' outta the back of your head."

When she said it, she glanced at Sam Taylor, who was standing nearby, a worried look on his face. She knew he was waiting to get a chance to apologize for breaking the stock of his rifle on the back of Logan's head.

"That oughta be good enough," Logan insisted, and tried to get to his feet while ignoring the pounding in his head. "I'm all right now."

Daisy wasn't so sure, but she tied a knot in the bandage and stood back to let him get to his feet. "That's what I thought," she said when he staggered sideways, trying to keep from falling. Ox quickly stepped up to support him. "Take him in the house, big boy," Daisy said to Ox, "and set him down on that sofa in the parlor."

Still protesting, Logan was helped into the house. Daisy followed right behind with the repentant Sam Taylor lagging after her. As soon as they got Logan settled on the sofa, Daisy ordered him to stay there while she went to get some clean cloths.

"Keep him there, Ox," she said, and turned, almost colliding with Sam. "Damn it, Sam, I'm gonna run you over if you don't get out from behind me. Go on and say what you wanna say to Logan, then get outta the way."

"Yes, ma'am," he said, and stepped up cautiously by the sofa. Logan looked at him, still in a slight daze. "I know I done the wrong thing," Sam started. "But I'm hopin' you'll understand we was all fooled by that Quincy Smith, or whatever his name is, and I thought I was doin' the right thing. I'm just as sorry as I can be."

At this point, Logan blamed himself for his carelessness more than he blamed Sam, and his only concern was to clear his head so he could get on Quincy's trail.

"Just take care of my horses and we'll be square," he said.

While Logan was being restrained in the Three Widows, Quincy and Lonnie were over two miles away, following a trail beside Spearfish Creek. Pressing their horses hard for speed on the snow-covered track, they followed the creek into Spearfish Canyon, hoping their lead would be too much to overcome.

After another mile in the rugged canyon, they were forced to let up on the horses for fear of breaking a leg on the icy trail. Quincy, leading the way, pulled up to a stop when he reached a small clearing protected from pursuit by several large boulders. When Lonnie came up beside him, he stepped down and reached for Hannah.

"Come 'ere, darlin', I know you been wishin' you were ridin' with me."

She tried to fight him, but Lonnie pushed her off the horse and she landed on the ground. Frightened for her life, she scrambled up, slipping awkwardly in the snow, but managed to keep her feet and started to run back the way they had just come.

"No, you don't," Quincy yelled, and ran after her, only to find that the blow he had received from Logan's boot still caused him too much agony to chase her.

"Damned if he didn't pretty much geld you, didn't he, cousin?" Lonnie sneered when he saw how Quincy was favoring his injury. He had no patience for Quincy's lusty notions at a time like this. Having already taken control of their escape while Quincy was incapacitated, he did not intend to endanger it now. He wheeled his horse and easily overtook the terrified woman within a couple of dozen yards, pulling the horse around to bump her backward onto the snowy ground. Taking his time, he casually stepped down and dumped her on her backside again when she tried to get up. He stood over her and pointed a threatening finger in her face.

"You get up from there and behave yourself. I'll tell you when you can go." He reached down, grabbed her wrist, and roughly helped her to her feet. Then he herded her back to the clearing, where Quincy immediately grabbed her and pulled her tightly against him.

"We ain't got time to play no more of your little games," Quincy told her while she struggled to free herself from his embrace. "You've been wantin' to be with me ever since we came to town."

"Let me go!" she pleaded, terrified. "You told them you'd let me go!"

Quincy laughed scornfully. "I've told a lot of people a lot of things."

"We damn sure ain't got time for you to fool around with that woman while we've got a posse to worry about," Lonnie said. "Hell, you couldn't cut the mustard right now anyway. We'll take a minute or two to make sure that bunch ain't ridin' hot on our heels. Then we'll let her go, just like I said we would."

"When in hell did you start givin' the orders, cousin?" Quincy demanded, still clutching Hannah. It had always been understood that he was the boss, and he didn't like the notion that Lonnie evidently had decided he could tell him what to do.

"When you started sniffin' around that damn woman like you was a hound dog, and she was in heat," Lonnie told him, "at a time when it might cause me to get my ass shot."

"Well, suppose you get your ass up on that rock and take a look down that trail to see if they're comin' after us or not?" Quincy said, taking command again.

Lonnie, who had already been in the process of climbing up on the rock, didn't bother to answer as he scrambled up on top, and stood looking down the canyon behind them.

"There ain't nobody in sight for as far as I can see,"

he reported. "So I reckon we can let the woman go, and we'll make tracks away from that damn town."

But now that he had his hands on her, Quincy was reluctant to let her get away. "I think maybe I've changed my mind," he said. "I think I'll take her with us. You'd like that, wouldn't you, honey?" he teased, and tried to kiss her.

She fought him with all her strength, determined to resist his advances, moving her head from side to side, until he became so frustrated that he struck her with his fist. Staggered by the blow on the side of her face, she sagged, dazed, and would have fallen had he not been holding her with his other arm.

"That's better," he said, gloating. "Now I'll have that kiss."

"Damn it, Quincy!" Lonnie railed. "We ain't got time for that. We've got to get goin' while we've still got a head start. Let the bitch go and they won't have no reason to come after us."

"Well, what about Jake?" Quincy demanded. "Are you sayin' we just ride off and forget about what that son of a bitch did to Jake? He's the only reason we rode up to this damn canyon. I ain't lettin' nobody get away with killin' my brother."

"I ain't sayin' we'll forget about Jake," Lonnie replied quickly, alert to the possibility of one of Quincy's fits of anger. "I'm just sayin' the time ain't right now. Too much has gone against us. We had half a dozen men when we came out here. Hell, that was before we picked up Lacey. Now there ain't but the two of us. On top of that, we got the whole town of Spearfish after us now." It would be better to come back for Logan Cross when all this cooled down a little.

I ain't about to lose those two sacks of gold dust we left under the bed back in that boardin'house, either, he thought. *That's too much to leave behind, but we have to wait till things cool down.*

Quincy was still reluctant to let her go, but he knew Lonnie was talking sense. "All right, damn it!" he replied angrily. "I'm lettin' her go." He pawed over her body for a few moments but finally let her drop to the ground. "Maybe I'll come back to see you sometime," he said to her, then left her there and went to his horse.

Hannah walked for half an hour before seeing Jace Evans round a bend in the creek with half a dozen men behind him. Thankful to see her walking toward them, Jace pulled up to her and dismounted.

"You're hurt!" Jace exclaimed, concerned by the obvious evidence of Quincy's blow to her face.

Faint with relief upon seeing the riders, Hannah said, "That'll be all right. I'm so glad to see you. I'm more worried about freezing to death."

Three of the town men started shucking their coats immediately, but Jace was the first to drape his heavy woolen coat around her shoulders. "We brought an extra horse for you to ride," he said.

Jim Bledsoe rode around the others and brought a saddled horse up front. "She's a right gentle little mare," he said to Hannah as Jace helped her up into the saddle. "I don't think she'll give you any trouble." He remained there with Jace and Bob Whitley while Fred Ramsey led Hannah and the others back down the trail to Spearfish. They watched the men from town escort Hannah away, and then Jim asked the question on all three of the Triple-T riders' minds. "You thinkin' about goin' after those two skunks?"

"I've been thinkin' about it," Jace replied after a

moment's hesitation. "There's no doubt they need somethin' done about 'em, but I'm halfway thinkin' we ain't got the time to chase after 'em, when we've got our own work to tend to. I told Mr. Towson we'd be right back after we told the people in Spearfish the truth about Quincy Morgan."

"Well, we made a bargain, even if it was with a couple of outlaws," Bob said, "and it looks like they're keepin' their end of it. They let her go."

"Even if they did whomp that poor lady on the jaw," Jim said. "I reckon it's enough for the town that the two of 'em are gone from here."

"I reckon," Jace agreed. "Let's get on back to town."

After following the creek for about five miles, the two outlaws came to an old game trail leading up between two mountains on the eastern side of Spearfish Canyon. They were not sure where it would lead them, but they decided it might at least take them in the direction they wanted to go, hoping to eventually find their way to Deadwood.

They had decided that Deadwood would most likely be the best place to wait out the winter for several reasons. They were not ready to abandon the gold that they had left in the room at the Three Widows. And the towns in Deadwood Gulch were bound to offer many opportunities for two ruthless outlaws to prey upon the efforts of the hundreds of placer miners who might have struck solid color.

In spite of that, they could never be assured of striking a payday to equal the gold they had already found and had hidden in the Three Widows. At the heart of these reasons, however, was Quincy's unrelenting passion that would not be satisfied until Logan Cross was dead. It was a near-constant obsession in Quincy Morgan's mind, and an irritating failure that needed fixing in Lonnie's. There was a firm commitment in the minds of both men that sooner or later Logan Cross would die by their hands.

"Damn that son of a bitch," Lonnie swore when he thought about it. "We've got to get back there before somebody stumbles on those sacks under that bed."

"There ain't much chance of it," Quincy said, although every bit as concerned as Lonnie. They had loosened the nails in a couple of floorboards under the bed in guest room number one, Quincy's bedroom. Lifting the boards just enough to stuff the gold sacks underneath, they had carefully replaced them. "Somebody would have to know that dust was hid in that room somewhere, and be lookin' real hard for it. We'll just let the town cool down. Then we'll go back and get it."

"That might not be so easy," Lonnie said. "We'll liable to get shot on sight the minute we show up in that town now."

Chapter 15

"You got banged on the head pretty good," Mae Davis said when Logan got to his feet and had to grab the wall to keep from swaying. "Sam busted the stock on that Henry rifle of his."

"It sounded so loud," Daisy commented, "I wasn't sure if it was the rifle stock or your head that cracked." She stepped forward and placed her hand on his arm. "Why don't you sit back down on that sofa? You don't need to be in a hurry to go anywhere till your brains calm down."

"I need to get after that pair before I lose their trail," Logan insisted. "I'll be all right as soon as my head stops spinnin'."

"Shoot," Daisy scoffed. "You'd fall offa your horse." She poked him in the chest with her finger, causing him to have to sit down again on the sofa. "You might as well quit arguin'. You ain't goin' nowhere tonight. It's already too late to be tryin' to follow anybody up that canyon anyway. If you just can't stand it till somebody's shootin' at you, you can go out after those two bastards in the mornin'. Maybe you'll be over that swimmy-headed spell by then."

"You can stay here tonight," Mae suggested. "It just so happens that I've got two rooms come vacant today, and they're paid for, too."

"That's right," Daisy chimed in. "And they're in pretty good shape right now. They didn't have time to mess 'em up before they checked out."

Logan didn't argue the point any further. He had realized when he tried to stand that he was going to have to let his head settle down before he could rely on his body to do his bidding. When he had no longer insisted on leaving, the two women left him for a while to tend to other chores left in the wake of the confrontation in their dining room.

It was difficult to put their minds to the mundane work of clearing away all the uneaten food left on the tables when they were anxious to hear news of Hannah's fate. Fully aware now of the deceitful practices of Quincy and Lonnie Morgan, and the extent of their evil intentions, they feared they might never see Hannah again.

"They were damn fools to let that pair ride away with Hannah," Daisy said.

"What else could they do?" Mae asked. "He had a gun under her chin. He woulda killed her."

"Somebody coulda got a shot at him when they rode outta the stable," Daisy insisted. "If I'da had a rifle, I'da shot the son of a bitch."

Mae knew the cynical young woman was just talking, because she had felt helpless to do anything to prevent Hannah's abduction.

"Well," Mae sighed, "there ain't nothing we can do

but wait and see. So we might as well clean up this mess they left on the tables." She walked over to look at the tables turned over in the back corner. "Least-ways, this is the last mess we'll have to clean up after Marshal Smith and his hounds."

"Amen to that," Daisy said, and started collecting dishes.

The two women worked away in the dining room, with Daisy periodically looking in the parlor to make sure Logan was still propped up on the sofa. When they were almost finished with the cleanup, they heard the sound of horses's hooves in the front yard, caus-ing them both to run through the parlor to the front door. Logan was already on the porch when Jace Evans and his rescue party pulled up before the hitching rail. They breathed great sighs of relief when they saw Hannah perched atop the little mare that Sam had saddled for her ride home.

With Hannah safely back, the second most import-ant thing on Logan's mind was the two outlaws who had abducted her.

"What about the Morgans?" he asked Jace. "Did you catch up to them?"

"No," Jace answered. "We met Hannah on her way back, after they let her go." He paused, waiting for Logan's response. When there was none, other than a pensive look of concern, he said, "We thought about some of us goin' on to try to catch up with them, but it didn't make much sense. It was already gettin' dark in that canyon, and I didn't wanna lose anybody in an ambush."

"I reckon not," Logan said.

Jace evidently felt he should have to make an excuse for not going after Quincy and Lonnie, but Logan knew that the task was his alone. He turned to greet Hannah as Mae and Daisy led the shivering woman up the steps to the porch.

"I'm sorry you got caught up in this," he said to her. There was no time to say anything more, as Mae and Daisy hurried her into the house to change out of her wet skirt. She smiled at him before she was whisked away.

With Hannah in good hands, Jace turned to Logan to find out what he had in mind. "You look like you're still a little shaky," he said, noticing that Logan was holding on to the rail for support. "Whaddaya got on your mind? You ready to go on back to the Triple-T and get to work?" He asked the question with a fair idea what the answer might be.

"I don't know, Jace," Logan replied after a long pause. "I kinda feel like there's a job that ain't finished, one that needs finishin'."

"Kinda thought you'd say somethin' like that," Jace said. "Tell you what, why don't we go inside and see if Mae wouldn't mind buildin' us a pot of coffee, and we'll talk about this job that needs finishin'? That all right with you?"

Logan shrugged. He knew he wasn't going to start anywhere until morning anyway.

Jace turned to Bob Whitley. "Bob, why don't you and the boys go on over to the saloon and have a drink while Logan and I have a little talk? Tell Cecil I'll buy one round. I'll be over to pay him in a little bit."

"Yes, sir," Bob replied, and turned to get on his horse. The other men, having heard Jace's suggestion, were already mounting up as well.

"And, Bob," Jace called after him, "I said one round. Anything after that, you're liable for yourself." He looped his reins over the hitching rail and stepped up onto the porch as his posse loped toward the Gateway Saloon. "I don't think a drink of liquor would do much good for that head of yours right now," he said to Logan. "Let's go inside."

Although the women were in the midst of cleaning up the dining room, they were glad to oblige Jace's request for coffee. All three of them felt that they owed Logan Cross a whole lot of making up for the low regard they had credited him with. Mae interrupted her cleanup to put a fresh pot of coffee on the stove while Hannah sat Logan and Jace down at a table at the side of the room.

"You might give 'em some of those biscuits you're so proud of, too," Daisy suggested to Hannah. She paused, hands on hips, while she took another look at Hannah. "Maybe you oughta set yourself down with 'em. The side of your face has got a good-sized knot on it now. You sure you're feelin' all right?"

"I'm all right," Hannah insisted. "It's just a little tender to the touch. I think that long, cold ride back here mighta helped it."

The sudden frown that wrinkled Logan's forehead when Hannah's injury was mentioned did not go unnoticed by Jace. He knew it provided another reason for the determined young man to go after Quincy Morgan, but he didn't say anything.

"What is it you wanted to talk about?" Logan finally asked when it appeared that Jace was content to merely take his ease in the warm dining room. But Mae appeared at that moment with two large mugs of fresh coffee and a plate of biscuits that had been warming in the oven while the coffee perked.

"I wish ol' Spud, back at the Triple-T, could make

coffee that tastes as good as this," Jace said, after a sip of the hot liquid, still making small talk. "Nobody makes a better cup of coffee," he said, smiling at Mae, who answered with a smile of her own.

When Mae returned to her chores, Logan pressed, "I know you've got somethin' on your mind besides havin' a nice cup of coffee. What is it?"

"Yeah, we might as well get right to it," Jace responded. "You figurin' on goin' after Quincy Morgan right away?"

"I told you that," Logan replied.

"Yeah, but that's the thing," Jace said, trying to find the right words. "What's the use of goin' after those two saddle tramps? Ain't you killed enough men to make up for all they've done to you? It's over and done. Those two have hightailed it outta here. They ain't comin' back. They'd be crazy to, after the trick they pulled on the whole town." He paused to study Logan's reaction to what he was saying, but his words appeared to have no effect upon the determined young man. He continued to try to reason with him. "From what you told me, Quincy's brother, Jake, and two other men, shot your brother. You killed all three of them, right?" He paused but Logan did not reply. "And then, when Quincy and Lonnie came after you, you gunned down their whole damn gang. Now they've had enough, and they've been run off for good." He paused again. "Logan, you've avenged your brother. Everything else is just senseless killin'." He was interrupted then when Daisy brought the coffeepot out to refill their cups.

Logan took that moment to think about what he had said, but he was still not convinced Jace was right. "I don't know," he finally said. "It's just that somebody oughta stop those two from doin' any more harm."

"Maybe so," Jace replied. "Maybe somebody should,

and maybe they will . . . but it don't have to be you. What if you catch up with 'em, and you come out on top? Sooner or later, the word's gonna get out that Logan Cross killed Quincy and Lonnie Morgan, and the whole damn Morgan Gang, to boot. Then, my young friend, you ain't gonna be able to go anywhere without makin' sure your back's to a wall, lest some gunman out to make a name for himself takes a shot at you. Is that what you want?"

"Damn, Jace." Logan hesitated. "I don't know. I don't reckon anybody wants a life like that."

"Well, that's what it would be. I'm tryin' to tell you there's a place for you on the Triple-T. In the short time you were with us, every man you've worked with says you know workin' cattle inside and out. I'd like to see you stay on with us and help Mr. Towson and me build this ranch into the biggest in the territory. Whaddaya say?" When Logan seemed to weaken for a moment, Jace joked, "Hell, even Ox has taken to you like a brother, and Ox don't like nobody." He studied Logan's face intently. "Whaddaya say? To hell with those two bastards. We've got work to do on the Triple-T."

Daisy, who had managed to stay close enough to overhear most of their conversation, came by one more time with the coffeepot. "Listen to what Jace says. You're a damn fool if you don't," she offered to their surprise. She filled their cups and walked away without saying more.

Their advice only served to make him unsure. What Jace said was true, he had killed those who had taken Billy's life. But Quincy Morgan had caused him a great deal of trouble and turned a whole town against him, with his charade.

More than that, however, he and his men had hunted him with the intention of executing him. How could he not seek vengeance? If he listened to Jace's advice, he could forsake the constant hunt, and the ever-present danger of being ambushed, and go back to working cattle. But how could he be sure that Quincy was done with it?

I can't, he decided, *but I don't want to spend my life with a target on my back, like Jace said.* He looked up from his coffee cup to meet Jace's gaze. "I reckon I'm ready to go back to work," he said, "if you meant what you said about havin' a job."

Jace nodded, pleased. "You're makin' the right decision," he said. "You can ride back with the rest of the boys tonight, if your head's feelin' all right. Or wait till mornin', and come on when you're ready."

Logan thought about it for a moment. His head still felt as if it were splitting open with the headache from the two solid blows to his skull. And the thought of a seven-mile ride didn't appeal to him at all. "If it's all the same to you, I think I'll wait till mornin'—see if I can get rid of this damn throbbin' in my head. Mae offered me a room, so I think I'll take it."

"Not a bad idea," Jace said. "It's settled, then." He got up from the table. "I'd best go get the boys before they get so drunk they'll have to stay here with you tonight." He started for the door. "How much do I owe you, Mae?" he asked when she came out of the kitchen.

"Nothin'," she said. "It's on the house."

"Thank you kindly," Jace said, and continued toward the door, calling back over his shoulder to Logan, "Don't go changin' your mind, or I'll have to send Ox after you."

After Jace had gone, Mae came over to the table. "You want some more coffee?"

"No, ma'am, I reckon I've already drank a gracious plenty."

"Like I told you, you're welcome to stay here tonight," she said. "Whichever room you want, one or two, they're pretty much the same. But let me know which one, so Daisy can change the sheets on the bed."

"I'll just take number one, I guess, and I sure do appreciate it, but you don't have to go to any trouble about changin' the sheets—couldn't be much worse than sleepin' in the stable with my horse."

"I wouldn't be too sure about that," Mae said. "We'd best change them. We're gonna have to fix some kind of supper, even after all the excitement we've had today. It'll be something quick and simple, so if you're hungry, we'll have it ready in about an hour."

"I probably will be by then," he said. "I wouldn't pass it up, even if I wasn't hungry." He got to his feet. "I'll go on over to the stable and get my saddlebags."

Already feeling somewhat more steady on his feet, Logan walked into the stable, startling Sam Taylor. "Logan!" Sam exclaimed. "I didn't hear you come in."

"Didn't mean to scare you," Logan said. "I just came to pick up my saddlebags. I'm gonna leave my horses here tonight."

"Sure thing, Logan," Sam replied quickly, "and there won't be no charge."

"Why, that's mighty neighborly of you, but if this is about that knot you put on my head, you've already apologized, and it's over and done, as far as I'm concerned."

"That's mighty Christian of you, Logan. I can't tell you how sorry I am for bein' such a gullible jackass, but he had everybody fooled."

"Forget about it," Logan said. "I'm surprised you ain't come after me to pay for that rifle stock I broke. We'll call it even."

Sam's second apology was one of several from other citizens of the town, who had bought Quincy Morgan's story. Fred Ramsey came by when Logan was at the supper table to say he was sorry to have believed the accusations made by Quincy and Lonnie. Cecil Grant sent an apology as well, saying he couldn't tell him in person, because he had to tend bar at the saloon. Logan appreciated their concern, but it was beginning to make him feel uncomfortable, and he wondered if he'd made a mistake in remaining in town for the night.

One person who felt especially guilty was Hannah, for she had spent more time alone with Logan Cross than anyone else. She should have known the man was honorable, yet she had allowed herself to be taken in by the handsome image of a U.S. Marshal. She was thoroughly ashamed of her treatment of Logan when he tried to tell her the truth. In her defense, she told herself that Mae was equally taken in by the ruse. The only person who was not convinced was Daisy. She somehow had seen through the slick image that Quincy Morgan had painted. But Daisy was always cynical about most things, so it was not so unusual that she had not fallen in line with everyone else in the small settlement.

Anxious to get away from the apologetic citizens of the town, Logan headed out early the next morning to return to the Triple-T, leaving Hannah disappointed that he had not even waited to have breakfast in the dining room.

The next few days that followed the exodus of Quincy and Lonnie Morgan from the town of Spearfish were a period of much-needed relief for Logan Cross. Back into the business of winter chores on a cattle ranch, he found that he was rapidly settling again into a satisfying role as a cowhand. Concerning himself with nothing more than finding strays and protecting the cattle from predators, he felt as though he was at home again.

He was not overly surprised to find that he was most often paired with Ox Russell when riding the perimeter. The oversized man had somehow been transformed into a gentle giant. Bob Whitley was of the opinion that Ox felt a responsibility for his safety, because Logan had told him that he had saved his life by catching him at the attempted hanging.

Whatever the reason, Logan didn't mind having the simple man as his constant companion. Ox didn't talk much, and he didn't require anything in return. Logan didn't give it much thought, but if he had, he would have realized that he was enjoying the first peaceful time in his life since Billy's death.

Chapter 16

"Ha! Quincy Morgan! I heard you was outta prison."

Quincy turned in reaction to the booming voice behind him, thinking he recognized it. "Mike Swann," he huffed when he saw the hulking man dressed like an Indian in animal skins and wearing a red bandanna wrapped around a full head of long dirty black hair. "Damn, you ain't any better lookin' than the last time I saw you."

"That would be Oklahoma Injun Territory, if I recollect rightly," Swann said. "Last I seen you, you was hightailin' it down the center of that gulch with two Choctaw Lighthorse policemen hot on your tail. Did they catch up with you?"

"Nah, but a damn deputy marshal did after I ran my horse till he foundered," Quincy said. "Set down and have a drink." He nodded at Lonnie. "You know my cousin, Lonnie?"

"Can't say as I've had the pleasure," Swann said as

he pulled a chair back and sat down. "You wasn't with Quincy that day back in the Nation, I don't believe."

"No, I was in Witchita, doin' a little cattle business," Lonnie said.

He knew of Mike Swann but had never had any dealings with him, as his cousin had. Quincy had pulled a couple of jobs with Swann but was never interested in forming a lasting partnership. According to Quincy, Swann was a crude, brutal man who took too many chances.

Turning back to Quincy, Swann said, "If you'd hid in the back room of that bank with the rest of us, you'da got away." He grinned wide. "But you ran out the front and they saw you." He laughed. "Them Choctaws took off after you and gave us a chance to ride off real peacefullike. Never got the chance to thank you for that till now. I'd be happy to give you your share of that bank money, but we spent it." He enjoyed a good laugh over the incident before continuing. "So I reckon that's when they sent you to prison."

"No," Quincy answered. "I said the deputy marshal caught up with me. I didn't say he walked away from it." His remark brought on another roar of laughter from the crude man. "What are you doin' out in this part of the country?" Quincy asked. "You finally get run outta Oklahoma?"

"I just come out here for my health," Swann said, and winked at Lonnie. "It was gettin' a little too warm for me back there."

"You still livin' with that Choctaw wildcat?" Quincy asked.

"Nah, she got to where she was gettin' into my likker too much. I come in one day and caught her on her back with Skinny Tarpley in the saddle. You remember

Skinny—used to ride with me? Anyway, I cut her throat." He laughed thinking about it. "That's the reason I come out here for my health. That bitch musta had a hundred relatives, all wantin' my scalp. Yes, sir, it was gettin' a mite warm back there." He shook his head thoughtfully in recalling. "Skinny's still with me. He was too good a man with a gun or knife to get rid of."

"Are you doin' any business out here?" Quincy asked.

"A little," Swann replied. "Most of it small stuff. There's plenty of miners all over these hills, but ain't many of 'em findin' no real color. Grub money is about all it amounts to—ain't run across no big score yet."

Quincy picked up the bottle and poured Swann another shot. Lonnie could tell at a glance that he was doing some serious thinking, and he was afraid he knew what he was thinking about. And he wasn't sure he went along with it, so he frowned at his cousin, but Quincy only winked in return, then proceeded to make Swann a proposition. "You and Skinny just might be glad you ran into me and Lonnie," he said.

"How's that?" Swann replied, immediately interested. "You got somethin' goin'?"

"As a matter of fact," Quincy said, "we've got a little chore up in Spearfish we're fixin' to do. We've been holdin' back on it, 'cause there ain't but the two of us. But with four of us, it oughta be a cakewalk. Right, Lonnie?" He looked at his cousin for support, but Lonnie was not enthusiastic about sharing the gold left behind at the Three Widows. Quincy continued to ignore the signals sent his way.

"How much is in it for me and Skinny?" Swann asked.

"Gold dust worth about five thousand dollars, just settin' there where we hid it. All we got to do is go up there and take it, and we'll split it down the middle, twenty-five hundred for you and Skinny, the same for me and Lonnie. How's that sound to ya?"

"Well, you damn sure got my attention," Swann said. "Whadda we gotta go up against? You said you was holdin' back when there was just two of you."

"Just a few townspeople," Quincy said. "But it'll just be easier with four of us. They won't give us no trouble atall. They'll be too scared to. If it was just me and Lonnie, somebody might try to take a shot at us." He went on to explain the situation in Spearfish, what had happened there, and where the money was hidden.

"What about that posse that stopped the hangin' you was fixin' to have?" Swann asked.

"You ain't gonna have to worry about them," Quincy assured him. "They were from the Triple-T Ranch, seven miles away."

Swann didn't have to take any time to decide. "All right," he said. "We're in. When do you wanna get started?"

"You think you gotta talk it over with Skinny first?" Quincy asked.

"Nah, I can speak for him. He's upstairs with that big ol' whore, the one with the wart on her chin." Swann laughed. "He's partial to big women. I told him one of these days he's gonna be with the wrong woman and the next feller will shoot him instead of the woman."

"Good," Quincy said. "We'll start out in the mornin'. I don't see any sense in waitin'. We'll meet you for breakfast in the hotel. I'll even spring for it."

They had a couple more shots of whiskey, and then Swann left to tell Skinny the news. When he had gone, Lonnie spoke up for the first time since the crude man had joined them. "Five thousand, huh? We figured them two bags are holdin' more like ten thousand each. We might not ever get a shot at that much again."

Quincy grinned. "I don't think Swann needs to know that. Hell, it might be worth more than that. We just gotta make sure me and you are the only ones to handle those two bags. I figure it'd be worth twenty-five hundred to have two extra men to help us. We'll see how it goes—might not even cost us the twenty-five hundred." He gave Lonnie a wink. "We'll tell 'em somebody musta got away with half of it. Don't worry. We ain't gonna give away our fortune."

"I'm glad to hear you say it," Lonnie said. "I sure as hell don't wanna give up that money to the likes of Mike Swann. I didn't like the idea at first, but you're right about one thing, nobody's liable to try to put up a fuss if there's four of us."

"Good Lord A'mighty!" Fred Ramsey blurted as he stood looking out the window of his store.

"What is it, Fred?" Martha Ramsey called out from behind the counter where she was arranging a stack of dish towels she hoped to sell.

"They're back!" Fred answered, scarcely able to believe his eyes. "Ridin' down the middle of the street just like they owned it."

Struck by the urgency in her husband's voice, Martha hurried to the window to see for herself. The sight caused her to catch her breath in alarm. "Oh my Lord," she gasped. "They've got two more of their kind with them." She clutched Fred's arm in fear. They had never expected to see Quincy and Lonnie back again after the loathsome pair had been driven out of town. "What should we do?"

"Hell, I don't know," Fred answered. "What can we do?"

"Why do you suppose they came back here?"

"I don't know," Fred repeated. "They sure came back with some fearsome-lookin' help—came to get even, maybe. I'm damn glad they passed us by. I sure as hell don't wanna be the one to tell 'em they're not welcome here." They continued to watch the four riders as they moved on past the saloon, walking their horses four abreast. When they passed by the stable, Fred exclaimed, "They're headin' for the boardin'house."

"Oh my goodness," Martha gasped, "those poor women."

Fred made up his mind. "The best thing for us is to close up and go to the house till they ride out again." He immediately pulled the shade on his front door and bolted it. "Hurry, now. I don't have any idea why they came back, but I know it ain't gonna be good for anybody in town." He walked by the window again and paused when he looked across the street at the harness shop. "Ralph's thinkin' the same thing. He's turned his OPEN sign around."

There were similar reactions from the blacksmith and the barber at the menacing sight of the four outlaws boldly entering the town. Quincy had been right in estimating the intimidation caused by the sight of four gunmen to deal with. No one in the town was willing to take the risk of shooting at them. Anyone happening to be on the street quickly found the first convenient door to slip inside until the riders passed. Quincy grinned at Lonnie when the whole town seemed to button up and the residents scurried to their holes like frightened insects.

"The damn town's ours again," he couldn't help commenting.

"We'd better cook the rest of these potatoes," Mae said. "They're goin' bad awful quick. I ain't sure they'll be fit to fry in another day." She carved off about a fourth of the one she was holding. "That's plumb rotten, and I don't know when we'll be able to get some more this winter."

"We'll just serve more beans," Daisy said. "As long as we give 'em plenty of meat, they don't—"

Mae turned to see why Daisy had not finished her comment and found her staring wide-eyed at the dining room door, dumbstruck by the vision of Quincy Morgan standing there. Never far from finding her voice, however, Daisy demanded, "What the hell are you doing back here?"

"Why, we came back here to call on you charmin' ladies," Quincy said sarcastically. Coming in behind him, the ominous figure of Mike Swann filled the doorway, causing both women to automatically take a step backward. Lonnie and Skinny came after him, completing the promise of evil to follow. "We left in such a hurry that we plumb forgot to get all our belongin's outta our rooms," Quincy went on.

"You didn't leave anything in those rooms but a few filthy clothes," Daisy said, still the only one of the two women who could talk. "I threw them in the wash and put 'em in the closet at the end of the hall. I'll get 'em for you so you don't have to waste any more time here."

Quincy chuckled, pleased by the apparent fear he saw in the women. "There damn sure better be somethin' else in my room, or I'll burn this damn house down. Now, suppose you rustle up some coffee for my two friends here while me and Lonnie get the rest of our belongin's. And maybe some pie or somethin' to go with it. That'ud be all right, wouldn't it, Swann?" Skinny and Swann looked at each other and nodded. "Just set yourself down and these fine ladies will bring you somethin'," Quincy said. He looked toward the kitchen door then and asked, "Where's Hannah?"

"She ain't here," Daisy said. She had a pretty good idea that Hannah had heard what was going on in the dining room, and was probably hiding in the pantry. At least, she hoped she was.

"Where is she?" Quincy asked again.

"She went to the store to get some things," Mae answered, having recovered enough to speak. "Daisy and I can help you get your things. We don't wanna hold you up."

"You better not be lyin' to me," Quincy threatened. "Now, get your ass in the kitchen and make some coffee for my friends. Daisy can help me and Lonnie with our stuff."

Perfectly content to sit down at the table to await a cup of coffee, Swann and his wiry companion made themselves comfortable, unsuspecting of any double-crossing from their partners. Back in the hallway, before the door to guest room number one, Lonnie asked Daisy, "Who's been in here since we left?"

"Nobody," Daisy said, seeing no reason to tell him that Logan had spent one night there. "I told you I put your stuff in the hall closet."

"Not all of it, or you're gonna be in more trouble than you ever saw before," Lonnie said, and opened the door. "Grab the end of that bed." He took the head-board while Quincy stood at the door to keep an eye on the hall, in case Swann got curious. "Walk it over a piece," Lonnie instructed Daisy, and they moved the bed several feet.

As soon as they set it down, Lonnie pulled his large bowie knife and went to work prying up one end of a floorboard. It came up fairly easily, to Daisy's surprise. Lonnie pulled it up about a foot from the floor, then did the same to the board next to it.

"Safe and sound," he announced to Quincy, still standing at the door.

Astonished, Daisy watched as Lonnie pulled two heavy canvas bags from under the floorboards. Quincy walked over then and hefted the bags to make sure they were not lighter than when first hidden.

"I need a couple more sacks, stout ones," he said to Daisy.

"We ain't got any sacks," Daisy said.

"Pillowcases will do," Lonnie said, and grabbed the pillows off the bed. "They're strong enough," he said, after testing them. Working quickly then, they transferred part of the gold dust into the pillowcases. "Now get them clothes you said we left," he told Daisy.

Dazed by the thought that so much treasure had been hidden right under her nose, she went at once to the closet to fetch the few articles of clothing they had left behind. Lonnie stuffed them into the heavy pillowcases in an attempt to disguise the actual contents.

"I reckon that's about the best we can do," he said. "I'll tote these, if you'll tote the rest of it." They started out the door.

"How 'bout fixin' the floor you just tore up?" Daisy said, becoming more perturbed now than afraid.

"How 'bout fixin' it yourself?" Quincy said with a sneer.

"You no-good bastard," she responded, earning a hard slap across her face.

"I never did like you very much, you mouthy bitch," Quincy said. "And if you open that sassy mouth of yours about what's in them pillowcases, I swear I'll shoot you down on the spot. You got that?"

"I got it," Daisy replied, rubbing her stinging cheek. "What do I care if you cheat that scum you're ridin' with?"

Back in the dining room, Swann and Skinny got to their feet when Quincy and Lonnie walked in, anxious to see the gold. "Here it is, boys," Quincy announced, and dropped the two canvas sacks on the floor before them. "Just like we left 'em, they oughta be about the same weight, so take your pick, and me and Lonnie will take the other'n."

Swann and Skinny immediately opened the two sacks to inspect the contents. If there was any question in their minds about the pillowcases Lonnie was holding, they made no comment. The payday was definitely larger than one they could have expected before running into Quincy and Lonnie.

"Which'un you want, Skinny?" Swann asked. When Skinny simply shrugged indifference, Swann picked one up. "We'll take this'un." Although simple, Swann was not stupid, so he posed a question to Quincy. "You didn't have no need for me and Skinny to help you fight these two women. You ain't payin' us this much just for our company, so what the hell are you payin' us to do?"

Quincy smiled. "I told Lonnie you was smart enough to know there was more to it than this. I figure you'll earn your pay by doin' what you do best."

Swann grinned smugly. "Somebody needs killin'," he said. "Who, and how many are you talkin' about?"

"Ain't but one man," Quincy said. "But he might have a few friends with him. That's why I need you—to make sure his friends don't get in my way."

Swann looked at Skinny and nodded. Then back to Quincy, he said, "Let's get to it, then, so we can get busy spendin' some of this gold."

"Hold on just a minute," Quincy said, then turned to Mae. "How long's Hannah been gone?"

"She left just a minute or two before you got here," she said.

A slow grin began to form on Quincy's face. "Now, why do I think you're lyin' to me, bitch? If she'da gone to the store a minute before we got here, we'da seen her on the street. Now, where is she?"

"She ain't here," Daisy said. "Mae told you that."

Quincy grabbed her by the front of her blouse and jerked her hard up against him. "I've done told you to quit lyin' to me, but you don't learn too quick, do you?" He shoved her hard enough to slam her against the wall. "Now, I think I'll take a look in the kitchen."

He charged through the kitchen door, looking expectantly from right to left. Mae and Daisy both gasped in fear. When he saw no sign of Hannah, he went to the only place for the woman to hide.

"No!" Mae exclaimed without thinking, knowing that Hannah was in the kitchen when they came in. With a satisfied smirk, he grabbed the doorknob and flung the pantry door open to bang against the wall.

He stood there for a long moment before turning around to face Mae. "Where is she, damn it?"

"I swear, I don't know where she is," Mae said, as

surprised as he to find she was not there. "I told you, she went to the store. I don't know why she didn't come back. Maybe she saw your horses and ran. Least, I hope to hell she did."

Determined to find her, Quincy stormed out of the kitchen and marched down the long hall to Hannah's room while his three partners watched in amusement at his frantic antics. "Damned if ol' Quincy ain't got the itch bad," Swann said.

"She must be somethin'," Skinny said. "I'd like to get a look at her." He looked around toward Daisy. "I wouldn't throw that one outta the bed." He smiled when the comment made Daisy cringe.

Outside the kitchen door, Hannah could easily hear Quincy's loud remarks of frustration. Hearing the conversation coming from the dining room earlier, when she was hiding in the pantry, she decided it was not a safe place to hide. Now, outside, with her back pressed tightly against the back of the house, she knew it only a matter of minutes before he looked out there, and she would be discovered at once. With no other choices, she decided to run to the outhouse, hoping he wouldn't think to look there.

Stalking out of Hannah's empty room, Quincy opened all the other bedroom doors on his way back to the kitchen, then went straight to the back door. There was no one in the backyard, so he turned to come back inside, pausing when he thought of one other place. With a victorious grin on his face, he went straight to the small privy beyond the washhouse and yanked the door open. His grin was replaced at once by a dark frown of anger when he discovered that the outhouse was empty. He slammed the door shut and strode purposefully back to the house. Behind him,

Hannah released the breath she had been holding and thanked the Lord she had hidden behind the outhouse, instead of inside it.

What to do now was the question in Hannah's mind. From the talk she had overheard when still in the pantry, Quincy was planning to go in search of Logan, now that his gold was recovered. She did not have to think about it long, for she knew that Logan needed to be warned. She owed him that. She looked across the fifty yards of open expanse between the house and Sam Taylor's stable. Could she possibly cross it without being seen?

Well, I can't stay here forever, she told herself. Sooner or later Quincy was bound to look behind the privy. She got to her feet and started running, afraid that the longer she waited, the harder it would be to make herself do it.

Back in the house, Lonnie was getting impatient with Quincy's lust for the young woman. He finally expressed it when his frustrated cousin came back from the outhouse. "How much longer are you gonna chase around here like a rutty boar? I thought we was gonna go settle up that debt we've got with Logan Cross. Or have you forgot about Jake?"

Already angry, Quincy jerked his head around to glare at Lonnie. "You ain't got no call to talk to me about killin' Logan Cross. I'll kill that son of a bitch—you don't have to worry about that." Lonnie's words had the desired effect on him, however, for Quincy remembered the dark rage that had possessed him since his brother's death. "We're goin' after him in the mornin'," he said, "and any of that crew that gets in the way." He looked at Mae then. "So you women best get some food started, 'cause we're gonna need some supper. Maybe your partner will be back to help you cook it." It was not the decision Mae was hoping he would make.

"How 'bout it, Lonnie?" Swann asked. "We stayin' here tonight?"

"Looks that way, don't it?" Lonnie answered, not happy with the decision.

"Suits me," Swann said. "Might as well go take a look in that saloon back up the street after we put the horses up in that stable across the yard."

"Spend some of that dust in this here sack," Skinny said with a rare showing of enthusiasm.

"All right," Quincy said. "Lonnie, why don't you take the horses down to the stable with Swann and Skinny? I'll stay here and keep an eye on our gold."

"You don't understand," Hannah pleaded. "He's come back to kill Logan. Somebody has to go tell him."

"I understand," Sam Taylor insisted. It was the last thing he wanted to hear when Hannah had run breathlessly into his stable. "But it ain't gonna be me. I can't run off and leave my stables for them to do whatever they please." He knew that he wouldn't be able to prevent them from doing anything they pleased even if he was there. But he didn't want to tell Hannah that he was afraid of what they might do to him if he tried to warn Logan Cross.

"Well, saddle a horse for me!" she exclaimed. "I'll do it, but I've never been to the Triple-T. I don't know if I can find it."

"I can tell you how to find it," Sam said, eager to help her now. "I'll saddle that little mare from before. You did all right on her, didn't you?"

"Yes, I guess so," Hannah said. She paced back and

forth near the door, watching the house for anyone outside. "Please hurry!" Sam worked quickly, saddled the mare, and led her out of the stall. *Why am I always caught outside without my coat?* Hannah thought. "Do you have a coat I can borrow?" she asked.

"Yes, ma'am, I do," Sam replied, and went to the tack room to fetch a heavy blanket coat. She slipped into it gratefully. Ready to ride then, she climbed aboard and walked the mare out the door. Armed with Sam's rough directions, she rode off into the fading light of day in search of the Triple-T.

Sam watched her until he could no longer see her, feeling less of a man for letting her make the ride, but telling himself that he had a family to consider.

Chapter 17

"What you starin' at, Lou?" Bob Whitley asked when he walked up from the streambed after rinsing out his cup.

"Yonder," Lou answered, and pointed, "where that old dead tree's leanin' over the stream. That's somebody ridin' this way." The tree was about three hundred yards from where they now stood.

"Who is it?" Bob asked. "Can you make 'em out?" If it was one of the men from the ranch, he would hardly be coming from that direction, so both men stood staring until the rider came close enough to identify.

"Well, I'll be . . . ," Lou started. "It's a woman, looks like."

When she came a few yards closer, Bob said, "It's Miss Hannah. What the hell is she doin' out in the middle of the prairie?"

"Somethin's wrong," Lou said. They walked a few yards forward to meet her.

"Where's Logan?" Hannah asked anxiously as she pulled the mare up before them.

"Why, he's back at the ranch, I expect," Bob answered her. "He rode night herd last night. Is somethin' wrong?" It seemed obvious to both men that something was.

"They're back, and they're coming to look for Logan!" Hannah exclaimed. "He's got to get away from here!"

"Who's back?" Bob asked, picking up her urgency. "That phony marshal?"

"Yes, him and Lonnie, and they brought two gun-men with them!" Hannah said. "They're coming to kill Logan."

"Did you look for him back at the ranch?" Lou asked, still wondering what she was doing out there on the prairie.

"I was trying to go to the ranch," Hannah replied frantically. "But I guess I got lost. I've never been there before. I'm just thankful that I met you."

"It was pretty lucky," Lou said. "Because if you hadn't, the way you were ridin', you wouldn'ta found nobody before you struck the Belle Fourche." He and Bob looked at each other, knowing they had to act, but not sure how. "I reckon we'd best get back to the house and let them know what's goin' on."

"I reckon," Bob agreed. It sounded as though there was a war about to happen. He turned to Hannah. "We'll saddle up and head back to the ranch." He paused then to take a look at the mare to determine how hard the horse had been ridden. It looked as though it was in good shape and he considered the fact that the point where they now stood was no more than three or three and a half miles from town.

"We can get goin' right away," he decided. He looked

at Hannah, perched atop the mare, bundled up in an oversized coat. "Are you all right? You ready to ride?"

She nodded vigorously in reply.

They were met by Jace Evans, coming from the barn. He stopped, astonished to see his two men riding up with Hannah. He didn't have time to ask the reason for her visit, for she excitedly repeated the story she had told Lou and Bob even before she could slip down off her horse.

"Logan's in the bunkhouse," Jace said to Lou. "I think that's where he went after supper."

"I'll get him," Lou said, and hurried away.

Turning his attention to the lady then, he asked, "Are you all right, miss? Would you like somethin' to eat, or some coffee?" She declined both, saying she was fine. "How soon are they comin'?" he asked.

She could not say, having been at the stable when Quincy said they would leave in the morning. "I don't know. I just heard them say that they were going to find Logan. I was afraid they would catch me before I got here."

Jace's first thought was to prepare his men to defend the ranch, expecting an outright attack by the four gunmen. "Bob, you'd better go up to the house and let Mr. Towson know we got trouble headin' this way. Then tell whoever else is in the bunkhouse to get down here so we can decide what we're gonna do."

Turning to Hannah again, he said, "I expect it would be best for you to go to the house until the trouble is over." Seeing Logan and Lou approaching then, he turned to face them.

"I heard," Logan said when he walked up. Wearing

his sidearm and carrying his Winchester rifle, he looked ready for action. He looked to Hannah first. "Are you all right? Why did you have to ride out here to tell us? Couldn't somebody else have done it?" She hurriedly explained the circumstances that had led to her ride, and the fact that it was necessary for her to escape as well. Like Jace, Logan wanted to know how far behind her the gunmen were, and Hannah apologized again for having no idea.

"We'll get everybody here in a minute," Jace interrupted. "Some of us can pick a spot around the barn, and I'll put a couple of men to guard the house."

"You ain't got enough men to cover every spot on the ranch," Logan said. "Hannah says there's four of 'em. I would expect they'll work in from four different directions and wait for a chance to pick us off, and that ain't no good. This is my fight. The only reason they're comin' is to get me, but they don't care how many of your men they have to kill in the process. So I'm aimin' to ride out to meet 'em before they get this far."

"You don't have to take a chance like that," Jace protested. "You're a Triple-T man, and we take care of our own."

"I ain't gonna take the time to argue with you, Jace," Logan informed him. "There's a right and a wrong about this thing, and I don't intend to bring my trouble down on you and your men. I've got more on my conscience already than I care to have. I ain't willin' to add more. You just set your men up to defend this ranch, take care of Hannah, and I'll do what I can to stop Quincy Morgan and his bunch before they get this far. Your first responsibility is the men and the ranch."

"What if he sees you before you see him?" Ox

wanted to know, troubled by the solution Logan suggested.

"Then I reckon that'll be one way of settlin' it," Logan responded. "If he gets me, then he's got what he wants, and he won't have any reason to bother the Triple-T." He turned and went to the barn to get his saddle, having wasted enough time talking.

"This ain't right," Bob said to Jace while Logan saddled the big gray gelding. "Him goin' up against four hired gunmen."

"I know," Jace replied, his mind still churning with the issue of what was best for the owner and the men who rode for the Triple-T. Logan was right in telling him his primary concern should be for his men and the ranch. Added to that, there was now the responsibility of keeping Hannah safe. He wasn't comfortable with Logan's solution for the problem, but he had to agree that it was the best for the Triple-T. "But he knows what he's doin'," he finally said.

Logan slipped his Winchester into the saddle scabbard and stepped up on Pepper as Thomas Towson came running from the house. With a nod, perhaps of farewell for good, to Towson, he turned the horse toward the wagon road to Spearfish, pulling up when Hannah ran to stop him.

"Logan, are you sure this is the right thing to do? These are dangerous-looking men he has with him. You should get away while you still have time!"

"And let them come down on the Triple-T? You know I can't do that."

"I know it, damn it," she said. "Please be careful."

"I will," he said, and started out again, leaving Jace to scatter his men to take up defensive positions behind him.

* * *

A large yellow moon rose over the crest of a distant mountain, illuminating the wagon track that led to Spearfish. With his concentration focused entirely on the farthermost point of the road that he could see, he rode on, intent upon being as far away from the Triple-T as possible when he encountered the gunmen. There was still no sign of Morgan and his killers by the time he saw the faint lights of the town. Could he have missed them? He immediately discarded the thought. If they were going to the Triple-T, the road was the way they would have come. Maybe Hannah had been wrong, and they planned to wait until daylight.

Well, I'm here, he thought. *We might as well get this thing settled once and for all.* He was weary of the hunt.

Sam Taylor's stable was closed, with no horses left out in the corral, when Logan walked Pepper slowly past. He paused briefly before the Three Widows Inn, but decided to ride on after a moment's thought. The whole town appeared to be buttoned up, no doubt because of the sudden return of Quincy Morgan. The one exception was the Gateway Saloon. Logan doubted that Cecil had much choice in the matter. He figured this was the most likely place to find Quincy and his gang this time of evening, so he continued along the street to the saloon.

He chambered a round in his rifle before stepping up on the boardwalk before the saloon, then slowly pushed the door open. Looking the room over before stepping inside, he saw only one customer, a large man, dressed in animal skins. Instead of a hat, he wore a red bandanna around his head and was seated at a table against the wall. He was a stranger to Logan, but was he one of the two men who had come to kill him? There was only one way to find out, so he pushed on through the door and walked in. He glanced quickly at Cecil behind the bar when the startled bartender dropped a glass he had been drying, stunned by the sudden appearance of Logan.

Mike Swann noticed Cecil's shocked reaction, too, but he made no indication that he had. Instead he smiled at Logan and said, "Come on in, stranger, and have a drink." The man holding the rifle seemed a bit too cautious. Swann had a feeling.

"Uh," Cecil stammered, "Lila's upstairs right now. I expect you'd best come back later."

"What?" Logan asked, confused. "Lila?"

Then in the silence of the almost empty barroom, he heard the soft metallic clicking he instantly identified as the sound made by the cocking of a hammer. With no time to think, he spun around, raising his rifle, and fired at the man standing at the top of the stairs. Skinny Tarpley doubled over and fell forward down the stairs, firing harmlessly into the steps beneath him.

Already too late, Logan turned back to find Swann's .44 aimed at him. He ejected his spent cartridge, bracing himself for the impact of the bullet he knew was coming. He heard the shot, but felt nothing.

To his astonishment, Swann fell back against the wall and slid down to the floor, a black hole through the red bandanna, in the middle of his forehead. Logan spun around toward Cecil, but the frightened bartender had both hands on the bar, with no gun in either. Logan looked quickly toward the door then. Seeming to fill the doorway, the imposing hulk that was Ox Russell stepped inside, cocking a Spencer carbine that looked like a toy in his huge hands.

Every nerve in his body tense from just having looked death in the eye, Logan stood for a moment staring in disbelief. "What are you doin' here?" he finally asked.

The big man shrugged. "It was crazy, you ridin' in here to take on four men, so I followed you. Thought you might need some help." He grinned. "I snuck off again without tellin' Jace. You're glad I did now, ain't you?"

"Partner, I damn sure am," Logan said.

"How'd you know that one was at the top of the steps?" Ox asked, pointing his carbine at Skinny.

Logan nodded toward Cecil. "When he told me Lila was upstairs, I guess I just naturally looked up there when I heard him cock that pistol. Tell you the truth, I didn't have time to think about it."

Cecil shook his head, still shaking from the incident. "I didn't know any other way of tellin' you," he said, "without gettin' shot myself."

"I expect we'll have company pretty soon. They were bound to have heard those shots," Logan said. "Have you seen Quincy and Lonnie?"

"They were in here—left about thirty minutes before you came in," Cecil said. "They're stayin' at the Three Widows again."

Logan was right—Quincy and Lonnie had heard the shots fired in the saloon as they sat in the dining room now empty of all customers.

"Not but two shots," Lonnie speculated. "Whaddaya s'pose those two jaspers are up to—just scarin' hell outta Cecil Grant?"

"I wouldn't be surprised," Quincy said. He glanced at the door again, looking for Hannah to come in.

"Where in hell is that bitch?" With their table right beside the kitchen door, he was ready to grab her if she tried to sneak in through the back door.

"I hope to hell we ain't wasted our gold on those two," Lonnie said, ignoring Quincy's question, having heard it repeated more than once. "They're liable to sit up in that saloon and drink likker all night—won't be much good to us in the mornin'."

"They'll be ready," Quincy assured him. "That damn Swann lives offa whiskey." He gave Lonnie a smug grin. "Besides, I ain't plannin' on wastin' an ounce of that gold on Swann and Skinny. I'm just lettin' 'em hold it for a little while till we get the job done. Then I expect they'll meet with some bad luck." Then he turned his attention to the two women seated across the room. "Get up from there and make me some coffee," he ordered.

"We've already cleaned up the kitchen," Mae told him. "And the fire's about gone out in the stove anyway."

Her answer did not please Quincy. "Maybe you need to get your ears cleaned out. I didn't ask you if you would do it. Now get up off your lazy ass and fix me some coffee."

"I'll do it," Daisy volunteered. "There ain't no good in arguing with him." She got up and went to the kitchen. After a moment, Mae got up and followed.

"Now you're startin' to get a little smarter," Quincy said. "It ain't no good arguin' with me. Just do what I tell you." He turned to Lonnie and laughed, only to wonder at the expression of shock on his cousin's face. "What the hell ails you?" Then he turned to follow Lonnie's stare toward the dining room door.

He was there, standing in the doorway, his rifle leveled at them, waiting for Mae to clear out of the way.

Lonnie's reaction was automatic; he plunged through the kitchen door to save himself. Almost falling in his haste to escape, he flung the back door open and collided with the massive hulk of Ox Russell. The collision drove the frightened man to the floor. His attempt to draw his pistol was a wasted motion since Ox already had his out.

Inside the dining room door, Quincy heard the shot that killed Lonnie, as did Mae. Unfortunately for her, she recoiled by jumping back a step, presenting Quincy with a desperate chance to save himself. He grabbed her and pulled her up before him as a shield. "Now, by God, I'll kill her," he threatened, reached for the .44 on his side, and jammed it up against her head. He pulled her back away from the door.

"Lonnie!" he called out. "You all right?"

"He can't answer," Ox called back from the kitchen.

Frantic then, Quincy exclaimed, "You come through that door, and I'll kill her!"

"Let her go," Logan said. "It's down to just you and me. Let her go and we'll settle it between the two of us."

"The hell I will," Quincy quickly replied. "There's two of you."

"There's just you and me," Logan repeated. "Ox will stay out of it. You hear that, Ox?"

"I heard," the big man replied.

"You've been doggin' me all over these hills," Logan said. "Now you've caught up with me, so let's get this thing done. We'll take it outside and finish it."

"All right," Quincy said. "Lower that rifle and ease the hammer down."

"Just as soon as you holster that .44," Logan countered.

They stood there, glaring at each other in what amounted to a standoff with neither man trusting the other. While they were locked in the tense situation, Daisy came out of the kitchen. Without hesitating, but with an unhurried air of casualness, she walked up beside Quincy, whose gaze was riveted on the rifleman facing him.

From the folds of her skirt, she brought a pistol up to rest against Quincy's temple and pulled the trigger. It was done in one continuous move, too quickly for Quincy to realize what she was doing. He slumped to the floor immediately, without even the reflex action of pulling the trigger of his weapon. She looked at Logan, who was stunned, scarcely believing what had just happened.

"He mighta killed you," she said, as casually as if she had swatted a hornet. She turned to Mae then. "You all right?"

"Well, that ain't something that happens to you every day," Mae said, still shaking a little. "I think I mighta peed myself."

"Sorry about the floor," Daisy said. "I didn't think about his brains flyin' all over the place." She turned when Ox walked over to look at Quincy's body. "Here," she said, and handed him his .44. Looking to Logan next, she asked, "Do you know where Hannah is?"

When he told her that Hannah was safe at the Triple-T, Daisy nodded. "Well, I reckon we can get this place cleaned up and back to where it was before you and those phony marshals hit town."

"I reckon," Mae said while Logan remained standing there, astounded by the young woman's callousness. "I think maybe I could use a cup of coffee myself," Mae said.

"I'll build up the fire in the stove," Daisy said. "You and Ox drag those two buzzards outside," she said to Logan, who was still standing dumbfounded, not sure he could believe what he had just witnessed. The realization that it was all over finally struck him, although it would be a while yet before it really sank in that there was no longer anyone seeking to kill him.

Bringing his thoughts back to the moment, he discovered that Daisy was studying him intensively.

"Help Ox drag them outside," she repeated softly. "Then we'll sit down and have a cup of coffee." He nodded and turned to do her bidding.

Daisy paused a moment, watching him walk away. She had not hesitated to assassinate Quincy Morgan. The world would not judge her harshly for her actions. Quincy needed killing, as much as any ruthless murderer, and she had not been willing to risk losing Logan Cross. He was a good man. She had formed that opinion on the first day he had come into town.

And unlike everyone else, she had not changed her mind when the whole town thought he was an outlaw. She figured, like Jace Evans, it would not be good for Logan to have killed Quincy Morgan in a gunfight, consequently earning a reputation to be challenged by every two-bit gunman in the territory.

I've got plans for you, Logan Cross, she thought. *Hannah had her chance, but she hasn't done anything about it. And I intend to go after what I want.*

Read on for a look at
the next thrilling adventure
from Charles G. West,

SLATER'S WAY

Available now from Berkley.

It was altogether fitting on this spring day in 1864 that the muddy streets of Virginia City were awash with a flood of water from a violent thunderstorm.

Nothing good can come of a day as dreary as this, Leona Engels thought.

The heavy dark clouds hovering over Alder Gulch erupted again late in the afternoon and threatened to continue their assault of thunder and lightning into the evening. The disagreeable weather had not been sufficient to keep John Slater Engels and his longtime friend and partner, Henry Weed, from their usual visit to the Miners Saloon. It was a ritual that John's wife loathed, since the little bit of pay dirt her husband and Henry were able to pull from their claim in Daylight Gulch went straight into Gil Mobley's pockets at his saloon, but she was too fearful to complain about it.

As darkness began to gather in the gulch, Leona became more concerned, for it was well past the time when the two men usually came home for supper. She walked to the door of the rough cabin once again to peer out into the rain. There was still no sign of her husband and his partner. Finally, she turned and called to her fifteen-year-old son, "Jace, come here, boy."

John Slater Engels Jr. was originally called J.S. by his parents, but in a short time the initials evolved into the nickname of "Jace" since the sounds were not that far apart. The boy carefully put the shotgun he had been cleaning aside and came from the kitchen.

"Ma'am?" he replied.

"I'm startin' to worry about your pa," Leona said. "Him and Henry are usually through with their drinkin' and card playin' by now. I want you to go down to Virginia City and tell them I'm gonna throw their supper out the door if they don't get theirselves home."

"Yes'um," the stoic young boy replied.

With no sign of emotion, he turned and went to the front corner of the cabin, where he slept on a bedroll, and picked up his hat. It was not the first time he had been sent to find his father and his hard-drinking friend, and it was a chore that he didn't much care for. It would be a year this month since they had come to the gulch in search of gold. So far, it seemed the main thing his father had accomplished was to garner a reputation for himself as a drunk and a brawler.

There wasn't much law enforcement in most parts of Alder Gulch. Outlaws and hell-raisers were ultimately dealt with by the vigilance committee, and Jace felt sure they were keeping an eye on Weed and his father. He was disappointed that his father lacked the backbone to resist the temptations of the lawless crowd. The family had fled Kansas after his father and Weed were identified by witnesses as the men involved in a bank holdup. That holdup was Weed's idea, and he talked Jace's father into it. It seemed like every scrape his father found himself in could be traced back to some illegal scheme that Henry Weed had come up with. Mostly, Jace was ashamed for his mother and the abuse she sometimes suffered when his drunken father came home after a night of gambling and dallying with the *fancy ladies* at the saloon.

On this day, the rain had started in the morning and his father said it was too wet to work their claim. But he and Weed decided it was not too wet to ride over to Alder Gulch for a drink of whiskey and maybe a hand or two of poker. When Jace asked how the rain could hurt the gold they were looking for in the water, he received a backhand for his sarcasm. And then, off they went, riding to Alder Gulch in the rain after a casual promise to be back by suppertime.

With his hat pulled low to help shield him from the rain, Jace plodded along the trail that led to Virginia City. His coat was soon soaked through, but he ignored the discomfort, concentrating more on what he would say to convince his father to come home.

When he reached the point where the trail ended at the main street, which traced the length of Alder Gulch, he was immediately aware of an event going on beside the Miners Saloon. A sizable crowd had gathered to stand in the rain, ignoring the occasional flash of lightning and rumble of thunder. When he came closer, he realized they were there to witness a hanging. As curious as anyone, he edged up through the noisy circle of spectators to see for himself. There was no tree next to the saloon, but it was not the first hanging that had taken place there. One single pole served as a gallows. Approximately fifteen feet tall, the pole had been notched near the top so that a rope could be tied and secured to support the unfortunate victim as he dangled at the noose end of the rope. With his hands tied behind his back and his feet bound together, the victim hung motionless, his head cocked to the side by the heavy noose around his neck. In the darkness, it was hard to see the man's face, but from the excited conversation he overheard around him, he learned that the man had been hanged because he killed a fellow he had argued with in the saloon.

Since he didn't see his father in the crowd of spectators, he decided he'd best look for him instead of gawking at a dead man. So he started to turn away and head for the saloon when he was startled by a sudden bright flash, followed almost immediately by a loud clap of thunder. In those few seconds, he was stunned to see the grotesque features of his father's face in the flash of lightning.

"That's the Good Lord saying thank you for riddin' this world of troublemakers like John Engels," he heard someone say. It was followed by a hardy chuckle from someone else.

Jace felt his body go numb, and his legs threatened to deny him support as he pushed blindly through the crowd of men standing around the pole. Confused and horrified by the terrible scene he had just witnessed, he didn't know what to do. After making his way through the mob, he leaned against the wall of the saloon until he could think clearly once again. His father was dead, and that was the only thing he knew for sure.

Weed, he thought, then. *Where is Henry Weed?*

He decided he should find him, so he left the side of the building and started searching through the crowd again. Weed was nowhere to be found, so he went inside the saloon to look for him there, but to no avail. He was left with no choice but to return home as fast as he could to take the terrible news to his mother. Running almost all of the two miles back to the camp, Jace was surprised to find Weed's and his father's horses standing beside the cabin. Weed had evidently started for home shortly before the boy arrived at the scene of the hanging and had somehow circled back on the trail Jace had walked. Perhaps Jace would have seen him if he had not been walking with his head down in the driving rain.

So Ma already knows about Pa, he thought as he opened the door.

He walked into the cabin to find his mother sobbing in Henry Weed's arms. When she heard Jace come in, she turned and beckoned to him. He went at once to comfort her. She put her arm around him and pulled him close to Weed and herself.

"Oh, Jace," she wailed, "did you see your pa?" When he answered yes, she sobbed again. "You poor boy," she cried. "I'm so sorry you had to see him like that, hung on a post."

"There warn't nothin' I could do to help him," Henry Weed said. "He got into a tussle with some feller we was playin' cards with, and before I knowed it, they was goin' at each other with their guns. John was faster'n that feller, and shot him through the chest before he ever cleared the table with his six-shooter. Then a bunch of fellers that had been standin' at the bar, drinkin', took your pa down before he could get off another shot. They said they was on the vigilance committee and they was fixin' to put a stop to all the lawlessness in town. I got back here as fast as I could. You don't have to worry. I'm gonna take care of your ma."

"I reckon I can take care of my ma," Jace said.

"Why, sure you can," Weed said, "but I expect I'd best be the one to take care of both of you."

Leona stopped crying then. "Henry's right, Jace. He's offered to stay with us and take care of us now that your pa's gone. We'll talk some more about it later on tonight."

"What about Pa?" Jace wanted to know. "We've got to go get him down from that pole and bury him proper." He looked at Weed, waiting for his answer.

"I don't know if we can do that," Leona said.

"Why not?" Jace asked.

Weed answered for her. "They ain't likely to let us take John down from there for a while yet. They'll most likely want him to hang there to let other folks know what happens to troublemakers in Virginia City."

Jace couldn't believe the indifference on the part of his father's wife and his supposed best friend. "How can you just not care what happens to Pa's body?" he charged. He turned to look into his mother's eyes. "We've got to take care of Pa."

"We can't," Leona said. "It's best to just do what we can to carry on now without him. I knew it was gonna come to this. It was just a matter of time."

"The hell we will!" Jace exclaimed.

"Now, don't be gettin' yourself riled up about this," Weed said. "It's over and done with. Your pa's gone, and I reckon it was bound to happen—the way things were goin' and all."

Jace made no response other than the angry glare he cast in Weed's direction. His pa wouldn't be dead if he had never crossed paths with Henry Weed. After a moment, he shifted an accusing gaze at his mother, who was no longer crying but stood wringing her hands in apparent distress. It infuriated the boy that Henry

Weed was acting as if John Engels was the wild, hard-drinking troublemaker, and he was no more than an innocent bystander.

Some friend, he thought, glaring at Weed again.

He made up his mind then that he was going to cut his father down from that pole, no matter what his mother or Weed said. He had never had a particularly close relationship with his father, but he was his father, and Jace didn't intend to leave him hanging as an amusement for the miners in Virginia City.

"I'll put the horses away," he volunteered, and headed for the door.

"That's a good idea," Weed said. "There're some things I wanna talk to your mama about while you're doin' that."

Outside the cabin, Jace paused to study the nighttime sky. The rain had slackened considerably as the thunderstorm moved across the gulch, though the clouds were as dark and thick as before. He led the two horses behind the cabin to the simple shelter that served as a stable for them and the two mules. Having already decided what he was going to do, he left the saddles on the horses, then tied a shovel to the saddle on Weed's horse. Next, he checked the Henry rifle riding in the sling on his father's saddle to make sure it was still there and had not suffered any from the rain. Satisfied that Weed would not likely take the trouble to check on the horses, he returned to the cabin.

When he walked in the door, he found the two of them standing before the fireplace, facing the door as if waiting for him. "We need to tell you somethin'," Weed said. "We decided that with the way things are, the best thing is for me and your mama to live together as man and wife."

Jace recoiled sharply. Seeing his reaction, his mother tried to soften the shock. "I know it's kind of sudden, but I think John would approve of it. He and Henry were such close friends."

Unable to speak for a moment while his brain spun wildly, Jace finally blurted, "Pa ain't even in the ground yet! It didn't take you long to jump in bed together!"

"Jace!" Leona scolded. "You watch your mouth! It ain't like that at all."

"Your mama's right," Weed said. "It's just the best thing to do. I've always had a fondness for your mama, and I intend to make it right when we can stand up before a preacher. We'll make a new start. Me and John had been talkin' about movin' on, anyway. We ain't found much of anythin' in the sluice box for a while now, so I think it's best to leave our claim and head up to Helena. There's a new strike at Last Chance Gulch and we can make a fresh start there—might have a little better luck. There ain't no reason me and you can't get along, as long as you mind your ma and me. Whaddaya say?"

"Sounds to me like it don't make no difference what I think," Jace replied. "You and Ma have already decided what you're gonna do."

Tired of trying to solicit the boy's cooperation, Weed smirked and said, "That's about the size of it, boy, so you might as well get used to it."

Anxious to avoid a conflict between Weed and her son, Leona spoke up then. "Let's sit down and eat the supper getting cold on the table. No matter what's happened, we need to eat."

Jace still found it hard to believe his mother's apparent acceptance of his father's death and her immediate acceptance of Weed's proposal—not much different from changing one horse to ride another when the first one got tired. But he said nothing more. He sat down at the table with them and ate the supper she had cooked. When he was finished, he excused himself to make a final check of the livestock before going to his bedroll in the front corner of the cabin. "We'll start a new day in the morning," his mother said to him as he pulled the quilt that served as his bedroom wall across his little corner.

"Yes, ma'am," he mumbled.

He lay there on the thin pallet for what seemed hours, listening to the whispered conversation between his mother and Henry Weed. Finally the talking stopped. Even then, he continued to lie there until he felt certain they were both asleep. As quietly as he could, he pulled the edge of the quilt back far enough to peek into the main room. Weed was sprawled on the pallet he had been using before, snoring lustily, the alcohol he had apparently consumed earlier finally rendering him unconscious. Jace slipped outside the quilt and paused to watch the sleeping man. There was no sound from the bedroom.

At least he ain't already jumped in the bed with my mother, he thought and tiptoed to the door.

Outside, he went quickly to the stable and led the two horses out, walking them up the path until certain he was away from the cabin without anyone aware of his departure. Jumping up into the stirrup, then, he headed back to Virginia City, his father's cartridge belt around his waist and his Henry rifle riding in the saddle sling.

The storm had spent its energy and moved on, leaving a dark and damp night. He had no watch to tell the time, but he knew the hour was late when he reached the ridge overlooking the gulch and the lusty town that never slept.

Nudging his father's sorrel gelding, he descended to the noisy street below, riding along unnoticed by the drunks coming and going from the saloons. He pulled the horses up when he got to the harness shop next to the Miners Saloon, thinking he was prepared to see the grisly sight of his father's lifeless body dangling from the solitary pole again. He was wrong, however, for the sight of his late father jolted him as before. The crowd that had been there had dispersed, returning to the saloons of their choice to talk about the shooting and the hanging that had followed. At the present, there were only two spectators standing at the foot of the pole, gazing up at the late John Slater Engels. Jace remained in the saddle and waited until the novel sight of the dead man yielded to the craving for another drink of whiskey, and the two men walked back toward the Miners Saloon.

Jace nudged the sorrel, anxious to do what he had come to do before someone else showed up to gawk at the hanged man. He felt the blood in his veins go as cold as ice when he pulled up beside the corpse. While he was seated in the saddle, his eyes were even with his father's belt. With his heart pounding inside his chest, he forced himself to remain calm and do what he had to do.

"Easy, boy," he said softly to the horse. "Steady now," he said softly as he pulled his feet from the stirrups and carefully placed one foot on the saddle. Then, using his father's body to steady himself, he stood up on the saddle. As he pulled himself up, he almost lost his footing when he brushed against his father's face and looked into the sightless eyes staring grotesquely at him as if already suffering the fiery coals of hell. Forcing himself to look away from the cruel face, he pulled the skinning knife from the cartridge belt and sawed furiously at the rope above his father's head. It seemed the rope was never going to part, but finally the last strands were severed and the corpse dropped to the ground. Rigor mortis having already set in, the body landed feetfirst and, rigid as a pole, fell face-forward into the trampled mud.

Jace dismounted and stood staring at the body for a long moment. It would be no easy task to get the corpse across the saddle. He was still contemplating the job when he was startled by a voice behind him. "Hey, boy! What the hell do you think you're doin'?"

He turned to find Arlen Tucker walking up behind him. Tucker, a blacksmith and a prominent member of the vigilance committee, was no doubt instrumental in the hanging of Jace's father. "I'm takin' my pa for buryin'," Jace answered.

"The hell you are," Tucker said. "Nobody told you you could cut that murderer down. Now you can help me haul him back up that pole. I oughta give you a good whippin' for pullin' a stunt like that."

Jace gave no thought to his response to Tucker's threat. As he stood beside his father's horse, his face was no more than a foot from the butt of the Henry rifle riding in the saddle sling. Following his natural reaction, he pulled the weapon from the scabbard, cocking it as he brought it to bear on the surprised blacksmith.

"I wouldn't advise you to try it," Jace said. "You look like a pretty stout feller, so I reckon you oughta be able to lift my pa up across that saddle."

"The hell I will," Tucker responded. "Boy, you'd better put that rifle down! If I have to take it away from you, I'm gonna break it across your backside." He threatened, but he made no move toward the determined boy.

"I reckon you could try," Jace calmly said, "if you think it's worth gettin' shot over."

Tucker hesitated, measuring the cold, ominous look in Jace's eyes. He decided it not worth the risk to test the boy's resolve. "You're makin' a helluva mistake," he said. "You're gonna wind up with the same reputation your pa had."

"Pick him up and lay him across that saddle," Jace said, motioning with his rifle. "I ain't waitin' around here all night."

"All right, all right," Tucker replied. "Just don't get careless with that damn rifle."

He took hold of John Engels's shoulders and stood him up. Then he bent down, put his arms around his knees, and lifted him up as though hoisting a log. Henry Weed's roan was not sure it wanted the body across its back, and it sidestepped nervously when the corpse landed on the saddle. The sudden motion caused Jace to quickly grab his father's shoulder to keep the body from sliding off the saddle. Tucker saw it as his chance to act. He pulled the .44 he wore, to his instant regret. Due to the stiffness of the body, John Engels's feet kicked up to spoil Tucker's aim when Jace pulled on his father's shoulder, causing Tucker's shot to miss. Jace took no time to think. Holding the nine-pound Henry in one hand, he pulled the trigger and cut Tucker down with a slug in his belly.

Staring in disbelief, the blacksmith sat down heavily in the mud, clutching his stomach. Equally surprised, Jace paused only a moment to consider what had just happened. Someone was bound to have heard the shots, so, in a panic, he grabbed the horses' reins and turned to discover a witness staring at him, seemingly in a drunken stupor. Until that moment, he had not noticed the man slumped against the side door of the saloon, obviously having gotten no farther after leaving the saloon. Although he continued to gape openly at the boy, the drunk didn't move, and he said not a word. Jace paused for only a moment before leading the horses around behind the saloon to secure his father's body across the saddle. Working as quickly as he could, he bound the body with a rope, hearing voices from the side of the saloon. Thinking the man sitting against the side door was no doubt telling them what had happened, he climbed up into the saddle as fast as he could and rode down the alley behind the stores, leading the roan behind him. When he came to the first trail that led up from the gulch, he followed it out of Virginia City and into the hills beyond. His only quest now was to find a place to dig a grave. It didn't matter where, as long as it was not easily seen. The burial itself was not as important to him as the removal of his father's body from public display. So when he came to a grassy ravine with one solitary spruce tree standing as a grave marker, he decided to bury his father there instead of taking him back to Daylight Gulch.

When the grave was done, and his father's body was in the ground, Jace stood looking at it for a long moment. It was customary to say something about a person when they were buried, talk about all the good things they had done before they died. He continued to stand there while he thought back over his short life and the relationship he had had with his father.

Finally, he said, "I can't think of a damn thing he ever did for me and my ma except make life hard for both of us. Amen."

Ready to find
your next great read?

Let us help.

Visit prh.com/nextread

Penguin
Random
House